With very [...] wishes

UNTOUCHED DEPARTURES

Olga Merrick

Olga Merrick

chadgreen books

First published 2015

British Library Cataloguing in Publication Data
A CIP record for this book is available from the British Library

ISBN 978-0-9929577-4-2

Chadgreen Books are published by Chadgreen Publishing,
Telford, Shropshire

Printed and bound in Great Britain by BookPrintingUK,
Peterborough, Cambridgeshire

Dedicated to the memory of my mother,

Rosa Marie Merrick

Acknowledgements

I am indebted to my partner and editor, Geoff Thatcher, for his tireless encouragement and support in helping me shape these words into a finished novel, and pouring me the welcome glass of wine at the end of each working day.

Untouched

Departures

1
Early Morning

She remembered that day in the pub, the tiny hilltop one on the edge of town. It was the day Carl's murder was planned. She and Gerald sat in a secluded corner, away from the bar where beer barrels perched on the counter, like fat egg-laying hens. The barrels were covered with clean red-and-white checked tea cloths and she thought they looked a bit like headscarves. The Three Tuns had no cellar, only this single room, with its wooden bar counter, and a nook-and-cranny seating area. She and Gerald were meeting some man there, not a nice man she suspected, but one who could 'do things, get things done' and 'get someone done over'…

Thinking about that day, she fingered her chin, her cheeks, under her eyes, and round both sides of her nose. Now she had unblemished skin, no black eyes, no bruised jaw and no broken teeth. No fear either. Her mind flickered back again. She recalled how Gerald had stood up when the man came into the tiny bar, to the private corner where they were seated. The two men shook hands and Gerald said, 'What'll you have my friend?'

'Scotch,' the man had replied, adding 'Large one'

in a gruff, untutored voice. No please. And no thank you when Gerald returned with the glass of amber-coloured liquid. She had watched the man down it in one. Seen him stare at her face, examining the injuries.

'You all right?' he had said to her.

She nodded, gave him a shy half-smile. 'Yeah, I'm ok, thanks.' She took his query to be a kindness. Apart from Gerald, no man had shown her that for a long time, certainly not Carl. She had sat quietly, sipping a half of shandy, not much of a drinker in those days. Carl preferred to go to a pub without her. That way he could meet up with his mates, have a laugh and swap bawdy jokes, and eye up the tarts in their short skirts that were more like wide belts (so he said). Then come home and show her who was boss, be it in the bedroom with his spiteful and cruel sex, or with a storm of blows to her body and face if she dared complain. She learned not to, but it didn't stop the bullying. She likened it to a kind of addiction, that he got pleasure from, hitting her and counting the bruises when they appeared. He never said sorry afterwards, never showed remorse or regret.

The Three Tuns was definitely not Carl's sort of pub. Or his drinking buddies. Really, she supposed, it was more of a tourist pub. Once an old brew house, the pub was famed as being the smallest in

Hampshire. A novel sort of hostelry, where tourists looked around the quaint room with curiosity and a faintly condescending amusement, and stood at the bar with a half pint drawn from one of the hen-like barrels, then ordered a glass of wine for their wives or girlfriends from the wall-hung refrigerated wine dispenser just behind the bar. It offered Sauvignon Blanc, Pinot Grigio and French Rosé in two litre bottles hanging upside down, with optics that poured medium or large measures. It also had space outside the refrigerated area for a bottle of red. Very space saving.

Perhaps the tourists chose to sit in one of the nook-and-cranny areas, as she and Gerald did that day. She could not imagine Carl or his cronies choosing such seating, too poncey they would have sneered.

Carl, her first husband, her teenage rebellion. Big mistake. Rough, uncouth, untutored Carl, who laughed too loudly at his own jokes. The brute who bullied his way through their four-year marriage, kept her incarcerated. If she dared to venture out without his permission, he would cudgel her with questions and his fists. She had scant life beyond the marriage, beyond the marriage bed. Often he forced his way into her body, once puncturing her with his unwanted seed. He gave her a clumsy child, Maria, shortened to Mia. Shortened life too. Less than one year. They, the hospital staff, blamed it on lack of oxygen at her birth. Left her brain damaged: no life expectancy, no skills or motivation.

She blamed him, Carl. Brainless man producing brainless child. Let him do the cuddling, the midnight feeds, the bathing and changing of this mewling creature. She wanted no part of it, no responsibility. She had no love for the baby who would not survive, not a baby that was *his*. Carl tried to persuade her to open her arms, her heart. 'Chrissakes Deelie, she's your baby. Ours.'

Mia died without her mother's love weeks before they were due to move into the flat above Gerald's stationery shop, the one that sold art materials as well. She would have liked to purchase brushes, canvasses, watercolour pads. But Carl's snide remark when she mentioned it, killed her enthusiasm. 'What bloody for? Who d'you think you are? Bloody Van Gogh?' He pronounced the Gogh as Goff. Surprising really that rough, untutored Carl even knew the name of the famous painter.

Gerald knew nothing of baby Maria, and Delia saw no reason to tell him... he was their new landlord, not a friend: the friendship would come later...

Gerald did not introduce her to the man. In fact, remembering the day, Delia realised no names had been used. Conversation was conveyed barely above a whisper, mostly between the two men, while she sat and stared out of a tiny porthole window, trying to see the world out there beyond its bevelled, distorted glass, and fingering her bruised cheek. She hadn't taken in the gist of their conversation, lost as she was in her own thoughts. More dreams really, she supposed, dreams of what might be if she was freed from the monster that was her husband.

A few days later Carl was dead, his throat slit from ear to ear. The weapon had been inserted with a twist, the detectives said. One of them actually likened the wound to the serrated teeth of a Halloween pumpkin. She had pasted a look of horror onto her face, but failed to ask if he would have suffered: an oversight perhaps, but she hadn't cared. She was only relieved that she was freed from his violence, from her fear of him. She did briefly wonder what the sky had been like then. She had this fascination for them…

By then her bruises were almost healed, practically invisible under her make-up. She had escaped to her sister's in Hereford when the murder took place. Left the flat while Carl was at work and took the coach north-west to that cathedral city. There was no question of her being involved.

Her sister, Saskia, was married to Gethin, a clever motor mechanic who serviced coaches for a private firm. They lived in a prefabricated bungalow, among a graveyard of old and broken coaches, on the outskirts of Hereford. Gethin fascinated Delia, perhaps she was even a little in love with him? When he came home from his workshop across the yard, dressed in his dark blue overalls, he smelled of engine grease. A tall man, with dark hair, deep brown eyes, and a kindness about him. He would pick up his and Saskia's two boys and swing them round and say, 'How are my two young heroes then?' in his deep nasal voice. Delia thought it sounded like he had an oily rag stuffed up his nostrils. She noted the grease under his fingernails and marvelled when he emerged from the bathroom, clean as clean, with barely a trace under them. She thought he must scrub them almost raw.

They were sitting down to dinner, beef stew and dumplings with lots of fresh vegetables that Saskia grew in their pocket-handkerchief garden, away from the graveyard of broken vehicles. A call came through from the Hampshire police. They gave Delia the horrifying news and told her she would be visited by local constabulary within the next hour. She was helpless, cried into a large white handkerchief that Gethin offered: she enjoyed being hugged by her older sister, and her two young nephews holding her hands. She couldn't eat any more of the stew, delicious though it was. Or rather, she thought it best to 'lose' her appetite.

An hour later two police arrived from the local station, a man and a woman PC. They briefly told her what had happened, patted her hand and said

'Sorry love' more than once. She said she would travel back in the morning and thanked them through her tears for coming to see her; promised to contact her local police when she got home, and no, she didn't want transporting back to Hampshire as her ticket was a return one.

'Should I wear black?' she asked her sister. 'Only I don't think I brought anything black with me.' Except the remains of my black eye, she thought.

'He is… was… a gambler,' she later told the Hampshire detectives, when they were trying to find a reason for the unexplained murder. 'Maybe he owed money to the bookies.'

In the end, they put it down to just that, an angry bookie looking for his money and not getting it. No one was ever arrested, no bookie, or a bookie's runner as they called them then. They also interviewed Gerald, purely because he was acquainted with both Carl and herself, he being their landlord, and renting them the flat above his stationery shop in the small town high street. He knew several bookies but not, he said, any he imagined as would-be killers. He also, wisely, did not mention being aware of the beatings Delia suffered at Carl's hands. And, most definitely, did not mention the meeting in the little pub between themselves and the nameless man who drank large scotches and didn't say thank you.

After Carl's funeral, Gerald suggested it might be wiser if she moved into his flat, which was above his second shop, Manning Antiques, in a nearby village close to the town.

'You should have more peace there,' he said 'away from the press and the gawpers.'

She gratefully accepted his kind offer, moved her scant personal belongings into his guest room and in weeks, not months, these few items were gradually transferred to the main bedroom and herself to Gerald's bed. A year later, they were quietly married. Gerald sold his two shops, and they moved away from Hampshire to Kent. They never went back...

Husband Gerald: quiet, polite, couth and tutored. Bookish Gerald, whose lovemaking was done with his eyes shut until he ejaculated. Then he would take two large, white cotton handkerchiefs from his bedside drawer, wipe between her legs with one of them and his flaccid, spent penis with the other, before kissing her and whispering goodnight and thank you. They only ever had sex at nighttime, in the dark, and rarely more than once weekly. Gentle Gerald who, later, diffidently infused her with twins...

Now she was looking out of her bedroom window at a tentative sky, dawn just breaking over the new day.

What do you mean by tentative, she thought, and proceeded to have a little discussion with herself. (It was something she often did.   She certainly considered her own opinions better than most people in her acquaintance). *Well, there's those little orange wispy clouds, capped with frowns of grey: behind them a limpid blue sky.   Will they fuse together and threaten rain? Or will they skip happily along, a heavenly meadow of gambolling swirls within the sunshine? Oh very pretty, Cordelia. Going in for purple phrases are we?*

She sipped her tea, watching the sun gradually rise as she dissected these memories, then filed the pieces into separate folders of her mind.   A few minutes later, she tried to remember the man's face, the possible killer of her brutal husband all those years ago. His features remained a blur. She could barely remember what Gerald had looked like back then.   Gerald, who died ten years later - of pneumonia, leaving her to bring up their twins on her own.

She remembered Carl's face though, etched as it was, deeply and painfully, into her psyche. It was one she would never forget. That boorish face, with its flared nostrils and overhanging eyebrows: Neanderthal. He was older than her, not as old as Gerald, but old enough to have a cunning that she was too young and naïve to possess. When they married, he was twenty-eight to her eighteen. Had done a bit of boxing in the army; knew where to punch that didn't always leave physical marks, kidney blows that left her gasping in pain and wanting to vomit. Blows that scarred her mind with fear and loathing.

Of course, they were diminished now, those scars, probably gone forever or at least pushed far enough back in her lifetime of memories to mean nothing to her any more. Her life was so different now...

Half an hour later, she came back to bed, after replenishing her cup. It was still only 7.30 am. Coffee this time, she preferred it to tea, liked its pleasing aroma and slightly bitter taste. She leaned back on the pillows and became aware that she knew the man's name, had probably known it all those years ago. It was when Gerald had said goodbye to him: adding the man's name, Denny, short for Dennis she supposed. Denny, she thought now, sounded like her son's name, Danny but with an 'e'. Though realising she knew his name, and had always known it, did not conjure up a picture of him. Try as she might, she could not recall the colour of his hair. Was it long or short and his eyes brown or blue? Was he tall, short or medium height? She remembered his voice, the one thing he had said to her, 'You all right?' Not a cultured voice, and no 't' on the end of 'right', or one that betrayed a local accent: more like London, East End London.

Whatever else he said was spoken in a kind of gruff whisper to Gerald. She had turned to the porthole window of the tiny pub, played with her hair – she remembered doing that – tried to imagine what was out there through the distorted glass: who had passed by and in what direction. She only looked up when the man shook hands with Gerald and half smiled in her direction as he left them. He had not shaken her hand.

She wondered if he, this Denny chap, was still alive, still 'got things done'. Then, mentally, she shrugged her shoulders. Even if he was, he'd be at least in his sixties now. Perhaps he had a son. Again she shrugged. If he did, was he the same as his father? A man who 'got things done'? Even so, how would she know where to contact him? Where did he live: London maybe? But London was a huge city. She smiled to herself. *Excuse me. Do you know a man called Denny and his son? They live, I think, in London.*

Yes lady, so do about ten million other people...

The duvet moved as the person next to her stirred, turned to face her and mumbled, 'Morning gorgeous.'

'Morning,' she said, briefly smiled and patted his bared shoulder. 'Sleep well?' All thoughts of the past had gone now. They would return only when she could be private, alone to recall, analyse, assess. 'Coffee? Or tea?'

He licked his lips, let his tongue get between his

teeth and the inside of his lips. Pulled a face. 'Coffee I think.' Then, 'Did we have a lot to drink last night?'

'Fair amount I suppose. I think you carried on after me.' *Of course he had*.

He yawned, 'Yeah, maybe.' He caressed her arm, ran his hand up and down, felt her breast.

'Coffee would be good.' He grinned in a suggestive way. 'Before? Or after?'

On the following morning, the first light of day simpered its way into the bedroom. Today, the sky was not tentative, she thought. Once again, she sat up in bed, once more on her second cup of coffee, again recalling a death. The clouds out there looked angry, at best grumpy. They were lumped together horizontally, yet separated into layers. Why this absorption with clouds, with the sky? Did they, it, mean something to her? Were the clouds sort of indicating the passage of time, like they did in screenplays when they raced across a sky? Of time moving on, no matter where it was going? Did they recall something from her childhood? Something that was buried deep inside her? She shook her head: too deep, philosophy was not her forte.

'What time is it?' The sleepy head next to her spoke. She glanced at the clock on the bookshelf beyond the bed end.

'Seven-thirty.'

'Any tea going?'

She was tempted to say, 'Get it yourself,' but years of submissiveness within her three marriages inhibited her from giving that answer. She shifted in the bed, pushed back the duvet and swivelled round until her feet touched the floor.

'I'll get you some.' It was said without a trace of resentment in her voice but it lurked, irritated in her mind. She went downstairs minus slippers. The stairs were carpeted, and the old parquet flooring in the inner hallway as she passed through to the kitchen at the back of the house, did not feel unbearably cold. She filled the kettle, flicked its switch, put a teabag into H's oversized mug, added two teaspoons of sugar and waited for the kettle to boil.

'Any toast going?' he called down. A moment's annoyance flickered across her face like a screen in a darkened cinema. It took only an instant to slot two slices into the toaster, to get the butter from the fridge, the thick-cut marmalade from the cupboard, but each operation was done with irritation. She was annoyed at herself, at her automatic obedience. Plus she was now beginning to feel cold in the chill morning air, having no slippers on her feet and no dressing gown wrapped round her.

Once again, she thought about Carl and his bullying power over her, his sudden violence when he accused her of annoying him. Only she did not know what annoyed him and what didn't with his unexpected mood swings. And Gerald. He too, in his quieter, more genteel way, had exercised a power over her. His had been the power over her gratitude, her acknowledgement of being freed from Carl. Only that freedom had proved to be short-lived. Soon they were living together in Gerald's house. Living like man and wife, almost immediately getting into a domestic routine. The affectionate term *darling* quickly lapsed to *dear*. At least on Gerald's part. She did not quite know how to address him, and soon realised he was not a man who used the word 'darling' habitually; he lacked the passion the word implied. In any case, she did not love him.

Next had come the bonds of that second marriage, of moving from Hampshire to Kent, motherhood, ten years of routine, followed eventually by widowhood. The widowhood brought about by murder, in a way, or an untouched departure as she preferred to consider it. It was not as if she had smothered him with a pillow. No, no, no. In fact, people had said she'd been wonderful the way she had nursed him, a devoted wife. Gerald fell ill that winter, with a severe chest infection that savagely attacked and weakened his lungs. He took to his bed within days, coughing up vile-smelling, yellow sputum into his large white handkerchiefs that she preferred to launder separately from the family wash. She moved out of their bed, unable to cope with his sweats and all-night cough. Eventually she persuaded him to let her call their GP.

After Dr Oldham's first visit, they waited for Gerald's condition to improve, but it didn't. Delia said, 'I'm going to call him again. The tablets aren't working.'

Gerald had no strength to argue, just looked up at her with an expression of weak gratitude. She thought he was not attractive in any way. Her feelings for him had waned, like a disappearing moon in a darkened sky.

'You'll need to keep a goodly eye on him,' the elderly doctor had warned. 'I've already given him a strong dose of antibiotics, but they're not being as effective as I'd like.' He had added, 'I'll leave these stronger ones with you, though he might have to be hospitalised if the infection worsens.'

'What d'you mean?' she had asked.

The doctor shrugged. 'He's got the beginnings of pneumonia. Keep him warm' he cautioned and patted her on the shoulder. 'Make sure the room is light and airy, m'dear, but never cold.'

He had emphasised the word 'never'. She nodded her acquiescence and followed him downstairs.

'Thank you, Doctor,' she said as she let him out of the street door.

Danny and Tilda were at school, both practising for their Christmas Nativity that was taking place the following week. She went into the kitchen, made tea and a small dish of porridge for Gerald. She drizzled some honey on it, guessing it would soothe his aching throat, and put the new box of pills beside his cup and dish.

An icy wind had blown quite strongly in from the sea when she let the doctor out. She remembered his parting words. 'Make sure the room is light and airy.' Mm... Gerald was asleep when she returned to the bedroom, his chest making wheezing and gurgling noises. She was minded of a stew bubbling on the stove. She paused, looked at him, saw an unhealthy line of perspiration on his forehead. She listened to his laboured breathing and slowly shook her head. Best to be kind...

Putting the tray quietly down, she crept to the bedroom window, opened it wide and shivered as an icy wind bullied its way into the room. At the same time, she turned the radiator beneath it down to zero. She shivered again, despite wearing a heavy-knit polo-necked sweater and corduroy pants. Before she left the room, she very gently pulled back the duvet from her sleeping husband's body. 'You might get too warm,' she whispered. Just as silently, she shut the door behind her, leaving him and the untouched tray of tea and honey-drizzled porridge to the bitter cold. She shoved her own freezing hands into her trouser pockets and continued down the stairs. Winter was not her favourite time of year. Never had been.

Later, she turned off the radio in the warm kitchen where she sat. It had been on quite loud: some Christmas carols were being played, sung by cathedral choristers. She liked those. Also a dramatic rendering of the final movements of Swan Lake. There had been no sound from the room upstairs. If there had, would she have heard? Probably not. The music and closed doors would have stifled any call from the bedroom, where Gerald lay wheezing and gurgling. She went upstairs slowly, deliberately, and glanced at her watch: ten past three and time to fetch the twins from school. Best close the bedroom window first and turn the radiator back on.

Gerald had stopped wheezing. In fact, he was making no sound at all, as she tiptoed past the bed towards the still-open window. The room, no longer light and airy, was gloomy, damp, and freezing. Daylight, even before three-thirty, was swiftly diminishing. As she glanced at her husband, she thought he looked a bit like all three: gloomy, damp and freezing. She closed the window, straightened the net curtains, turned the radiator on full, and listened to it gurgling through the pipes. She examined Gerald's face. It had taken on a pale, waxen tinge, and his lips were blue, like his closed eyelids. She covered him again, touched his hand, nodded to herself and gave a slight shudder. Yes his hand was cold too, icy cold, *dead* cold. He was not breathing, she was sure, but there was no time now to test with a mirror to his face. The twins would fret if she was late. They would have much to tell her about their day and how the play was progressing. Maybe she would take them to Kate's Kafé for afternoon tea. Chocolate brownies and homemade flapjacks with tall mugs of hot chocolate. A treat for all their hard work with the Nativity play. They would like that, especially as Kate had decorated the café with a pretty tree and lots of Christmassy baubles hanging from the ceiling.

She closed the bedroom door, went downstairs, shrugged on a warm coat and wound a long scarf round her neck. She ran to the school, only two streets away, fearing to be late. But it was fine. The children were just spilling out of the school's main entrance: a sea of felt hats and striped scarves, of caps and duffle coats, the outer uniform of Reeves' Prep School.

After hugs, kisses and 'How was your day?' she shepherded them towards the tearooms.

'How's Dad?' asked Danny.

'Is Daddy ok?' echoed his sister.

'He's asleep at the moment,' she told them. 'You can see him later.'

Only they didn't. She couldn't allow ten year olds to view a dead body. It would be too upsetting.

She did of course allow them to attend their father's funeral. It looked good, she thought, the two of them clinging to her arms, all three of them crying into large handkerchiefs as they followed Gerald's coffin into the church. She went alone to their school Nativity, clad in deep-mourning black, a very young widow, barely into her mid-thirties. The other parents squeezed her hand and gave her looks of sympathy. She smiled her gratitude at them, the smile almost glued to her face, thankful these sympathisers could not read her mind.

Christmas following was hardly a happy time, but she did her best: indulged Tilda and Danny with extra presents and a visit to the pantomime in Canterbury. (Gerald had left her more than comfortably off). Saskia wrote, asking her to bring the twins for New Year, but she declined. The journey would seem non-ending all the way from Kent to Hereford. They hadn't attended Gerald's funeral anyway, said Gethin could not get the time off work and the boys were poorly. Why should she make the trip there?

2

Maybe H should be number three. He was getting to be so tiresome: still acting like he was half his sixty years. Flamboyant and handsome – yes, still that, with his thick grey hair expertly cut, his smart-casual clothes and his charm. Oh yes, he could charm the ladies and display a unique confidence among men. H, her third husband for five years now. Not brutal like Carl, or bookish like Gerald: he was more like an aging poser who was beginning to bore her…

But he wouldn't be really, would he, be number three of her contrived eradication? Not if she was honest with herself. What about Tilda's unsavoury boyfriend? The one her daughter had met at Art College? Must be ten years ago now. Long hair, smelling of sweat, wearing scruffy clothes: had no ambition to get a job, and every other word was like or man in that twangy, nasal voice. He and his stupid dialogue had so irritated Delia when Tilda brought him home for the weekend. Definitely not the sort of young man she wanted in her daughter's life.

Damien had inadvertently devised his own death, should have stuck to smoking pot to give him his weird pleasures. Pity about the 'magic mushrooms'. Delia hadn't shown or told him where they grew. Well, maybe just a thrown remark about her walks in the woods and what strange little toadstools she had discovered one morning by the farm gate at the forest edge. Plus showing him the wrong page in her fungi book, which described very similar looking ones as edible.

The sky, on the morning Damien ate poison and died, she remembered, had been a clear azure sky, bright enough for him to see where the ominous little grey mushrooms grew on the edge of the woods. She had read it would only take two or three to prove fatal. Damien was greedy, wanted a free breakfast. He had grinned as he piled them onto his plate, with toast and huge blobs of tomato ketchup. Revolting... and manners to match.

Death by misadventure was the verdict, through his ingesting the tainted mushrooms. Renal failure happened rapidly, apparently. They told Delia, away from Tilda, that the boy had died very quickly. But as she held her weeping daughter by his bedside she had said, cuddling her daughter close, 'Poor lamb, he must have died in such agony, renal failure... dreadful way to die.'

Tilda had been inconsolable... well for six months. Then Michael came along. So much better for her, Delia thought. Such a lovely boy. And the perfect wedding a year later, with her brother Danny giving her away, and memories of Damien gone forever.   She had said on the day, 'How proud Daddy would have been of you all.'   Even managed to squeeze a single tear into her lace hankie as she cuddled her beautiful daughter and kissed her handsome son-in-law.   Such a pity that Tilda could not have children.   Still they might adopt one day… one day, and make her a doting granny.

Later there was Danny's flatmate in Highbury, a real gangrel.   She liked the old-fashioned word, loosely suggesting a villain or drifter.   Had discovered it in the history novel she was reading at the time.   Wasn't quite sure that it had anything to do with ganglions which was quite close to it in her dictionary, both words certainly sounded like morbid complaints.

Tim Cadwallader was undoubtedly a bad lot, a gangrel.   Not one she wanted Danny mixing with. Oh, he was charming all right; had that engaging smile that attracted you to him.   In the same way a moth is attracted to a flame, a trout to a lure, man to woman, woman to man. Delia did not think Danny's attraction to Tim Cadwallader and vice versa was a healthy one, or a natural one.   She did not want to accept that Danny might be gay.   Not that.   Not ever.

Tim would have to go.   It took a good deal of planning, of imagination and lots of false smiles when she visited them in their St Pauls Road flat just off Highbury Corner.

'Let me cook for you, Mrs Manning,' Tim said

when she visited. 'I'm pretty handy in the kitchen.' Poncey little toad, she thought. Vain too, 'pretty handy in the kitchen.' So? At least he wasn't camp, didn't don a frilly apron, walk in a mincing way, or talk effeminately. If anything, he was very manly, extremely handsome and muscular. She imagined he looked good in swimming trunks, like Tom Daley, the Olympic diver. Tim's very masculinity made her want to gag. What did that make Danny if Tim was the macho one? What part did he play in the relationship? Did she want her mind to travel that route? Not really, not ever, not at all. It made her shudder to think about their bedroom activities.

'But I want to take the two of you out,' she had insisted. 'Danny tells me there's a new Turkish restaurant opened in Upper Street. I'd like to try it.'

'You *will* like it, Mum,' said her son. She looked at him with love. He was such a soft, gentle soul, much softer than Tilda, his twin. 'Timmy and I went there last week. Great wasn't it - mate?'

Was he about to say love or darling? Did he change it to mate to spare his mother? She pushed away lewd thoughts of an all-male double bed (although there were two bedrooms), and the disgusting scenes that might be played there. She was adamant they go out, and the treat was on her. 'Besides, can't a mother indulge her handsome son occasionally?' she asked and added a little slowly, 'and his flatmate?' emphasising flatmate.

She was determined to delve into this young man's background, find out where he worked and what days of the week. Did he have a car? Unlikely in London; parking cost a packet unless you had your own driveway, which they didn't, only steps leading down to the pavement. To her questions Tim had answered, 'I go by tube, only three stops to my office.' He was a designer/draughtsman she had discovered. *Good, you can design your own demise.*

That evening she sat between them at the small, round table for three, hoping they could not, would not, touch each other under the table. She stretched out her legs, not very ladylike perhaps, (the sort of pose Ann Cleeves' detective, Vera Stanhope, might adopt) to prevent it happening. She played tennis with her eyes, trying to intercept any secret glances between them, any nuances that were supposed to go over her head. She could not, however, diminish the electricity or quash the chemistry. A thought occurred. Danny would not make her a grandmother if he was gay and Tim was his love buddy. It gave her a keen sense of loss and more than a modicum of anger. Yes, Tim would have to go, and soon. She could persuade Danny that it was just a passing phase, a sexual experiment. She imagined herself saying to him, 'Chrissakes, darling, we've all been there, seen that, got the t shirt etcetera. Heavens, I had a crush once myself.'

'Yeah, on the gym mistress I s'pose' would probably be his response. And she would deny this, invent a best friend that she had experimented with, lived with before she met Dad. The twins knew nothing about Carl, nothing about her life before Gerald.   It had simply never cropped up in conversation. Danny would not know whether she told the truth or a lie…

The food was good and the ambience very pleasant with lots of candles and tea lights everywhere: some hanging prettily from the ceiling, some in Turkish brass pots with star shaped holes where the light shone through. There was a rather pleasant variety of Middle Eastern music playing in the background and shouted orders in a language unknown to her. The lack of pleasure regarding the evening was only in her mind: well hidden, she hoped, from these two. She drank more than she had intended. Or did they deliberately get her inebriated? Was it planned so they could sleep together, make *lust*, while she snored away on the sofa bed?

3

She took the tray of tea and toast upstairs, left her memories downstairs.

'Hiya gorgeous,' H said. He was sitting up, bare-chested, the duvet pushed down to where his abdominal and pubic hairs began. For sixty, he continued to have an amazing physique and Delia wished she could still find him attractive. Well she did really, but five years of almost daily sex had left her bored with his love play, wanting a rest or a change. She didn't have anyone in mind, had not met someone, no secret lover or an assignation. Just bored with him. Time for a replacement maybe.

She smiled, manoeuvred the tray between the books and table lamp on his bedside table. 'There you go, tea and toast with marmalade.'

'Crumpet first or after?'

Again she smiled, but not with her eyes, walked round to her side of the bed, obediently slipped out of her nightdress and slid under the duvet. Best get it over with then she could return to her thoughts, her plans, and her strategy. I wonder if they would call me a serial killer, she thought. But each departure (she preferred that term to murder or killing or death) had been different. Surely serial killers employed the same *modus operandi,* or killed the same type? Her victims were certainly different, quite an eclectic variety really... interesting.

H crunched noisily on his toast and slurped the tea, eyeing her body as he did so. He licked his lips and replaced the mug and plate on the tray. 'Thanks sweetheart, that was lovely. Now,' he added. 'How about me eating you?'

Half an hour later she was standing in the bath, letting the shower wash away the last of H's sex from her body. She hummed a few tunes as the hot water targeted her skin with fiery needles. The songs were fragmented, unconnected, like the thoughts that trickled through her mind. She finally drifted back to Tim Cadwallader, the late Tim. Sad the way he went in the end. Under a tube train, Dan had told her in between his sobs. Hard to believe that such a macho guy could even contemplate suicide, let alone commit it. But she'd asked Danny that question anyway.

'No way, Mum. There's no way Tim would have committed suicide. We... he had so much to live for.'

She suggested he come home for a few days, at least until the coroner's court sitting. 'I'll come and fetch you if you like.'

'Let me think about it.' She could hear his sobs and yearned to hold her boy, cradle away his deep unhappiness. She herself had no sadness, only a quiet satisfaction.

The verdict had been an open one. Did he fall or was he pushed? CCTV was unclear. Because the platform was so crowded at that time of day, eight fifteen on a weekday morning, it was difficult to decide what, or even who, had caused the sudden surge of people towards the track. Delia had known of course, the crowded platform of mixed cultures and backgrounds, and costumes. Several Muslim women in burkas, at least four of them fully covered including the niqab, invisible except for their eyes. Delia had been one of the fully covered Muslim women, at least three people back from Tim. She had worn special contact lenses that changed her blue eyes to mid-eastern brown. And she had briefly stumbled, causing the others in front to stumble as well, in a forward direction, like dominoes. Tim had virtually flown onto the line, winged his way into a violent impact with the front of the train and under its grinding, screeching wheels. Perfect timing, messy death.

The line, of course, had been closed for several hours, the train evacuated of its shocked passengers, and the platform emptied except for police and ambulance personnel. Unseen by the CCTV cameras, a Muslim woman with her face covered by a niqab had left the station and walked to nearby public toilets. She was invisible to others in the ladies' room. It was London, few looked at anyone else in the big city. The forty-something lady who emerged from the cubicle, ten minutes later, toted a large carrier bag decorated with the logo of an expensive store. She wore a light coloured coat, neutral coloured shoes, dark glasses and a fairly large straw hat that covered much of her face. If she had been stopped and questioned she would have denied being in Highbury Station, certainly not on that particular platform, where the tragedy had taken place. The contents of her bag might have taken some explaining... but no-one could have said differently about her being down there, or the cameras catching her in their lenses.

Leaving the area of the station behind and walking towards Upper Street, she decided to travel by road to Victoria and hailed a cab. When she was set down outside the station, she took a train to northeast Kent. She had discarded her carrier bag in a skip before hailing the cab. It would seem the burka, folded inside the carrier bag, stood an excellent chance of not being discovered, more likely lost within the pile of rubble being thrown on top of it from the premises that builders were renovating. She had previously cut the niqab into pieces and flushed it down the toilet.

Her coat was reversible. After half an hour, she moved along the train through to another carriage, and turned the coat inside-out in the cramped toilet. The hat she threw out of a window between carriages, and her sunglasses she tucked into the clutch purse that she had secreted in a pocket of her coat. She fluffed and readjusted her hair. If anyone had seen her on the train, they would only have had a full view of her face from Faversham, a town she often visited. No one would know she had been to London. On her way out from Birchington she had alighted from the very early morning London-bound train at Faversham, visited the toilets, and a Muslim woman, fully enclosed in a black burka and niqab had emerged and gone to the ticket office with a badly written note that said *London Victoria* return on it. She nodded her voiceless thanks at the ticket clerk, paid cash and walked back onto the platform to 'begin' her journey... to London.

Hours later, when Delia finally got back to Birchington, she relinquished her return ticket from Faversham, walked over the bridge to her house, found her front-door key in the clutch purse, walked through to her kitchen, and switched on the radio: just in time to listen to the lunchtime news.

'A man died this morning in Highbury tube station. Apparently, he fell off the platform into the path of an oncoming train. The station was closed for several hours while the ambulance and police services retrieved his body. The Police say they are examining CCTV coverage of the platform. Carnegie Farrow, the train driver, was taken to the

Whittington Hospital and treated for shock.'

Delia smiled and made herself a nice cup of tea... Later, months later, Danny met Ray, lovely Ray with his floppy, blonde hair, his sunny smile and endearing lisp. By this time Delia had come to terms with Danny's sexual preference. There were one or two partners before Ray, men she preferred not to meet. She was right too, they had not lasted long. Just as well for them, moving on before she made a terminal judgement on *them*. She would not harm Ray, or wish harm to him. Her Danny was happy again.

Six months later, she married Henry Oliver Fontaine, known universally as H. But not before she had a short dalliance with Caius Hennessey: a very short dalliance. Caius, who she met at the art class that she had recently joined in Margate. A man who fascinated her the first time she was introduced to him. She was intrigued by the island of calm that seemed to surround him. When she set her easel next to his it was as if she was drawn in by this peace, and she became conscious of a tranquillity that was pleasant if slightly puzzling to her. He was, she discovered, an ex-priest who had discarded his black soutane but kept his God. He dressed more colourfully than when he had worn the priestly clothes, preferring purple corduroy trousers and pink shirts with colourful neck ties.

Did he excite her sexually? She wasn't sure. She was attracted to his soft Irish brogue and the way he phrased his remarks. 'Would you know it, I've created a cloud dabbling my fingers on the canvass.' He pronounced *I've* almost like *Oive*. His blue eyes, gazing occasionally at her during class, seemed to pierce her thoughts, laying them bare for him to interpret. Strangely, this didn't make her feel uncomfortable: if anything it added a frisson of excitement. About three weeks into the art classes, Caius asked her out to dinner, to a restaurant she had not heard of, near the Cliftonville end of Margate.

'We'll walk there if you like,' he said. 'And leave our cars here at the college. It's not far.' And he grinned. 'It'll give us the appetite, don't you think?'

She wondered which appetite he meant. It had been a long time since she had thought about sex, or sampled it. Gerald had been dead now well over ten years, and bringing up the twins had shed any thoughts of a relationship outside motherhood. Perhaps she was being a bit ahead of herself. Maybe Caius, yes very probably, was referring to their stomachs and not lower down their bodies.

'Fine by me, I like walking.'

He slipped his hand into hers quite naturally, as if they had been friends for years. They chatted easily. About the art classes and their fellow would be painters. About the fearsome tutor, a Norwegian lady called Ingeborg.

'I swear she owns a Viking helmet complete with horns,' he said and laughed. He asked her gentle questions about her life and she told him about Gerald, and widowhood, and bringing up the twins. She neglected to mention Tilda's first boyfriend, Damien, or Danny's friend Tim, only to say that both her children were happily married.

'And you?' she asked. 'Have you any family?'

'A sister and a brother back in the old country, Ireland, if you haven't already identified my accent,' he grinned as he spoke, displaying brilliant white teeth. 'They're both married with large families, so plenty of nieces' and nephews' birthdays to remember.'

She was about to ask him whether he had children of his own, until she remembered he'd been in the priesthood for most of his adult life. Reaching the little restaurant precluded any more in-depth conversation, which, she supposed, was just as well. Caius held open the pale blue-painted door for her to be transported into a typically Greek environment with hanging vines, marble statues and soft, tinkling background music. A little man, with a ring of black hair and wearing a white tuxedo, greeted them with 'Kalispera' and swept them to a table in the corner of the room. He greeted Caius with a handshake and a beaming smile that included her as well.

'Your coat, kyria?' She looked slightly puzzled until Caius whispered to her, 'It means madam.'

When they were seated, and a bottle of Thymiopoulos opened and poured for them, they studied the menu.

'Heaven and earth,' he said.

'What?'

'It means heaven and earth – Thymiopoulos.'

'Mmn, nice name. Hope it tastes heavenly.' She sniffed her glass. 'Smells good, anyway.' And, 'Yep, it tastes good. Don't know about heavenly: that's more your department.'

He smiled, crinkling his very attractive blue eyes. 'Not anymore. I spend more time painting nowadays than praying. Besides,' he added. 'I think the name refers to the mythical Greek heaven of their legends, when gods like Zeus ruled the Earth.

She enjoyed the food and the conversation in addition to the wine, and was not completely surprised when the evening finished in Caius' modest flat, above a florist near the old Nayland Rock Hotel, and in his bed until breakfast time.

The lovemaking had been a revelation. So long since her body had been subjected to such pleasant attention, it was only practicality that sent her home after breakfast. She needed a shower and fresh clothes, and time to digest a new relationship after so many years.

He kissed her goodbye on the doorstep. 'Will I see you again soon?'

She considered the question. 'Before next week's

art class, or during?'

He grinned as the sea breeze whipped his hair. 'I'd prefer it to be sooner. How about later on? Or tomorrow, or the next day?'

'You're a swift worker, Mr Hennessey. I don't think my feet have touched the ground yet.'

'Then stay in the air until I catch you.' He played with her hair, stroked her cheek, until they kissed a final goodbye. And that was exactly that, a final goodbye. The art classes were suddenly cancelled for no apparent reason. At least, no apologetic explanation was given when they each received letters informing them of the cancellation. To add to this disappointment, Cordelia realised she had not given Caius her address or phone number and she did not have his. Something held her back from going to his flat and, as the days passed, he all but faded from her mind. Especially as she met H soon after and, in next to no time, became Mrs Fontaine...

4

Delia made a serious decision. This had to be her last undertaking. She was running out of ideas for 'untouched departures'. First, Carl's throat being cut by an unknown assailant, then Gerald's unfortunate and fatal pneumonia, Damien's deadly mushrooms, and Tim's terrible train accident. All these distant history now, but memories of them could still be dredged up and relived as if they had happened yesterday.

For the past month, she had sat up in bed reading Ann Cleeves, Ian Rankin, and the extremely violent Stuart MacBride books. But they were of no use, all having clever detectives: Rankin with Rebus, MacBride with Logan McRae, and Cleeves with Vera Stanhope. Poor Vera, with her bare legs and her eczema, stomping about highlands, lowlands and moorland, in sandals. Delia admired her tremendously for her toughness and fortitude, just wished she and the two male detectives would occasionally let someone commit the perfect murder. Not that she wanted to *commit murder*. Good Lord no… *untouched departure* was her forte. Only she was running out of departures, or ideas and the modus operandi for them.

During this past month she had risen, made coffee, tea, toast, gone back to bed for the dutiful sex, and what she secretly described as H's half hour. She had seen him roll over afterwards and climb out of bed, making first for the bathroom to have his shower, then hear him pad downstairs and go into the little back room behind the lounge that served as his office. There he would pick up the phone, do an hour or so of City dealing. Sometimes, if he left the door open, she could hear him shout 'Buy' or 'Sell'. Whatever he was instructing the person at the other end of the phone to do seemed to bring in an agreeably acceptable income.

She would doze, for perhaps half an hour, then get up and go downstairs. After his brief City dealing, H would get changed into his fishing clothes, waders and a waxed jacket. If it was cold he wore thermal long johns and a long-sleeved vest, thick woollen socks, fingerless gloves, and a military-style bush hat. Next he would load his rod bag and fishing box into the back of the car, while she prepared sandwiches and a thermos of coffee for him.

'Be back in…' he would glance at his watch, 'about three hours.' A quick kiss and he was out of the door and into the car, his work done and her – as he often put it – dutifully serviced.

During those hours of H's fishing time, Delia washed

up the breakfast things, filled the washing machine, did a little ironing, and vacuumed the lounge that used to be the shop she and Gerald had opened: where they sold antiquarian books and items of family history. She had closed the shop upon his death, choosing instead to devote her time to bringing up the twins on Gerald's considerable life insurance.

She watered the houseplants, made a shopping list, half-planned lunch and dinner, and thought about this, her fifth and – hopefully - final untouched departure.

There would be time for a shower after the housework. Time, also, to continue her plan of action. Pity H wasn't a diabetic. She had heard that you could overdose on insulin and die quite easily. He had mild blood pressure, so did most men of his age, women too she supposed. She wouldn't know: visits to the doctor were not in her remit.

Sometime later, she was busy towelling herself down after her shower when the doorbell rang. Whoever was there would have to wait. Annoyed, she wrapped herself into her towel robe, slipped on fluffy mules and almost stomped downstairs as the doorbell rang again: an insistent ring, as if whoever was there was not going away. Delia virtually yanked open the door and said 'Yes?' with an aggression that nobody knew she possessed. Her mouth fell open, Denzel Black, her next-door neighbour stood there, his arm protectively supporting H.

'Sorry to disturb you, Delia, found H when I was walking the dog down Minnis Bay. He collapsed. Couldn't move, could you mate?'

H gave a sick smile; his face had taken on an unhealthy reddish tinge.

'Come in, come in,' she said, and held the door open wide. She took hold of H's other arm, hoping her robe would not fall open, and guided him towards the leather sofa. 'Sit down, darling.' She took off his jacket and her next door neighbour helped divest H of his waders. She then left him with Dez while she ran upstairs, to fetch a duvet from the spare bedroom, hurried downstairs again and covered her husband, tucking the duvet round him. She examined his face and turned to her neighbour, 'What happened exactly?'

Denzel shook his head. 'Dunno really.' He left H to explain, pulled the dog closer to him and told it to sit.

Delia turned to her husband. 'What happened?'

'Don't really know, one minute I was feeling all right, the next I felt dizzy and fell down.' He touched his leg under the duvet. 'Think I cut myself, or grazed it or something, probably on those rusty old railings.'

She pulled back the duvet, swallowed. 'Mm... you've grazed your knee. Don't know how you managed that under those wader things.   I'll get something to wipe it.'

'Hope they're not torn. Are they?'

'I'll have a look in a minute.'

Denzel hovered. 'Anything I can do?'

'No, you're fine.   Thank you so much for bringing him home.' It was a dismissal and he gladly took the hint, backed out of the room towards the front door, pulling the dog with him.

'Yeah, well let me know if we can help... Jess and me.' He threw H's car keys onto a small side table, making Delia wince, and said, 'I drove the car back, it's parked outside.'   He gave an awkward salute and shut the door behind him. Delia was glad when he left and took his aging pooch with him. She wasn't really into dogs, thought they were smelly creatures, and left their hairs everywhere...

'Shall I get you some tea? Coffee?' she asked and added, 'Perhaps I ought to ring the doctor?'

'No, don't do that love. I'll be ok. Coffee would be good, black, one sugar.'

As if I don't know how you take it, she thought. She smiled, one that did not reach her eyes.

'Coffee coming up... d'you want a biscuit with it?'

'No thanks, just the coffee.' He stuck his injured leg out. 'And maybe a plaster for this knee.'

She looked at it again, now it was cleaner, paled slightly and hesitated. 'It'll need more than a plaster, that's quite a deep cut. Plus you've taken the skin off your shin, several layers I would think... all that ancient pipe-ware down there on the front.' She made to move off. 'I'll get another bowl of water and bathe it properly. You don't want any dirt to get in there.'

H's knee healed, eventually, though it took over three weeks and the same number of stitches before it looked anything like normal. His shin, however, developed an ulcer. Delia had seen ulcers before, on her father's leg before he died. Weeks and months they were there, never healing, weeping a disgusting ooze, and spreading if anything. She had once stayed in the room while the nurse dressed it and had almost gagged at the sight and smell of it. She hoped she would not have to dress H's leg.

Having these injuries seemed to age him; he had always been too macho for long-standing illnesses or injuries. The weeping ulcer seemed to drain the strength from him. He took to lying on the sofa, watching daytime television, limping about and generally getting in her way. She had laundered his thermal underwear the day after his fall and put it away in his chest of drawers, and there it stayed. Fishing was no longer the all-consuming hobby it had been. She was sure he did not even do much of his telephone dealing any more, lounged about instead in baggy tracksuit bottoms, with every other plea seeming to be for coffee, tea or a beer. After a while, Delia lost patience, 'for God's sake H, get up off your backside and make one for me for a change.'

He looked at her in complete shock.

'Well, sorry for causing you so much work, I only asked for a bloody cup of tea. Not too much is it?' He struggled off the sofa and limped towards the kitchen. 'Right, one cup of tea coming up.'

She listened to him banging about. Bad tempered sod. At least he didn't frighten her, not like Carl had. Something fell and smashed. She hoped it wasn't in pieces all over the floor. He swore and continued slamming things onto the work surface.

'Forget it,' she shouted. She went through to the hallway and slipped into her coat. 'I'm going out.'

H poked his angry head out of the kitchen door. 'Where are you going?'

'Out I said.' She did not wait for his reply. Let him stew for a while.

The door slammed viciously behind her. So what? She strode over the railway bridge, past low-bricked garden walls where daffodils waved in the breeze and down the slope towards the promenade. The wind blew up from the sea and tossed hawthorn and apple blossom from the trees, putting her in mind of paper flaking over a fire. It whipped her hair and encouraged flying salt spray to reach beyond the promenade, and even before she reached that wide walkway, it stung her eyes. Oh God, she was mad, angry mad, not insane mad. Or maybe she was a bit of both.

After perhaps half a mile of this livid striding, she calmed down. But not completely. A hundred mile walk and maybe she'd be all sweetness and light again. Hmm. She watched a few wispy clouds trot their way sedately over an otherwise blue sky and began to chant to herself, 'I walked and I walked and what did I see?' just like the schoolbooks that once taught you to read. 'I saw an aeroplane and it saw me.' Nonsense drivel: how could that little silver dart with its vapour trail up there possibly see her? Come to think of it, how many five year olds would recognise a word like aeroplane?

A low-flying seagull almost zapped her, causing her to duck. Must be breeding time. They did that if you got too close to their eggs, impossibly niched as their nests were up there in the chalk cliff. Delia didn't like seagulls: she shuddered, imagined their unleashed power if they collectively decided to attack the human inhabitants of the coastline.

Alfred Hitchcock knew the power of birds. Didn't he make a horror film about them years ago? She relinquished the concrete coastal walk to the gulls, climbed up a slope between the chalk cliffs and made her way slowly back over the daisy-filled meadow above them, felt the grass crunch under her boots.

The gulls were still there, screaming to each other, waiting for the mackerel to come in on the next tide she thought. That's what H did, waited for the maelstrom on the sea's surface that indicated a shoal was incoming. Only this time the gulls would have them all. H was not fishing, neither, it seemed, were any other anglers, his fishing buddies as H called them.

Delia had calmed down now. She felt hungry after her angry walk. A glance at her watch told her it was twenty to one. Perfect. Her mind went into catering mode. What would she decide for lunch? Something quick and easy for sure. Cheese and tomatoes on toast; the cheese grated, mixed with beaten egg and Worcestershire sauce, maybe a pinch of chilli flakes to give it extra zip, and thinly slice one of those delicious beef tomatoes. A shake of pepper, under the grill on toast and bingo, lunch. She would plan a more substantial dinner once she had eaten. And fed the brute.

H was in a drunken sleep when she arrived home. She guessed something was not quite right as she let herself in the front door. Music was blaring from the radio, too loud to appreciate what was being played. And she could smell strong alcohol, beer or scotch, as soon as she entered the lounge. H was laid out on the sofa, one leg sprawled along its length and the other, the bad one, dangled untidily over the sofa edge with his bandage hanging loose. She shuddered, totally unwilling to remove the bandage and replace it with a clean one; hated the idea of putting on a new dressing and seeing the oozing, malodorous substance.

H was snoring and dribble trickled down the corner of his mouth onto his chin then to his bare chest. She switched off the radio and shuddered again. Just look at you, she thought. You're getting fat H, getting a belly on you. She almost wished he would swallow his own vomit and choke to death. Not going to happen, he hadn't been sick and probably wouldn't. He stirred, opened red-rimmed eyes.

'Oh, you're back.' He sat up, and scratched his bare stomach. 'Your kid called.'

'Which one?'

'Erm, dunno. The girl or the boy/girl, hard to say.'

He really could be so nasty lately, all adding to her growing dislike of him.

'That's a bit below the belt, even for you.'

He spread out his hands. 'Ok, ok, so it was Danny Boy.'

'Did he say what he called for?'

H shook his head, slowly. Chewed his lips, ran his tongue over his teeth. 'No.'

'Well did he leave a message?' She was nettled

by now.

'Like I said, no.' He added, 'what's for lunch, I'm starving?'

'Champagne and fucking caviar. What d'you think's for lunch.' She even shocked herself, she wasn't really given to strong swearing. It's what he's doing to me lately, she thought.

'All right, all right, don't twist your knicker-elastic: wrong time of the month is it?'

He stopped scratching his stomach and fingered the bristles around his chin, sniffed and pulled a face. 'Enjoy your walk?'

She barely nodded and walked through to the kitchen, discarding her coat en route. 'Your mate Manda called as well, said she'd call you back this afternoon,' he shouted to her retreating back.

Manda, her one and only friend from Carl days. One who had despised him as much as she did. Manda knew about the beatings, knew her friend's fear. She was delighted when Carl died. Well-deserved she had said at the time. Whether she guessed his death had been contrived or planned, Delia never fathomed. It was something not discussed between them. The subject of Carl was dropped forever. Besides, they had both moved on, Manda to the Midlands to a job in television and herself and Gerald to Kent. They kept in touch, birthday and Christmas cards, presents for the twins, and the occasional phone call to her. Manda had come down briefly for Gerald's funeral, comforting her friend and cuddling the twins who were her god-children, but visits were few and far between. Delia wondered about the phone call. Unlike Manda to ring out of the blue.

Ten minutes later she took H's food through on a tray, quite happy to eat on her own in the kitchen.

'Any tea going?' he shouted. Sure you don't mean scotch or beer, she thought, and switched on the kettle. She looked forward to having a long chat with Manda, also wondered about Danny's call. Maybe she ought to ring him first. Hoped nothing was wrong between him and Ray.

A few minutes later the phone rang. She wiped away toast crumbs from the corner of her mouth before answering it. Danny. 'Hi darling, how are you?'

'I'm fine Mum, you? You sound a bit fed up. Anything wrong?' Trust Danny to pick up on her vibes.

'I'm fine son, honestly. How about you?'

'Yeah, I'm good, we're both good. Listen,' he added. 'I want to run something past you.'

Delia raised her eyebrows to the window opposite. 'Oh… what's that?'

'Ray and I are getting married,' he paused. 'Would you be ok with that?'

'Darling, that's wonderful news. When? Where?'

'Sometime soon. Where? Shropshire, at Ray's parents' home.'

She sighed. 'Well, it all sounds very exciting. Whereabouts in Shropshire?'

'Place called Ironbridge, near it anyway.'

'Yes, I know it, lots of museums there... Are Ray's folk pleased?'

'Yeah, they're fine about it… us.' He paused. 'D'you think H will come?'

She answered very quickly. 'Oh, I doubt it. He doesn't like travelling too far, especially since he hurt his leg.'

'Right,' there was obvious relief in her son's voice. 'How is he by the way? He sounded kind of… tired.'

'He probably was asleep, does a lot of that lately.'

'Right… oh, and we're thinking of adopting as well. Sorry, gotta go Mum, there's an international call coming in. Speak later. Love you.'

Delia made herself a cup of coffee and sat with it at the kitchen table, a smile on her face. Mother-in-law and grandmother-to-be, all from one phone call. She began to plan her outfit for the big day, then endless trips to 'Welcome to the World' babies' and toddlers' shop. Upmarket of course, it would cost her a fortune. But so worth it to cuddle a baby granddaughter or grandson.

Would they continue to live in London? They

ran their business from home, so she supposed they could relocate out to leafier suburbs. She smiled, seeing them both hands-on daddies. Or would it be Mummy and Daddy? She wasn't quite sure how these things worked.

The phone rang again, breaking into her musing.

'Delia speaking.'

'Hi sweetie. Manda.'

'Hi darling. Lovely to hear from you. Sorry I was out when you rang.'

'No probs, I had a brief flirtation with the gorgeous hunk. Sounded a bit pissed actually.'

'Probably was. We had a row and I stormed out.'

'Oh dear… honeymoon over?' Manda said and laughed.

'After five years? I think so.'

'Told me he has an injured knee, what's he been up to?'

'He fell over by the seafront, ages ago. It's healed up now. But he's got a leg ulcer that won't clear up.'

'Yuk! Horrible things. Poor him. Poor you… you don't have to dress it do you?'

'No thanks. A nurse comes in twice a week to do that. He's aged though, Manda,' she lowered her voice. 'More like seventy than sixty nowadays. *And* he's drinking more than he should… Anyway, nuff of H. Guess what? Danny and Ray are getting married.'

'Wow. When?'

'This summer in Shropshire, at Ray's parents' place. *And* they're thinking of adopting. You'll be there won't you?'

'Wouldn't miss it for the world. My godson's wedding. Not far from me, Shropshire. Whereabouts?'

'Ironbridge.'

'About thirty-five miles.'

'Great.'

'How's Tilda and Mike?' asked Manda.

'Yes, they're fine, off on holiday soon, climbing in the Lake District.'

'Mad pair. Wonder what she'll make of Danny adopting? Think it'll encourage her and Mike to consider it?'

'Don't know. She doesn't seem keen on babies. Quite happy with those two crazy Dalmatians and that bloody parrot.'

Manda giggled. 'What, the lovely Laura?'

'The very same. Can't stand the vicious sod, bit me once cos I wouldn't share a biscuit with her.'

'Pecked.'

'What?'

'Birds peck not bite.'

'Yeah, whatever.'

They chatted for another ten minutes, promised to meet up before the wedding, plan outfits and wedding gifts, until H called from the lounge.

'Any more tea going?'

Delia said a swift goodbye to her friend. 'I'll put the kettle on,' she shouted through. Then realised she hadn't asked her friend the reason for her phone call. She took H tea and a slice of fruit cake and picked up his lunch tray.

'What did the delicious Manda Panda want?'

'Just a catch up I think, didn't mention any particular reason. By the way,' she added. 'Got some news for you, Danny and Ray are getting married.'

He sat up. 'They're what?'

'Getting married. Up in Shropshire at Ray's parents' home.'

'How can two blokes get married?'

'Quite easily nowadays. Remember? We're in the twenty-first century now.'

'Hmm. When? The wedding, I mean.'

'This summer... they're thinking of adopting too.'

'That's nice for you, Granny at last.' She heard the sarcasm in his voice, noted he did not include himself as Grandfather. She knew H looked down on Danny's homosexuality, would probably never accept it. Well, tough. Neither had she a long time ago. Best not to think of that now.

'I don't suppose you'll make it to the wedding?'

'No, don't suppose I will. Did you want me to?

Delia did not answer. She almost regretted the way things were going wrong for herself and H, but could not think of a solution, had no idea how to turn things round, get back to a civilised relationship. Deep down she was not sure she wanted to. For a brief and unexpected moment she thought of Caius Hennessey and wondered what he was doing nowadays... If he had achieved the fame he sought, then remembered something she'd read about him being hung in The Turner Contemporary, near Margate harbour. Perhaps she could go and see some of his paintings: might even bump into Caius... She returned to the present.

'Manda's going,' she said. 'It's not that far from where she lives.'

'Mm. She's his godmother isn't she?'

'Yeah... it'll be good to catch up with her. Haven't seen her in ages.' Too busy pandering to you, she thought.

'What's the time?'

These kind of questions always threw her. Chrissakes, there was a clock only feet away from him. She looked pointedly at it and back to him. 'Two forty five, or quarter to three or even fourteen forty-five hours, whichever suits you.'

'Why are you so bitchy lately... starting the menopause or something?'

She shook her head, sighed. You really do have to go H, she thought.

5

Before it could happen, before she could plan his demise, his untouched departure, there was the arranging of a meet up with Manda prior to Danny and Ray's wedding. Delia smiled to herself, her bad mood temporarily dispelled, thinking of wedding gifts and outfits. She must get in touch with Tilda too. Oh, everything was suddenly exciting, things to look forward to. H disturbed her musing as he padded into the kitchen, tracksuit bottoms sitting somewhere under his newly acquired flabby stomach. He had a three-day growth and bad breath. Even at this distance, with the table between them, she could smell it. He, surprisingly, had brought in his empty mug and plate, ambled to the sink and plonked them on the draining board.

'You put any beers in the fridge?'

She thought 'please' wouldn't go amiss, or 'darling'. 'No, d'you want me to?'

'It's all right, I'm here now. I'll do it myself,' he said and limped out to the utility room where his crates were kept.

Big deal, she thought as she heard the clink of the bottles. She went back to her planning. The phone rang again. Tilda this time. 'What d'you think Mum? Great news isn't it?'

She realised her daughter was talking about the wedding.

'Yes, it's wonderful, exciting... and a bit unusual too.'

Tilda laughed. 'I know what you mean. It'll be the first same-sex wedding Mike and I will have been to. Do you know Ray's parents? Have you met them?'

'No, hope to see them before the wedding though, I'm meeting up with your godmother beforehand. We're going shopping together for outfits and presents. Any ideas about what to give them?'

'I think...' As Tilda paused Delia imagined her chewing on her lower lip, just like Gerald used to. 'They would prefer travel tokens, something like that. They're planning a trip to Las Vegas for their honeymoon. Besides they've got everything home-wise.'

Delia contemplated. 'Good thinking, I could get them some US dollars.'

'Yeah, why not?'

H continued stacking the fridge in his usual noisy way with several beers.

'What the hell is that?'

'It's H feeding the fridge with... beer.'

'Oh right.' Tilda paused. 'How is he, by the way?'

'Still breathing.'   She whispered it quietly into the phone.

Her daughter giggled.   'Don't suppose he'll make it to Shropshire.'

'No way.'   *Hope he won't make it to anywhere, definitely not if I have my way.*

They talked a little while longer, until H made it impossible for her to concentrate on her conversation.   'Best go, I'll call you soon, sweetie. Love to Mike.'   She sent kisses down the phone before putting it back on its cradle.

'Tilda?' asked H.

She nodded.

'How is the dear girl? Still in love with her dotty Dalmatians?'

'I expect so. We didn't mention them actually, we were talking about Danny's wedding.'

H grinned and started to hum "*Here comes the bride*". 'Wonder which one is the bride and which one the groom?'

She did her best to ignore his sarcasm, but added it to his growing list of faults... so many plans to be made, some good, some better.

'Why don't you answer me, bitch?'

She jumped, and shivered as she remembered Carl's violence those years ago. 'I didn't hear you.'

'I said... I need more beers and can you get me some when you next go shopping?'

'No *please* then?'

'Oh for fuck sake, don't be so fucking precious.'

She shrank back as he limped towards her, an uncapped bottle in his hand. She could scarcely believe what happened next: how he threw the bottle across the room, how it thudded as it hit her chair before smashing to pieces. The amber liquid was silent as it spread across the floor. He was silent too.

'I'll get a cloth,' she said. Not a word of reproach or anger. At the sink she rinsed a floor cloth under the running tap, squeezed it damp dry. H was picking up pieces of broken glass.

'Careful,' she warned, 'I'll sweep it up into the dustpan.'

He muttered something like 'Sorry, I shouldn't have done that.'

'No,' she said. 'You shouldn't.' She knew he watched her as she crouched and swept up the pieces, then mopped the floor dry. She wiped more beer from the chair leg before standing up and carrying the dustpan over to the bin and emptying the broken pieces into it.

'Shouldn't you have put that into newspaper or something?'

She laughed. 'Of course. Perhaps you'd like to take the stuff out and wrap it. *You* broke it.'

He held his hands palm up. 'Ok, ok.' He stood there looking at her. 'I've said I'm sorry. What d'you want me to do? Grovel?'

She took a deep breath, and turned away.

'Forget it…'

The next morning Delia once again sat up in bed. Again she drank coffee while H snored by her side. She was reading, without much enthusiasm, her latest crime novel. One that seemed to drag rather than flow. She yawned, paused in her reading and glanced up at the clock, on the bookshelf above the chest of drawers. Their bed faced two large sash windows that overlooked the garden, and the chest of drawers rested against the wall, midway between these two. They were heavy, Victorian windows and she often wondered how easy it would be to lift them open in the event of a fire. Or what damage they would inflict if someone's head was resting on the sill as they came crashing down with the swiftness of a guillotine. Best not think about it… although?

It was barely daylight outside. She guessed, even before she had looked at the clock, that it was about five thirty. A moment's irritation crossed her face, the clock's hands showed six thirty-five. Wrong. That bloody hour hand must be slipping again. She had tried pressing the two hands together under the central fastener. No good, it hadn't worked. The other night she awoke about three to go to the lavatory and the clock said six. So confusing and annoying, especially in the small hours.

It would have to go. The clock… and him. She put down the book that was boring her. Drank the rest of her coffee. Decided to go downstairs and make a second cup. It always tasted better than the first, she thought. Had no idea why.

She twisted round in the bed, put her feet on the floor and felt her way into her slippers. She shrugged into her dressing gown, shivered slightly in the chill morning air. The central heating wouldn't kick in for another half hour. She yawned again and felt pressure from her bladder. Best to go to the loo up here. Time she got downstairs, and walked through the kitchen to the downstairs lavatory, she'd be near to bursting.

Taking her coffee cup, she left it outside the toilet door while she went in to relieve herself. Then moved next door to the bathroom to wash her hands. Another thing to add to her annoyance. Why, when whoever had designed this separate toilet, had they not put a washbasin in there? All these petty aggravations, broken clock, boring book, bad designing... was it going to be one of those days? Very probably: it seemed her life was full of stupid problems, beginning and ending with H.

Yes, he would have to go. But how?

6

Six months later, her wish was granted. H died, very quickly in the end. A brain tumour, which was exacerbated and his death accelerated, after a terrible fall from the cliff top above his favourite fishing spot. Though why he was there, in the middle of the night, no-one quite knew. The doctors suggested a confusion. Cordelia told them that he had lately taken to sleepwalking and they accepted it could well have been his muddled mind.

But it was neither sleepwalking nor disorientation that caused H to walk over a midnight meadow towards the cliff edge. It had more to do with the alcohol she fed him in the guise of a particularly rich and tasty boeuf bourguignon.

'You're doing so well, darling,' she had told him that night. 'I know those silly old doctors said you mustn't drink at all, but I'm sure one glass of this excellent burgundy won't hurt.'

'You spoil me, sweetheart.' She ignored his ravaged face, saw instead something of his old roguish smile as they clinked glasses. 'These are good looking,' he added as he admired the extra-large goblets she poured the wine into.

'Mmn, yes. Got them in House of Glass, that

new shop in the High Street. Arm and a leg price but... different. Lovely quality.'

She neglected to point out that one glass, generously filled, held over 250ml or one third of a bottle. Or that she poured her own wine into a modest third of her goblet. In the end she poured him another and urged him to drink up, especially when she saw his eyes begin to droop. After dinner she allowed him a nap in front of the television then woke him and suggested, 'I think a little walk before bedtime might be good for both of us: just a quick stroll, down to the front and back. You can have a crafty puff on one of your cheroots then.' She gave him a wicked grin. 'Won't get much going down into your lungs in that breeze.' She hoped, though, it would further damage his brain.

He stumbled against her as they stepped onto the parking area outside the front door.

'Steady,' she whispered, and giggled as silently as she could. He managed a lopsided grin and she held his hand as they limped slowly over the railway bridge and down past the avenue of darkened houses on their way to the sea front, where distant lights of ships crossed the horizon.

'Why aren't we going down there?' He pointed down to the promenade below the cliff edge where they were standing. He was frowning and she could see, despite the darkness that surrounded them, a childish, crumpled look on his face. One or two ships winked their lights at them.

'Tide's in,' she said. 'Don't want to get soaked, do we?'

The bungalows edging the meadow where they stood were all in darkness. She knew the street lamps that sent a little light their way would also soon be extinguished. Council frugality on the street they called Bungalow City, where the average age of the residents, H had often declared, had to be nearer eighty than seventy. He branded them the wrinklies brigade, or the crumblies.

One push and he would become a crumbly.

Afterwards she worked her way down steps cut into the cliffs until she reached him. He lay still, yet she suspected he was still alive. Damn! Not to worry, she told herself, a night in that chill air would more than likely kill him off. Or maybe the high tide would wash him over the edge and, like Luca Brasi in *The Godfather*, he could sleep with the fishes?

Delia hurried back alone to the house, undressed and crept quickly into bed and, just as quickly, fell asleep. H was found a few hours later by an early morning dog walker who called for an ambulance on his mobile. He was identified by the hospital staff who had recently treated him for his brain tumour and they rang Delia. She answered in what she thought to be a suitably sleepy voice.

'Yes, who is it?' Then feigned surprise, shock

and horror; told them she would get there immediately and no, she had no idea how her husband should be where he was when the early morning walker found him. But she did mention his increasing confusion of late. Within minutes of the phone call she was dressed and on her way to the hospital, driving like a maniac, headlights on full beam and easily breaking the speed limit. She was hoping to be stopped by the police so she could plead with them about H's terrible accident and her need to be by his side. Not a police car in sight... Delia arrived at the hospital in record time.

Seven a.m. next morning. A vertical beam of sunlight shone directly onto her face. She moved to one side to avoid its blinding gleam. Like her sense of smell and sensitive hearing, she needed her sight. Could not imagine – with a shudder – ever being without these vital sensory powers. Or a sense of touch, freedom of movement. She thought of H imprisoned in his dying body, shackled to tubes and transfusion paraphernalia, bandages and an iron hospital bed. Lying there, in a shared ward of seven other like beds, with swishing curtains, uniform bedside lockers, and gliding, efficient nurses to refill water carafes, answer the dangling bells and bring disposable bedpans, penis-shaped bottles or boxes of tissues.

H, a prisoner in his own body, captive to the

murderous tumour in his brain. No humour, no pleasure left in his life, only pain with brief morphine-filled respites. And visits from her, cloaked with crooning, soothing words and gentle kisses on his poor damaged head.

Why did he have to go out that night? To the cliff's edge of all places? What confusion made him leave their warm bed, beside her sleeping form, and stumble over the edge to the harsh, unbending concrete walk below? Or had she told anyone that he slept in a bed downstairs now? *Must be careful, Delia, you don't want to contradict yourself.*

He died two days later, with her at his bedside, squeezing his hand, the one with the cannula in it, and spilling her tears as she saw the sac that held the dark red blood suspended above his bed, and his poor bandaged head.

'I'm here darling,' she whispered. 'I'll hold your hand as long as you need me.' She chose not to see the pain in his eyes, squeezed his hand a little tighter. He tried to cry out but had reached that final weakness when no sound could be made. He tried to slip his hand out of her strong grip. Only then did she glance down and seemed to become aware that it was the hand that had the cannula in it; the withered thin-skinned hand that was feeding him the vital red fluid.

She shifted swiftly on the bed. 'Oh sweetie, I'm so sorry. Did I hurt you? I wouldn't do that for all the world.' She quickly reached for his other hand, the one that kept stroking the sheet covering his ravaged body. He appeared to be trying to pleat it, the sheet. She remembered Gerald had done that the night before he died. Was it a death thing? Or just a coincidence?

'Shall I call a nurse? Did I hurt your hand?' Again she apologised, leaned over and gave him a tender kiss on his forehead. There was a distinct and unpleasant smell of sickness emanating from his body and she forced herself not to gag. H shook his head slowly from side to side. His good hand weakly gripped hers as he attempted a half smile. 'No nurse. Just you, Deelie. Love you.' He licked his poor cracked lips with a white-coated tongue and she hid her annoyance at him calling her that name, just like Carl used to...

'D'you want a drink? Some water?'

H shook his head. 'No thank you darling,' he croaked, then closed his eyes, slackened his grip on her hand and, in a few short seconds, gave her the freedom she so badly coveted.

At that point she did call the nurse. In a strangled, desperate cry. Two came running over to her, swiftly pulled the curtained screens around the bed. One led her away to their office at the corner of the ward, past other beds of men with tubes in their hands, up their noses, with bags containing disgusting looking fluids hanging at their bedsides.

In the office the nurse sat her down. 'Would you like a cup of tea, dear?'

'D'you have coffee?' she sniffed through her tears and sobbing. 'Was that… is that… the end? Has H gone?'

The nurse did not answer. Instead she busied herself with the kettle, spooned instant coffee into a mug. 'Do you take sugar, milk?'

'Milk, no sugar, thank you.'

'Would you like a biscuit, I don't suppose you've eaten have you?'

Delia glanced at her watch; it was coming up for six thirty am. She remembered the phone call she had received from them, round about five o'clock. She was already awake, strangely missing H by her side in that large bed they had shared for the past five, nearly six years. As soon as it had rung, she knew it would be them, telling her to come quickly, that he was fading fast. Now he was gone and she was being offered a biscuit. How bizarre was that?

'Thank you.' She nibbled on the proffered biscuit, sipped her coffee, conscious suddenly that it was too hot to drink yet. She licked her lips and sucked in air to cool the temporary scalding. 'What happens now?'

The nurse sat next to her and patted her hand. 'My colleague, out there with your husband, has summoned the doctor. He will be the one to pronounce that… H, do you call him? That H has passed away. Soon he will be taken to the chapel of rest and later you will be able to make your arrangements for his funeral. Do you have someone you can call, someone we can call for you?'

Delia took another sip of coffee and finished the biscuit, carefully wiping crumbs from her skirt. 'Erm, my daughter, Tilda, or my son Danny. No, not Danny. Tilda I suppose. H isn't their father,' she added. 'Stepfather, their daddy died years ago when they were just children.'

The nurse gave her a look of sympathy, said gently, 'Do you have her number on you?'

'Yes… on my mobile.' She dug into her bag for her mobile, switched it on and scrolled through to Tilda's number. She looked up at the nurse. 'Can you do it for me? Please?'

The nurse smiled. 'Of course.' She took the phone from Delia. 'Will she be awake, it's only just gone half past six?'

'Oh, I didn't think of that. Erm, yes, I expect she will, she usually takes her dogs out for a walk before she goes to work. Two Dalmatians. Crazy they are…'

Again the nurse smiled. 'I've got a little schitzu, he likes his early morning run.'

'Where is he now?'

'Oh, at home with my partner. She'll take him out.'

Delia thought of Danny and Ray, wondered

what role this woman played with her partner... dismissed it... irrelevant.

The nurse put the phone to her ear and waited for the call to be picked up.

'Hello, is that Tilda? Yes, I know this is your Mum's phone, she has asked me to call you... yes, she's fine... well, ok. No nothing has happened to her. It's your stepfather... yes I'm afraid so, he passed away about half an hour ago. Yes, your mother is here... ok, I'll pass the phone to her.' The nurse turned to Delia. 'She wants to speak to you, Mrs Fontaine.'

'Hello darling.'

'Mum, you ok?'

'No not really.' Delia sobbed into the phone. 'H died just now... not long ago.'

'I'll come down. Stay strong Mum, I'll be with you in a couple of hours.' Tilda said goodbye and told her mother 'love you', then rang off. Delia imagined her daughter going into immediate overdrive; getting dressed, packing a small overnight case, loading the crazy dogs into the back of the hatchback, and driving off with a piece of toast stuck in her mouth. She half smiled, relieved Tilda was coming. Should she ring Danny? Perhaps later, from home. She wanted to leave here now, go home, sit quietly in her kitchen and think things through.

Half an hour later, the staff nurse walked her to her car, carrying H's belongings in a carrier bag (she hadn't thought to bring a holdall in the panic of getting here). In the plastic bag were his clothes and a pair of sea-water stained shoes. She also handed Delia a walking stick.

'That's not his, H doesn't have a walking stick,' she told the nurse, suddenly conscious it was didn't not doesn't, past not present. H was gone...

'Oh, ok, probably one left by another patient.' She took it back with her, waved a sympathetic goodbye and disappeared inside the hospital without a backward glance.

Delia drove slowly home. *Poor H, if only he had heeded the advice of the doctors and stopped smoking and drinking, he might be alive today. But he wasn't drinking, was he Delia? Not really... the odd glass of wine you persuaded him to have with dinner, making it larger and larger over the weeks: the occasional glass of cold beer on a hot day, maybe two, three at most. Hardly call that drinking, would you? You surely could not count the small amounts of alcohol you added to the dinners: chicken in a brandy sauce, lamb in dark rum, and pork in calvados? Well you had to make the meals tasty, didn't you? H was going off his food and he needed sustenance to help him get better: anything to change his pasty yellow face to a more robust colour. The best one, his favourite dish, was sausage and mash in onion gravy. What had he said one day? 'Not too much Deelie, can't eat a great plateful.' You complied, only gave him a child's portion really. Even decorated the mashed potato with a funny face, just to cheer him up. It was the onion gravy though, you made so special. Nearly a whole bottle of vodka... (you could use the remaining gravy to make into a delicious soup for his dinner), couldn't possibly taste it with the onions and the flavoured corn flour could he? Well, could he? Didn't he say how much he enjoyed it and could they have it again? Didn't he fall asleep again so quickly after lunch? Slept peacefully too, didn't he? Just that funny little intake of air in his throat each time he took a breath. You watched and listened for every single one. Even his colour looked better, slightly pink cheeks instead of that awful pasty yellow... Didn't even stay awake long enough for a quick stroll around the garden and a cheroot, did he?*

You never discouraged him from smoking either. As long as it was outside in the garden: even on chilly days, when he felt unwell, you wouldn't allow him to smoke those filthy cheroots indoors. Oh no. Even though he came back in shivering. Surely, you thought, smoking indoors would have been more damaging? All that toxic smoke lingering in the furniture, in your clothes, your hair? Much better, if he had to smoke, to do it outside... and walking in that savage midnight air... on the damp meadow grass... near the cliff's edge, his last night. Poor H.

But of course, the boeuf bourguignon was the final straw, that was what had pushed him over the edge, that and all the second bottle of burgundy, the one you didn't

add to the French dish.   What do you say?   You like the
pun?   Pushed him over the edge?   Poor H.

She drove through Margate on automatic, conscious
only once of her bearings when she passed the florist
shop and the flat above it where the Irish ex-priest
lived, Caius Hennessey.   A few minutes later, she
parked up outside her own house and let herself
indoors. So quiet, so spacious, so all hers.

She'd best wait until after the funeral to dispose
of his possessions. I could advertise the fishing gear,
she thought.   Maybe give his clothes to a charity
shop. Not here in Birchington, probably Margate...
no, Herne Bay, further away, or even Whitstable.
She didn't want to see anyone local wearing his
clothes. Thinking of them reminded her she had left
the bag, with H's possessions from the hospital, in
the car. She sighed. Let them stay there for the time
being. A cup of strong coffee was in order, also toast;
she felt as if she'd been up half the night and had not
eaten since her sparse share of dinner last night,
apart from one biscuit at the hospital. She walked
through to the kitchen, switched on the kettle,
spooned some coffee into the small cafetière and
popped two slices of wholemeal into the toaster.

The doorbell rang. She looked up. Who could
that be at this hour? Not Tilda, not yet, she would
have only just left London.   Better go and see...
might be the postman. No, it was Jessie, her next-

door neighbour, Dez's wife.

'Everything all right Delia? I saw you drive up just now, wondered where you'd been so early. Is it H?'

Delia held the door open for her and nodded. 'He's gone, Jess: died about six thirty.' She decided to tell her neighbour about H's midnight walk. 'He was either very confused or went sleepwalking. Remember I told you the other day how he's taken to these weird wanderings? Didn't even hear him get up,' she whimpered. 'Apparently, he fell... off the cliff top. An early morning walker found him, down on the promenade... called an ambulance on his mobile. The hospital called me.'

'Oh poor you, come here,' and Jess took Delia into her ample arms and hugged her. They walked through to the kitchen as the toast popped up and the kettle boiled.

'Sit yourself down, pet. I'll do your toast and coffee. Mind if I make myself some tea?'

'No, course not, help yourself.' Delia sat down and yawned. 'I'm so tired, Jess.'

'I expect you are, pet. Have you phoned the twins?'

She nodded. 'Tilda's coming down. I haven't rung Danny yet. Maybe Tilda will do that for me.' She yawned again; could feel her mind numbing. Jessie set down a plate of toast in front of her, rummaged round the cupboard for marmalade or something. She found a jar of manouka honey. 'This do you?'

'Yes… lovely,' said Delia. She accepted a steaming mug of coffee. 'No sugar,' as her neighbour poised with the spoon.

'Just have a little: the sweetness might do you good.'

'Ok, just a small spoonful then.'

The two women sat, quietly sipping their drinks. Delia did not know what to say. Neither, it seemed, did Jessie.

'Was he…'

'It didn't take long…'

'Sorry, you first,' said Jessie.

'It doesn't matter. He's gone. And no, it didn't take long, he was badly injured… his head. I held his hand…'

'Bless you. Well if Dez or I can do anything to help… you only have to say.'

'Thanks Jess, you're a good friend.' The tears welled again. 'I suppose I'll have to go and register his death.' She thought about the last time she had seen a registrar. Danny's wedding, barely a year ago. Such a perfect day it had been: warm sunshine, in the flower-filled grounds of a lovely hotel and that song playing, 'Perfect day…' Danny and Ray had faced each other to say their vows, both dressed in white suits with pale-blue ties, yellow-rose corsages and such loving expressions as they spoke the words to join them together. She could not remember their exact phrases, only the heartfelt promises to love each other until the end of time. Her daughter looking resplendent, in a pale-yellow dress, her hair decorated with tiny yellow roses, and her handsome husband by her side. Delia and Manda had looked at the four of them, held hands and sniffled happily into their hankies. Such a lovely day…

The next week passed in a haze of necessary arrangements, hushed whispers, lots of hand gripping and hugs from the twins and their partners, until Delia felt quite stifled. At least the funeral director took away a lot of the burden from her: such a quietly efficient lady, popping in suggestions and queries here and there. Delia decided on a low key affair. H hadn't kept up acquaintances with his business friends. It was as if he had sold them on with his business when he married and moved in with her.

'I can do just as much over the internet and phone from here,' he told her.

Whatever City dealing he did seemed to pay off and gave him plenty of income and ample free time to go beach-casting and sea fishing.

Hilary, the funeral director, suggested an advert in the Thanet Journal giving the venue, date and time of H's cremation. Delia agreed. At least anyone outside the family and neighbours would be more likely to include his fishing buddies. Fine, she could cope with them. She really did not feel able to handle any slick city types.

Manda came to stay a few days before the funeral: Tilda, Mike, Danny and Ray the evening before. Mike insisted on taking them all out to dinner. 'You don't want the bother of cooking, Ma-in-law. Far better if we let someone else do the pampering.'

Delia nodded. Fine by her. Tomorrow, she thought, would take care of itself. They walked to a new restaurant close by.

'I haven't tried it yet,' she told them. 'But it's had some good reviews in the Journal.' She briefly thought about the Turkish restaurant Danny and Tim had taken her to and just as swiftly dismissed the memory.

The evening passed quickly enough: pleasant company, good food and wine. They toasted H and Delia remembered he had died through her generous helpings of alcohol-fed meals as much as the fall. So what? The others did not know that and she had no intention of spoiling the atmosphere by referring to it.

The next morning was one of those warm, September mornings with a delicate breeze blowing in from the sea, and not a hint of approaching autumn or the October gales that swept this coast every year. The hearse pulled up outside the front door, carrying H's coffin that was covered with a simple wreath of white and yellow roses, surrounded with similar wreathes along each side. One of the attendants held open the door of the first car for her. She was joined by her two children and their partners. She watched from inside the darkened car as Manda, Jess and Denzel climbed into the second one. They were driven slowly through Birchington's high street, where a few older male residents stood at the kerbside and doffed their hats: not because they necessarily knew H, she thought. It was what they did. Tradition.

The funeral service was almost indecently brief, with a strange vicar intoning the funeral service and saying nice things about a man he had never met. Delia was not phased, would be quite happy when H's coffin slid behind the blue silk curtain and they could return home, to the buffet prepared and served by local caterers. There were a few unfamiliar faces in the congregation: H's fishing buddies, she surmised. Well, she'd invite them back to the reception as well.

She let out a huge sigh as the coffin began its final journey through the blue pleated curtains. Hid her shudder behind a man-sized hankie and managed to make it sound like soft weeping. Tilda touched her mother's arm and squeezed her hand. Danny, seated on her other side, put an arm around her shoulders. He whispered in her ear. 'Be strong

Mum, not long now. Love you.'

She smiled at them both in turn. Such lovely children, how blessed she was. And then it was over and they were being guided out into the bright sunshine by Hilary's black-coated funeral attendants: shown the row of wreathes and sprays as one of the men stooped to pick up the attached cards and pass them to her. She thought, what the hell am I supposed to do with them? She hoped Hilary had not read her mind as she coincidentally said, 'So you know who has given flowers.' She remembered then doing the same at Gerald's funeral, and nodded her thanks. Didn't remember Carl's funeral at all. Just as well... She turned to Tilda and Danny for support and the three of them led the others towards the cars that would take them home. She did not even glance back to say a silent farewell to H. She'd said her goodbyes in there, in the chapel that smelled so strongly of lilies. She hated lilies, always reminded her of death. In that case, they were in the perfect place...

Later Manda said, 'Would you like to spend a week in Portugal with me? 'I'm going down to the Algarve in a few weeks time, a little place called Alvor.'

Delia put her glass down. 'What a lovely idea, I could do with a break now.' Her face was pale and strained. Much as she had fallen out of love with H over the past few months, he hadn't been bad to her. He had often, especially in the beginning, made her laugh with his droll sense of humour.   But the relationship had soured, the attraction petered out. And those last weeks, the nursing, the constant visits to hospital, and her relentless thinking up new menus to titillate his appetite, and his so unfortunate death: it had all challenged her strength, leaving her drained. Yes, a holiday would be good.

The next weeks passed by in a kind of numbness, between Manda phoning her instructions and the final fleeting memories she had of H. Her friend arranged everything for their trip to Portugal. 'All you have to do,' she said, 'is pack your case and get yourself up here to Birmingham Airport for the 6am flight. Means we'll have to be at the airport,' she added, 'by 4.30am.'

7

About a fortnight before she was due to fly off with Manda, she sat at the kitchen table supping coffee and nibbling on a piece of toast. Her thoughts were varied and jumbled, bumping into each other with no apology. She was trying to picture the little fishing village they were going to visit, imagined herself and H being there, not Manda. Almost regretting, in fact, that she had agreed to go on the holiday at all. Manda, in small doses, was fine. She was not sure now, whether a full week with her oldest friend would be bearable.

The doorbell rang interrupting her flowing thoughts. Postman? Not more cards of condolence surely? Could she bear to read any more morbid verses of 'I am not gone, just resting in another room'? She stood up and moved towards the lounge and to the front door. Can't be just post, she surmised: the postman would just slip those into the letter box. Parcel? Who would be sending her a parcel?

She did not recognise the figure through the frosted glass. Looked like a man, but not the postie. She opened the door to face a young man who looked strangely familiar to her, uncannily familiar:

could even be a young H. Quickly she wiped away any toast crumbs from her mouth, secretly glad she was dressed and not walking around in a sloppy dressing gown like she had often been doing since H died.

'Can I help you?' She noticed the way he grinned when she wiped her mouth, a charming, mischievous grin, one so familiar to her.

'I'm Harry Fontaine,' he said. 'Son of H Fontaine.'

She stared at him, lost for words for a moment. 'H is dead,' she spoke abruptly and regretted it. 'I'm so sorry, I mean your father died last month, in hospital. The funeral was three weeks ago.'

'I know,' he soothed. 'I read it in the Thanet Journal. Leastwise, a mate of mine did. He lives in Margate. And he sent me a copy. I live in Telford.'

Quite near where Manda lived, and Danny's in-laws. What a coincidence. 'Would you like to come in?' She didn't consider it a rash decision, letting a complete stranger into her house. After all, he was H's son. At least, that is who he said he was. She had no reason to doubt it: he was the image of his father. She stood to one side, indicated the way through the lounge to the kitchen.

'I've just made coffee, would you like some? Or tea, if you prefer?'

He sniffed the air, an appreciative look on his face. 'Coffee's fine,' he said. 'Smells good. Kenyan or Arabic?'

She laughed, relaxed. 'Haven't a clue... just freshly ground. Would you like some toast as well?' she added.

'Thanks no. I've had breakfast with my mate in Margate. I travelled down yesterday.'

She placed a freshly poured coffee in front of him, then sat opposite, examining his face, noting the way he held the mug and drank from it, like H used to.

'When did you...?'

'I haven't seen my...'

They both spoke at once. 'Sorry, you first,' she said and gently laughed. He smiled, nodded his head and breathed deeply.

'I haven't seen my dad since I was thirteen. I'm twenty-nine now. He left us, my mum and me. Walked out the door one day and never came back.'

She calculated the sixteen years and felt relieved that her six- year marriage to H had not been the cause of Harry's parents' breakup. Realised that she knew little of H and this past life.

'I didn't even know he'd been married before. I hope they divorced,' she said and forced a strained laugh.

Harry smiled and shrugged. 'Couldn't tell you to be honest. Mum's dead too, she died five years ago... breast cancer... was only ill for months.'

'I'm so sorry.' She paused. 'And you? Are you

married?'

'No, not now. Was once, a couple of years ago... didn't work out, so we split.'

'Any children?'

'No, luckily. Wouldn't want any kid of mine to suffer what I did. Mum and I had some hard times.'

She could hear the bitterness in his voice. How could H do it to them? Just walk out and never go back?

'We got lucky though,' he said and gave a wide grin. 'Mum started to do the lottery and won £100,000 the second time she did it. Unbelievable.'

Delia felt a weight lifted from her chest. Even though she knew she had not been part of H's desertion, she felt a certain relief.

'How amazing; you hear about people winning large sums on the lottery but never anyone you know.'

Harry grinned, took another sip of coffee, and resettled himself in the chair. 'Yes, I know. Fortunately, nobody got wind of it. It's not as if it was the big one, the millions, but it was enough for Mum to purchase a modest house, two bedrooms, and still have a couple of grand left in the bank. I'd left school by then and started work.'

'What do you do, Harry… up in Telford?'

'I'm transport manager for a haulage firm, juggling men and lorries to different parts of the country and to Europe.'

She nodded, hoped she looked interested. 'Have you always lived up there?'

'No, no. Mum and I lived in Swanley, not that far from here really. When Mum died I sold our place, got a good price for it too: almost quadrupled what she'd paid for it. The firm I worked for moved up to the West Midlands, to Telford, and promoted me. They helped me buy a house there, helped towards moving expenses etc. I was quids in.'

'More coffee?'

'Thanks.' He held out his cup. She walked over to the dresser and poured them both a second one, added a little milk and one sugar to his.

'And you,' he said. 'Are you all right?'

'Yes, I'm ok. H left me a small life insurance and I have money from my parents' inheritance.' Where did that lie come from, she thought, then added. 'I expect I'll get a widow's pension or something. My son-in-law, Mike, is arranging everything for me. He's a treasure.' She thought she made it sound as if she was the helpless widow: didn't want him to imagine there were any rich pickings here for him.

'Did you and H have children?'

She laughed. 'Good Lord, no. I was turned forty when I married your Dad. I've two children from my first marriage, twins, a boy and a girl.' She did not mention Carl, or even name Gerald.

'Do you mind if I use your loo? Two coffees are going through me.' He gave her another H like grin.

He really was so like his father.

'Yes of course, there's one through there.' She indicated the door at the back of the kitchen. 'Round to your right.'

'Nice garden,' he said when he returned. 'I saw it through the back window.'

'Thank you. The garden's easy to maintain but it's a big house now I'm on my own.'

'Yeah, it looked pretty big from the outside.'

She sighed. 'It is. Four bedrooms and bath and toilet upstairs. I'm seriously thinking of selling up and moving nearer to my children.'

'Probably best.'

There was a lull in their conversation. Delia fidgeted. Perhaps he ought to go now? What to say to end this meeting?

'Erm, I still have your father's watch upstairs. It's a Breitling. Would you like it?'

'I haven't come to scrounge off you.'

'I know,' she soothed. 'It's just a token, his watch, and you *are* his son. It's only right you should have it.'

'Ok.' His eyes brightened. 'In that case…'

'I won't be a minute,' she got up from the table. 'I have it upstairs in H's bedside drawer.' She hoped it was where she said it was. Hoped, no she was certain, she hadn't got rid of it when she bagged up his clothes for the charity shop. Moments later she returned downstairs, clutching the brown leather strapped time-piece, a smile of relief framing her face.

'Here it is.' She handed it to the young man, to Harry, H's son.

He examined it. 'Great,' he said and laughed. 'They make such a fuss about Breitlings and Rolex watches. What's that other one? Pateq Phillippe? All costing an arm and a leg. But they are just a means of telling the time, just like Sekonda's or something. Don't get me wrong,' he added. 'I am really grateful for this. Nice to have something of my Dad's after all these years.'

She smiled one of her smiles that did not reach her eyes. 'I understand.' She chewed on her lip, ruminating. *What about H's car out there? Only cluttering up the miniscule driveway. Perhaps Harry would like his father's car as well?*

'I must be getting back,' he said. 'To my mate's place in Margate. I've left my things there. Need to head back to Telford today, some time.'

'Would you like your father's car as well?' She said it abruptly as if she was pushing it away, pushing it towards him. Really, she wanted nothing of H, save his generous life insurance. That would definitely come in handy. She almost grinned to herself: collecting husbands had proved to be lucrative and beneficial to her bank balance. She wondered, might there be a fourth?

'It's in immaculate condition. Only three years

old and regularly serviced.'

'Wow, that would be great. I didn't bring my car down cos it's on its last legs. Could've borrowed one from the firm, but decided to come down with one of our drivers heading for Dover. I planned to go back by train. Are you sure?' he added.

'Yes... I am. I don't need it, I've got my own car. I was planning to sell it... but I would rather it went to you. It's a Ford by the way, a Mondeo.'

'Yeah, I noticed it when I arrived. Nice colour, midnight blue I think they call it?'

'Yes, that's right.' She stood up. 'I'll go and find all the papers. They should be through there in H's office. She pointed through to the small hallway and the door off to the right.

Half an hour later he was gone, armed with the necessary documents and two sets of car keys for the Mondeo, plus the Breitling watch, and giving a vague promise to keep in touch. She doubted that.

Later, she walked through the house, upstairs and down. All mine again, she thought. She felt and appreciated the freedom, knew not the smallest pang of loneliness or sadness. H was gone, like Gerald and the Neanderthal Carl. Life was good... and sweet. And she had a holiday in Portugal to look forward to.

Mike and Tilda drove her to Birmingham Airport

and took her through to the terminal where she had arranged to meet her friend. It was a very sleepy Manda who greeted them.

'You look like no make-up and knickers to match,' said Delia.

Tilda giggled and nodded. 'About right, Aunt Manda.'

'Yeah, I know. Met some friends last night who thought it a good idea to give me a send-off. Haven't really slept,' she said with a yawn.'

Delia averted her face from her friend's stale breath that smelled strongly of alcohol. They said quick goodbyes to Mike and Tilda and trundled their suitcases towards the check-in desk. There, they were greeted by the smiling, fresh-looking, and newly made-up face of a stewardess and an extremely effeminate steward who said, in an impossibly high pitched voice, 'Hi girls, this way please,' and gave a curly wave towards a vacant desk.

'Thank God Danny's not camp like that,' whispered Delia as the steward minced away.

Manda smiled, 'He'd still be your son, my love.'

'Yeah, true.'

They were relieved of their hold luggage, wished a happy holiday by the girl at the desk, and wandered through to the security search area and on to the departure lounge.

'Coffee?'

'Coffee and a croissant,' said Delia. 'I'm starving.'

Despite the hour, all the bars and cafés were open, even the champagne bar. One look at her friend's pale and blotched face decided Delia against suggesting smoke salmon and scrambled eggs, washed down with a glass of bubbly. That could come later. Another day even… they were going to be in Portugal for the week. Instead, they sauntered over to a coffee bar, ordered two lattes and croissants, and sat at a table between two other tables, which accommodated men and their laptops.

'Don't they ever stop?' whispered Delia.

'Nah, they're like kids with favourite toys. Bet they're pretending it's business, and, really, they're playing solitaire or mahjong.'

Delia laughed and added. 'For sure.'

The coffee seemed to revive her friend.

'Just going to the ladies. Put on a bit of slap. Won't be long.'

Delia sat slowly sipping coffee and people-watched. Amazing how many of them buy best new outfits for travel, she thought. Even if it's a new tracksuit and matching trainers. Her eyes followed a middle-aged woman dressed in a grey and fluorescent yellow tracksuit with identical yellow stripes on her trainers. She shook her head, unbelievable. She watched as different age groups passed in front of her table: young couples with backpacks and pushchairs, elderly couples holding hands for dear life in case they got separated before boarding their plane.

There was a group of smiling black women in colourful clothes and full voice, singing Happy Birthday to one of their group. They added a second verse, 'God's blessing on you, God's blessing on you, God's blessing dear Anya...' and so on. Happy Clappies, H would have called them. Wonder if he is in a place called God's Heaven, she thought. But dismissed the idea. He was so many little granules now, total weight seven pounds, just like when he was born, and interred within the crematorium's rose garden.

Manda returned, looking distinctly unblotched and alert. Obviously, Delia thought, the coffee and her application of slap had improved matters considerably. They were informed over the loud speaker system that their flight was ready for boarding and would passengers please go to gate forty-seven.

'That's us,' said Manda. Delia nodded and picked up her cabin bag, passport and boarding ticket clutched tightly in her hand.

'I see you've booked us the leg-room seats,' she said to her friend.

'Too right, *and* there's only two of them either side of the aisle. No fatty wanting to squeeze by every five minutes, needing the loo.'

Delia grinned. Her friend thought of everything. 'You're amazing, Manda, leg room and no fatties.'

'More to come.'

'What?'

'Wait and see.'

To begin with, the flight was distinctly bumpy: ten minutes of sheer turbulence, thanks to the rainstorm, as they taxied away and rose up from Birmingham. Once the pilot had taken them up to 35,000 feet, they looked down on light fluffy, sunlit clouds and enjoyed a smoother ride.

'Time for the fizz,' said Manda and rang her overhead bell for the stewardess. 'We're ready now,' she smiled, and they were served chilled sparkling wine and smoked salmon Paninis. Both of them tucked in, enjoying both food and drink.

'Lovely start to the holiday,' remarked Delia.

Manda smiled, swallowed a mouthful of Panini and washed it down with a generous swig of Prosecco. 'Glad you approve.'

Three hours later they touched down onto a hot, sunny Faro airport, and half an hour later were whisked away by taxi to their hotel on the outskirts of the little town of Alvor. Manda flirted outrageously with their driver, completely ignoring the family photograph perched on the dashboard. Obviously him, with his wife, three children and Mama and Papa in the background. Delia pointed it out to her friend.

'So what? We're hardly likely to see him again, are we?'

'What about our return journey?'

'So?'

Delia gave up, realising that she too, was single again. It was a good feeling. Was she ready to go on the prowl yet? Ready to seek out male company? She shrugged her shoulders, bit soon yet, she thought: H was barely cold in that small patch reserved for loved ones' ashes. Nevertheless she told herself to keep an open mind... even thought about the guy who had sat across the aisle from them in the plane.

Part Two
DI Shackleton

8

Two good things had happened in D.I. Bob Shackleton's life. He had once won £250,000 on the Premium Bonds, enabling him to buy the five-storey house where he lived, in one of Westgate's respectable streets, and within walking district of the cliff top seafront. Even better, to have sufficient monies left over to convert it into four attractive flats. The ground floor and lower ground floor he claimed for himself. This included a pleasant, south-facing, back garden that was sheltered from the bracing north coast winds that blew incessantly along Westgate's seafront. Not a big garden, admittedly, but enough for him to enjoy on a rare, occasional day off from his job at Margate Police Station.

It was more of a large courtyard, with old-fashioned cobblestones and large urns he had bought at a nearby auction house. These were furnished, throughout the seasons, by an ex-lag turned landscape gardener, Ossie Whitchurch. Grey and grizzled now, after years spent in and out of prison, he had turned from house burglary to gardening, preferring the colours of flora to the drabness of life behind bars.

He planted daffodils and other spring bulbs to

flower in March and April, followed by pelargoniums, trailing lobelia and cushions of alyssum during the summer. In winter, Ossie made sure the stone urns decorated the courtyard with an array of colourful pansies, primulas, and cyclamen, with early flowering snowdrops to follow. There were waving bamboos in two large half-barrels on the back wall that Ossie had warned Mr Shackleton, 'Sir,' never to plant these invasive bastards in the ground. Bob had no intentions of planting anything, he assured his ex-lag friend. In between the waving bamboos was another half-barrel tub, planted with sweet smelling rosemary, pungent oregano, and purple flowering sage that thrived in the coastal garden.

The remaining three apartments were let to fellow police officers, only one of whom was married. To the Delectable Stella, a solicitor who commuted daily to London. He was Bob's sidekick, Phil Anderson...

There were no children or pets: not that Bob objected to either. Working, non-married policemen did not make the best pet owners, and would have been, at best, only part-time fathers from broken marriages. Stella could not, or would not, have children and her lifestyle meant no pets as well; far too busy to walk a pooch, and averse to the very idea of a cat-litter tray invading their pristine apartment.

The second good thing that had happened to Bob, he reckoned: was having never married; never had to make excuses or apologies to some long-suffering little woman for late nights away from home, investigating a murder case or planning a drug bust. He was hopeless at remembering birthdays, and wedding anniversaries would have been on a par. There were no stony silences in his life, not unless you included the flower-filled urns in the courtyard garden: any whining that might have occurred came through the front windows when the north winds blew.

All in all, Bob considered he had a satisfactory life. At fifty-five he was still reasonably fit, thanks to three sessions weekly in a local gym club. His doctor didn't approve, but had to concede reluctantly, that his five cigarettes a day were not as life-threatening as the forty a day many of his colleagues smoked.

Occasionally, he stayed behind and went for a drink in The Admiral with the boys, particularly when they celebrated the end of a case. The Admirable sold a very tolerable pint, and by the end of the evening, the pints would be washed down with Scotch whiskey or tequila shots.

Unbeknown to Bob, a bad thing was about to happen to him, at least within the next forty eight hours.

Bob awoke to the muffled sounds of Dvorak being played on a radio upstairs. He could only identify it as the piece once used to advertise Hovis bread. Classical music was not his forte. His bedroom, on the back ground floor, was directly under the kitchen on the first floor. The music came from Stella and Phil Anderson's radio in the flat above.

He squinted at his wristwatch, then turned over and saw the time on his bedside-table clock. Seven-twenty am. He blinked, looked up at the ceiling and let his imagination roam: pictured the Delectable Stella walking across the floor in some diaphanous garment that bordered on the indecent. Or maybe she was in the process of being half-dressed in bra, panties, and stockings as she switched the kettle on for coffee, made in their cafetiere. Maybe Phil had gone round to the baker's for fresh croissants. Bob could almost smell them and feel their just-baked warmth; savour the aroma of fresh coffee as Stella poured boiling water over freshly ground beans, still in her diaphanous garment.

He heard the street door open and shut, listened to footsteps along the Victorian ceramic tiled hallway, then the softer sound as the carpeted stairs were climbed to the first floor. Definitely Phil, getting the croissants for his desirable wife. Bob knew a moment of envy. The erection that had started, as he imagined a half-dressed woman above his ceiling, went limp. Unconsciously he massaged his crotch, sat up and climbed out of bed. He badly needed a piss, then shower, dress and go downstairs to his own kitchen, in the front of the house.

He and Phil were on the same shift today, nine o'clock start. They had both worked until gone ten last night, on the murder case that had taken place on a building site, close to where the old Lido had been, and not far from their nick as well. There, the body of an immigrant worker had been found, his body a sponge of multiple stab wounds. Later, Bob had said to Phil, 'coming for a swift half in the Admiral?'

His young counterpart hesitated, face unusually pale in the street lighting. 'Shouldn't really. Stella wasn't too happy when I rang her earlier to say I'd be late. Darling Daddy's turned up for the evening and she's planned a special dinner.'

Bob shrugged and hid his disappointment. He could do with company to talk over the case, try to make sense of the sulky wall of silence that the victim's fellow immigrants had built up.

'Well, you're a bit late for a dinner party. Another half hour won't make much difference, will it?'

Again Phil hesitated. He liked his boss, old warhorse that he was. Plus they lived in the same house: Bob the builder and Bob the landlord as well as Bob the DI.

'Go on then, two swift halves then it'll have to be home for me.'

'Done. I'll get them in... you better ring Stella again. Tell her you'll definitely be home by ten thirty.'

It was nearer eleven when Bob let himself into his front door down the concrete steps: when he had whispered 'g'night' to Phil. He heard the tap of his shoes as his young side-kick climbed the ground floor steps to the main front door.

For once, Bob did not envy the younger man. What was the old saying? Cold shoulder and tongue pie for supper? Yeah, that was probably Phil's lot tonight. He walked from the small hallway into his large, modern kitchen. A woman's dream kitchen, according to the designer. Poor sod had lost his son some years ago. Fell in front of a train on the London Underground. Yeah, a dream kitchen. Only there was no woman here to dream about it. He shrugged out of his Barbour and hung it on the back of a high-back chair, walked over to the fridge and fished out a large bottle of Bavarian beer. He found the bottle-opener in a top drawer of one of the units and plucked off the crown cork. It dropped onto the floor but he chose to ignore it as it rolled away under the table. There was always tomorrow...

The beer tasted good and cold as he took the first mouthful. He switched on the radio and played around with the tuner, wondering why he had never bothered to select three or four stations and put them on automatic. Couldn't be asked. He found at least three foreign stations, his house being so close to the

North Sea and the European mainland, before selecting one that was playing folk and country music, guitar, banjo, fiddles, and twangy, faux-American West accents. He yawned, scratched the back of his neck, thought briefly of Phil's frosty supper, wondered if Darling Daddy was still there, and then dismissed the thought, none of his business.

Stella took longer to get out of his head. Wonder if she's changed out of the black suit and white camisole top that does not quite hide her cleavage? The one that allows a hint of her nipples to show through the thin material? He felt suddenly hungry: for food or for sex? Or both? How long had it been since he'd eaten... or last got his leg over? Must be six months ago, the sex bit. When he went on that mini cruise that called in at Amsterdam, among other places. What was her name? Erica. Erica with the deep velvet voice, who rolled her r's as she said her name. She was a pretty good roll: in more ways than one, he seemed to remember.

9

Bob's Early Retirement September

'It's nothing personal, Bob. Come on, you've been a bloody good copper over the years. Well respected and a credit to the Force.'

Bob sat opposite his chief, his back to the window that overlooked the sea. It was the Super's privilege, the sea view, and the plants decorating his wide window sill, lovingly tended by the governor's aging secretary.

'It's these swingeing cuts we have to make, and you *will* be fifty six next birthday, am I right?'

Of course you're bloody right. Makes me three years younger than you, but you won't be taking early retirement or redundancy. Oh no, not you, the Big White Chief.

Bob kept the seething words to himself. Wouldn't make any difference, and he was buggered if he was going to plead. The Super had already hinted at a sizeable handshake: maybe not golden but at least solid silver. How many noughts he wondered? He had the house with its guaranteed rents coming in. There'd also be his police pension... Sure he'd manage. Might even enjoy the premature freedom for a while. No getting up in the morning after a late night on a case: no raiding the fridge for a lump of stale cheese and tomatoes with the fur on them. He'd have time to do a proper shop, time to go round to the Italian deli and pick up some of Angelo's real food…

'The other alternative…'

Bob let his mind come back into the room. What was the chief saying?

'The other alternative is a part time job here in the station, desk job, collating figures and facts etc.'

He shook his head. So hard it hurt his neck muscles. 'Oh no, not that… Sir. If I have to go, then I will. Leave and not come back. Give me some credit. Can you imagine a) me behind a desk, and b) watching my team go out on cases that I probably set up in the first place?'

The Chief Superintendent shifted uncomfortably. Bob saw him look at his watch. *Can't wait to get rid of me now, can you? How long have you given me? Fifteen bloody minutes for my thirty-five years policing?*

'If that's the way you feel about it Bob… Believe me I'm so sorry this has happened, but cuts have to be made and they're not,' he added, 'bringing in the new retirement age straight away, otherwise I might have been able to keep you on. Besides,' he soothed. 'You'll not be the only one leaving: Sergeant Joe Hargreaves and three of the civilian clerks will have to go too.'

Big deal, old Joe and three fluffy ladies. I'll be in good company. He stood up, wanting badly to ignore his boss's outstretched hand; realised it would be churlish and childish not to shake hands: beneath himself. He managed a strained smile.

'Right, Sir, see you at the leaving party. I presume I will at least have a farewell do?'

'Most definitely, Bob. I shall look forward to it.'

He closed the door quietly behind him, resisted the urge to slam it. As he walked along the corridor to his own office, he marvelled how life could change in such a short space of time. What was it his Dad used to say? 'You never know what's round the corner, Robert my boy.' *True Dad, you don't…*

Two weeks later he was on the plane to Portugal, to the little harbour town of Alvor on the Algarve. Thanks to Phil and Stella, or maybe Stella's Darling Daddy.

'Please take it,' urged Stella when she had heard his news. 'Stay as long as you like, Phil, and I won't be going there until after Christmas now. It's a nice little apartment, over a souvenir shop, and just a short walk from the harbour. Loads of restaurants and bars nearby.'

'Sounds ideal. Good idea, I think, to have a holiday now. Give me time to plan the rest of my life,' he grinned.

They had given him a great send off from the station: plenty of food and drink over at The Admiral and a thousand pounds worth of traveller's vouchers, interchangeable for air or boat fares and Euros or any other currency.

He stretched out his feet, having chosen a seat next to the emergency exit and saying a definite yes to the question 'Are you fit enough to help other passengers in the event of an emergency landing?' His adjoining-seat passenger already had his laptop in use. No conversation there then. Across the aisle were two ladies. Past the forty-five mark but still good lookers...

The trolley dolly had just taken his order for an in-flight meal and a small bottle of red wine, shown him a hidden table and how to slide it round in front of him, and then given him a smile to die for. Perhaps retirement was no bad thing. He glanced over the aisle at the two ladies laughing and sipping on glasses of bubbly. Definitely not bad lookers... and wondered where they were making for. He ignored the computer geek by his side.

10
Late October

Delia felt the chill in the air as soon as she woke. She must have flung the duvet off during the night and came to in a still-darkened room. There was the merest hint of daylight creeping in, through a gap in the curtains. No sun showed, only the gloom and a slight iciness. She quickly pulled the duvet back over herself, snuggled down with just half a face showing above the cover. She touched her nose, definitely colder than the rest of her body. She shivered and lay there thinking of the holiday in Portugal. Of meeting Bob the policeman (retired), grateful that he obviously preferred her to Manda. Manda always seemed to get first choice but not this time. She smiled, remembering how many times Bob accidently bumped into them, even though their hotel was a good half-mile outside the town and he was staying in a friend's apartment near the harbour. She thought about the afternoon she had gone alone to see him. When Manda was having her hair done.

'Can't abide this frizz,' she'd moaned.

'Price of being naturally curly. And staying by the sea, my love.' Delia showed Manda scant sympathy. Secretly she was glad to have an afternoon free of her often over-powerful friend. 'I'm going to take a wander down to the harbour and I'll meet you later by the taxi rank. Or we can go to a bar, before heading back to the hotel, if you prefer?'

'I prefer.'

So Manda suffered her hair straightening coiffure and Delia enjoyed her wander, a stroll that seemed to take her ever nearer to where Bob was staying. They bumped into each other, literally, as they turned a corner.

'Hey,' he said, a smile lighting his already-tanned face. 'What a delightful surprise, bumping into my favourite lady.'

'I'm flattered,' she replied. 'You've known me barely a week...'

He grinned. 'Doesn't take long to recognise class.' He took her arm. 'Fancy an afternoon glass of fizz or tea if you prefer?'

'Fizz sounds perfect.'

'As it happens...,' he paused. 'I've got a rather nice bottle chilling in the fridge upstairs. It's only a few steps away.' She liked the way his head went kind of sideways, indicating how close was a few steps and his cheeky, inviting grin.

'Be rude not to, I s'pose.' She only hesitated, she hoped, in her mind and did not betray her vacillation by body language. Briefly she wondered what would, or might, happen after the bottle of fizz. Her body felt a frisson of excitement. How long had it been since she'd last had sex?

She was late meeting Manda. Only by a few minutes. Enough to make her friend petulant, especially when she told her of bumping into Bob. She omitted to tell her where they had drunk the bottle of fizz, merely indicated they had had a drink together. The swift lovemaking she kept to herself. Swift it might have been, but delightfully satisfying. The only drawback was having to dress so quickly afterwards to meet her friend.

'You'll come here again, won't you?' Bob had said. He leant on his elbow... in bed... and watched her dress.

'Don't know. I want to, but I *am* on holiday with Manda. Might be difficult to get away again. Besides,' she added. 'We go back to the UK in two days.' She felt like a guilty schoolgirl, *except schoolgirls don't enjoy that mature kind of sex, do they?*

Bob made her promise to keep in touch, and was delighted to learn they lived so near to each other when they exchanged addresses and phone numbers. 'Have you got an email address?' he asked. 'I'll email you when I'm coming back.'

'Don't even own a computer - yet. It's next on my bucket list though.' There was H's old one but she had promised that to Jessie's granddaughter, just after the funeral.

'Maybe I can give you some computer lessons? About the only thing I can teach you,' he grinned.

Delia didn't see Bob again till they reached the airport for their flight home. He was there waiting for them in the airport lounge bar, a bottle of sparkling rosé chilling in an ice-bucket on the table. His thoughtfulness even brought a smile to Manda's face. She was in a fair mood anyway, having flirted outrageously with the owner of a tapas bar the previous evening, sending Delia back to their hotel by taxi, alone, while she stayed behind for 'extras' with Rodriguez. She had flirted again with their cab driver on the journey to the airport. Not the same one that brought them. This one returned the flirting.

'I could get quite used to these Portuguese delectables, sweetie.' Said Manda. 'Think we might have to come back soon...'

They enjoyed the wine until it was time to go through to the departure hall. Delia enjoyed a tongue exploring goodbye kiss from Bob, hoping her friend had not seen how deep their affection was, then thought *what the hell*.

She lay awake thinking about it now, stretched, smiled and curved her body again, pleased that Bob would soon be back in England. Soon, she hoped, to call round to see her. Should she get up and make coffee for herself and H? No there is no H any more, just herself and this bloody great house with its many rooms, four up here including the box room, plus the bathroom and toilet. She wished she had a walk-in shower... Downstairs there was the large front lounge that used to be her and Gerald's antique bookshop, the back room, once the store room, that she had given over to H for his office, and a huge kitchen at the back of the house, leading to a utility room and a small toilet. She could have a shower fitted there.

Her mind went into overdrive... the downstairs would make a lovely ground floor apartment for her... and up here? Why not a self-contained flat? The back bedroom would convert beautifully to a large kitchen, the front one could be the lounge. This room, also overlooking the garden, would be the double bedroom and the little front room, maybe, an office. She could let it out: only to professional persons of course, no DSS or whatever they called themselves nowadays. It would provide her with a comfortable income and H's life insurance would pay for any alterations and conversions. Plus she still had savings from Gerald's life insurance. None from her sojourn with Carl of course. There hadn't even been enough money for a funeral. Thoughtful Gerald had paid for that. Poor Gerald...

Her mind drifted on to memories of the holiday, and to Bob Shackleton. She felt her body respond. There had been an instant attraction, the meeting of eyes, and an electric handshake. Getting to know each other when exploring the little fishing town by day and a few shared dinners at night in different hostelries. She remembered that amazing afternoon in his borrowed apartment, and a few days later, their kiss goodbye at Faro Airport. Fleeting recollections. She wondered if he would call her when he returned. Sometime this month he had said. Or was it the beginning of next? She smiled again. Of course he would call her. She could return the compliment, invite him here. Have the fizz ready, and her bed...

Maybe she'd put the alterations on hold. Besides, did she really want to share the house with strangers? Perhaps just a makeover: redecorate, refurbish, stock up with good food and wine. Give it a wow factor to titillate her new ex-policeman friend.

The phone ringing brought her back to the present. She glanced at the clock. Nine o'clock and gone. She slid quickly out of bed and ran into the hallway to answer the phone before it went into voice message.

'Hello?'

There was a pause. 'Delia? That you?'

She recognised his voice, smiled. 'Yes it is. Bob?'

'Correct.'

She could hear the humour in his voice even though he'd only uttered one word. Or was that her imagination going into overdrive?

'Good to hear from you. Are you back in England?'

'Sure am. Close by as a matter of fact.'

'How close?'

'Doorstep close. Listen.'

She heard the bell go downstairs and grinned. That close.

'I'll be down in two ticks.'

She put the phone down, ran back into the bedroom for her dressing gown. Not the most glamorous of garments but perhaps he'd help her discard it. She slipped her feet into satin mules and rushed downstairs, anxious not to keep him waiting in the chill morning air. She could see his frame through the translucent glass, detached the safety chain and unlocked the door.

'Sorry I'm not dressed,' she apologised. 'Lazy morning lie-in.' She stepped to one side and waved him in, conscious of his fresh-air smell and tanned complexion. She prayed he didn't think her too bedraggled, and stopped herself from running her fingers through her hair. His raised eyebrows and the whistle through his teeth told her no, he didn't think her too bedraggled. She led him through to the kitchen, self-consciously pulling her tie-belt tighter and wiggling her hips as she walked. Well, why not?

'Coffee?'

'Sounds good.'

She turned to fill the kettle, switched it on and

turned back as he pulled her towards him and crushed her body against his. Their mouths found each other's and they kissed, a long lingering kiss, until the rattling kettle told them the water was boiled. She cleared her throat and disentangled herself from him.

'Fresh or instant?'

'Instant's fine,' he said. His voice sounded distinctly and attractively husky. She didn't dare ask where he would prefer to take his coffee. She knew where she would rather go.

They sat at the kitchen table in a sudden shy silence.

'How was the rest of...?'

'How was your flight...?'

They laughed together and Bob glanced down as her dressing gown came half undone revealing her nakedness beneath. He raised his eyes back to hers and lifted one eyebrow.

'Sleep in the altogether, do you?'

'Erm... yes... at least... sometimes.' She didn't know what else to say. Maybe it was one of those moments when conversation became unnecessary. The tingling in her body told her it was. His sudden caress of her breasts through the open dressing gown said yes as well. They left the coffee untouched and she took his hand, led him upstairs and into her still warm bed... hell it was good to have him home.

The next few weeks flew by, and grew slowly into months. They shopped for a laptop for her and, patiently, Bob gave her lessons in computer literacy. He did not, however, feel particularly patient when she rang him in the small hours to tell him her computer had crashed and what should she do? He was tempted to say turn the bloody thing off until morning. If they had been sharing the same bed, he would have thought of better things to do in the middle of the night. Instead he showed tolerance, reluctantly switched on his own laptop and talked her through the manoeuvres to solve the problem. Mostly he was rewarded the next day by a breakfast visit (in bed) or invited round to hers for the first meal of the day. They drank copious amounts of fizz to accompany their scrambled eggs and smoked salmon, usually after an extremely pleasant sojourn in one or the other's houses. He began to truly appreciate retirement. And being in a relationship.

She took out membership and joined him at his gym club: soon mastered the treadmill to a running pace and the rower to 750 metres in five minutes. Together they cycled for fifteen minute intervals, then onto the resistance machines and back to cardio-vascular for more running, cycling and rowing.

'Does this justify our champagne breakfasts?' she panted.

'Dunno. At least it keeps us fit in between our times of debauchery. Helps burn up the calories.'

'So does a session under the duvet... know which one I prefer.'

He had no argument with that, just a question. 'Your place or mine, afterwards?'

Delia also spent pleasurable weeks organising the makeover of her house, persuading Bob to help her choose decor, pieces of furniture, and soft furnishings. In between times she visited his house and let him introduce her to his tenants, his police buddies and Stella. At first, she was cautious and pretended a shyness to give herself time to weigh up these people, especially the 'Delectable' Stella, as Bob often referred to her, but not to the solicitor's face.

In time she introduced him to the twins and their partners. Which slightly puzzled him because she had not mentioned a family. It was only after he found a photo album, on a shelf in her lounge, recording the life of two children from birth to adulthood, that he discovered she was a mother. Delia, he thought, could be quite secretive at times. What did she have to hide? Then he would dismiss these suspicions, feel guilty, tell himself to stop playing the bloody copper. Wasn't she the best thing to have happened to him? Well, wasn't she?

One morning, as he sat in his kitchen, the phone rang.

'Hi scrumptious, it's me.'

'Hello you,' he grinned. 'What can I do for you

this lovely morning?' He hoped she wasn't going to suggest another shopping trip.

'My daughter, Tilda, and her husband, Mike, are coming to stay for a few days. Thought you might like to meet them at dinner tonight.'

'Be delighted to, lovely lady. What time would you like me?'

'Right now,' she laughed. 'Not for dinner at breakfast time of course, I can think of much nicer things... But not practical. I'll have to get their room ready, shop for the evening meal and put all precious ornaments beyond Dalmatian-dog-tail reach.'

'What?'

'They've two mad, spotty dogs who wag their tails at a hundred miles an hour, devastating everything in their path. Ornaments go up on the ceiling when they're around.'

'Got you. Ok, so what time shall I arrive?'

'Say sixish? Then you can get to know them over drinks, before we sit down to eat. Hopefully, they'll have taken the two hounds for a run down to the beach before then.'

'I'll look forward to it... Anything you want me to bring? Some beer maybe? What does Mike drink?'

'Not sure, to be honest. You and he can always pop over to the off-licence.'

'Ok, fine. See you at six. Love you, gorgeous. Bye.'

She wished he hadn't called her gorgeous. It reminded her of H and she didn't want to remember him especially. Not now... She shook her head, told herself not to be stupid and get on with the day's planning. Looked forward, instead, to her daughter's and Mike's visit. And for them to meet this latest man in her life. She so hoped they approved... and liked him.

11
The Wedding Plans

They sat drinking coffee and discussing guest numbers.

'Not many on my side,' she said. 'There's the twins and their partners, my friend Manda, and Jessica and Denzel next door. That's about it.'

'No-one else? No brothers and sisters?'

'No,' she hesitated. 'I was an only child. My parents died years ago, before Gerald in fact.' *Why did I just do that, deny Saskia and Gethin, and their boys? Was it because they knew Carl, and might bring his name up in front of the twins? But Manda knew Carl and she had never mentioned him to the twins, her god-children... so far. Wonder if the twins remember their Aunt and Uncle? Don't think so, haven't seen them myself since Carl's death... We don't keep in touch... not any more.*

Delia hadn't told Bob about Carl and hoped Manda wouldn't mention him either. She reminded herself to speak to her friend about it. But Carl was still no excuse to exclude her sister and Gethin from the wedding list. Now she regretted her denial but saw no way to tell Bob the truth after such a stupid lie.

'Gerald was the twins' father?'

'Yes.'

'Ok, so that's seven on your side.'

'What about you, darling? Who do you want to invite?'

'Erm, well I suppose my brother Eddie and his wife, Yvonne. They live in Norfolk. You'll like them, a great couple, and… the three guys and Stella.' (He remembered not to say the Delectable). 'That's Jay, Gary, Phil and Stella.' He counted on his fingers, 'That's six.'

'What about anyone from the station?' she asked.

'I don't think so. Been retired for six months now. I s'pose I could extend an invitation to Stella's father. If I hadn't borrowed his apartment in Portugal, you and I wouldn't have met.'

'Yes, why not?' she paused. 'D'you think we ought to invite anyone from the gym club?'

'Up to you, love. Anyone in mind?'

'Not really. I mean,' she added, 'they're a nice enough bunch but we don't seem to mix with them socially: not outside gym sessions, do we?'

'True. Ok, so that's fourteen and us two, sixteen. We could have the reception at the New Priory, I hear they do a pretty good bash there. Probably won't cost much more than hiring a hall and decorating it, plus caterers. What d'you think?'

Delia smiled. 'That would be perfect, the Priory. Right backdrop too for the outdoor photos… that lovely Virginia creeper climbing the walls and those wonderful gardens.' She thought about the venue, remembered going to one of H's fishing buddies' retirement party there; and the first floor restaurant and ballroom, how it was so beautifully decorated for each event. Yes, it would be perfect. Also, it had what she thought of as a Romeo and Juliet balcony. Yes, she and Bob could have some superb photos taken up there from down below in the delightful gardens… She sighed with pleasure, and more than slight amazement at the speed of their relationship, from lovers to getting married.

It had happened soon after Bob met Tilda and Mike, then Danny and Ray. Almost as if meeting her children was the catalyst for his proposal. Perhaps that was what Bob wanted in his life? Apart from herself of course. Family. She was pleased they all got on and looked forward to meeting his brother and sister-in-law.

Her mind went back to her weddings to Gerald and H, neither particularly memorable nor grand: one service discreetly held in Hampshire, the other in Ramsgate registry office, with a fairly quiet reception to follow. Just the twins, Mike, and Manda, at her wedding to H, with a lunch afterwards at an unpretentious little Italian restaurant away from the seafront. Genaro's.

There was only herself and Gerald, plus two of his staff, when they quietly married in Hampshire before moving down here to Kent. She was pregnant, not with the twins. There had been another baby, a two month embryo, the day they got married, and quietly terminated less than a month later.

Gerald was sad. He had really wanted a baby son or daughter. 'It doesn't matter which,' he told her. She did not tell him of her visit to the clinic. How she had told the doctor she had been raped and it was not her husband's child. He would be home soon from his tour overseas, she had sobbed, and he must never find out. The doctor she recalled, smiled sympathetically, patted her hand and said, 'Right, young lady, let's do something about it.' He was a fatherly figure, probably about Gerald's age…

A week later, the embryo was no more. Gerald had been away all day, at a book auction. When he returned, Delia was in bed looking pale and wan. She wept as she told him the news, that 'everything had come away, and there was no baby.' He had shown immediate concern and anxiety. 'Shouldn't you go to hospital? Have them examine you?'

'I've seen a nurse from the surgery,' she lied. 'She examined me, said I should be ok with a couple of days' bed rest. And I've to call her if anything happens, like a haemorrhage.'

Gerald knew little of these things and he believed her. He said, 'I should have been here for you. I'm so sorry.'

They did not make love for a month or more, then gradually went back to a once-weekly routine, nothing earth-shattering but adequate, until she fell pregnant with the twins, much to Gerald's delight. Delia enjoyed a perfectly healthy pregnancy and was secretly delighted the way Gerald fussed and worried for the four of them: him, herself and the two embryos. She went into labour at eight months, producing a girl and a boy, each weighing five pounds: a healthy enough weight for them to survive.

Gerald decorated the second back bedroom that overlooked the garden, as a nursery, with mobiles over two cots and a frieze of elephants around the walls. There were cupboards topped with fluffy toys, a soft pastel carpet and pale rainbow-coloured curtains. He added a further waist-high cupboard with a foldaway changing mattress on top and a wardrobe, filled with expensive baby clothes.

Delia knew they would want for nothing, these two, and be expensively educated. Gerald had already put their names down for Reeves. Sad that he did not see them grow up...

Then there was H. Best not dwell on him. And now, she thought, there is Bob, lovely chunky Bob.

'Penny for them.'

'What? Oh,' she laughed. 'Sorry, I was miles away. Yes... the Priory. Wonderful. We can get married there, too. They have a special licence to conduct weddings'

'Great, all the nitty gritty under one roof. We

can stay the night there before I whisk you off to Paradise: well the Algarve.'

She got up from her seat and went over to his, sat on his lap and kissed him. 'It all sounds perfect.'

He pulled her close, ran his hands over her body, a vessel for his love and adoration. He felt his erection rising. So could she, and moved her hand round to his crotch. 'Time for bed I think, Mr Shackleton.'

'But Mrs Shackleton-to-be, shame on you. T'is only half past three.'

'I know, I have no shame.' She stood up and pulled him to his feet. He was taller than her and she reached up to kiss him, teasing his mouth with her tongue. 'Come on,' she whispered. 'We can go over the plans later.'

She went to the fridge and pulled out a bottle of bubbly, grabbed two glasses from the cupboard and the teacloth hanging on its hook by the stove.

'Don't you just think of everything? he said, tantalizing her with more caressing.

'Just in case we get thirsty,' she said, and pulled him from the kitchen upstairs to the bedroom.

It was dark when they woke but she could see the time on her new bedside clock. Seven o'clock. Bob snuggled into her, enjoying their nudity. 'Mm... You smell gorgeous Mrs Almost.'

'Not so bad yourself, Mr S.' She enjoyed the

lingering scent of his aftershave, and his body smell.'

'Bloody hell!'

'What?'

'Just remembered we're supposed to be having dinner with Phil and Stella tonight. Seven thirty for eight, remember?.

Delia groaned but slid quickly out of bed. 'Ok, I'll go and shower while you call a taxi. We'd best not drive, not after that bottle of champers. You can have yours while I dress.'

'What... champers?'

'No, silly, your shower. We'll get there by seven forty-five.'

12

Later that night, after they left Phil and Stella's dinner party and were home in bed, not the one she and H had shared, her new bed, she thought again about her father. After H's death she had invested in a new one, a gondola the man in the bed shop had called it. She thought it was more like the sledge her father had made her, many years ago, when she was a little girl. It had curved ends, to stop her falling out, Daddy had said in his laughing voice. She felt a sudden twinge of missing him... and her mum. How many years had it been?

They could have stayed in Bob's flat, in his bedroom directly beneath Phil and Stella's apartment. Delia made the excuse that she needed to change clothes the next day and besides, she had nothing here to sleep in.

'What's wrong with sleeping in the altogether?' Bob said. 'You've got a toothbrush here and toiletries. We can pick you up a change of clothes tomorrow.'

She was tempted, but still felt the need to sleep in her own room, and wake up to birdsong, not Stella's tinny kitchen radio above the ceiling.

'Please?' she wheedled, and Bob easily gave in. He was enjoying the novelty and intimacy of their relationship too much not to indulge her. They didn't have to book or wait for a taxi: Jay and Gary came back from their shift at the station and Jay said he would run them back to Delia's place after the dinner. He and Gary were also invited to stay for the meal and Stella's father, another of the diners, was staying the night in the couple's spare room.

Perhaps it was being in the company of the older man, and hearing Stella calling him Daddy, that made her think of her father. She was introduced to 'darling daddy', and discovered his name was Stephen, the same as her Dad. Coincidentally, this Stephen had been to India, as had her father many years before. The name Tagore, a famed Indian poet cropped up.

'He won the Nobel Peace Prize in 1911,' he said.

Delia smiled. 'My father taught one of his descendants to play the Hawaiian guitar,' she told them at dinner.

'Really?' said Stephen. 'I visited Rabindranath's birthplace when I was out there, didn't realise he had relatives in this country. Fancy your father teaching one of his family. How did that come about?'

'Don't know really. I was only a kid at the time. Dad was a plane-maker by day and went to pubs and clubs at night to play his music. Maybe they met at one of these venues.'

'Hmm, interesting. What was he like, the young Tagore?'

'Very quiet, polite, reserved. Some of his friends that accompanied him were less reserved. Fun to be with and a novelty to have so many courtesy older brothers around. They spoiled me rotten, treated me like a younger sister, bought me lots of presents.'

Stella swiftly moved the conversation on to the present and directed towards herself. Bitch, thought Delia. *I expect she thinks I'm one too. Can't bear someone else to hog the attention of all these men, can you?* She struggled through the rest of the evening with a glue-fixed smile on her face, taking comfort in the knowledge that she and Bob would soon be home and away from here. Why did she so dislike the Delectable Stella? Logic told her she was no threat to her and Bob's relationship... as far as she knew. Could be her slightly superior air. Solicitor versus stay-at-home widow. So?

'What do you think, Delia?'

She blinked and returned a little shamefacedly to the company. 'Sorry, I was miles away. Didn't hear what was being said.'

She grinned and was relieved when they all laughed and suggested she was only hearing wedding bells.

'Sounds about right. Sorry.' She managed a convincing and meaningful yawn. Bob took the hint. 'Come on, woman, time I tucked you up in bed.'

'Did you say TUCK Bob?'

'Yes, Philip, I did. Ladies present and all that.'

When the time came to say goodnight, the two ladies airbrushed each other, then Stella lingered longer over her goodnight kiss with Bob, and Delia, piqued, did the same with both Phil and Stella's 'darling daddy'. She was slightly shocked when Stephen added his tongue to their kiss and hoped Bob did not notice.

Jay helped her on with her coat and Gary said he would come along for the ride. When they were all in the car, Jay said, 'Stella came on a bit strong tonight, or was it my imagination?'

'Mmn,' Bob agreed. 'Come to think of, it so did "darling daddy". Was it my imagination,' he turned to face Delia in the darkened car. 'Or was he trying to get his tongue down your throat?'

She was grateful for that dark interior. 'Not quite,' she lied. 'But he certainly wasn't past trying, dirty old sod.'

'Go on Bob,' laughed Gary. 'Go back and smack him in the mouth, dirty bastard.'

'Seems to run in the family,' Delia retorted. 'Stella was doing her best to eat you, wasn't she?'

Her fiancée's face was caught in the light from a street lamp as they passed it. She smugly noted he looked sheepish. Quid pro quo Robert... She dearly hoped he wouldn't ask the boys in for a nightcap, had had enough of their banter for one evening, enough of being pleasant to the Delectable Stella and her rakish father. God help us on the wedding day, she thought. What with them and Manda...

She need not have worried, Bob was more than ready to say goodnight to the guys as she and he climbed out of the car. He hesitated, as if decency decreed he at least invited them in.

'If you're about to suggest a nightcap. Forget it,' said Gary. 'We're both on early shift tomorrow. Phil too, come to think of it.'

'Right then. Thanks for the lift, Jay. See you guys soon. Bye.'

He put his arm around her. 'Come on woman, let's get to bed. Might still have enough energy for a swift tumble.'

'Bully for you. Hope I don't fall asleep on you, else you might refuse to marry me.'

'Don't worry darling, I'll pull your nightie down afterwards.'

She grinned. 'What nightie? Thought you preferred black bra and panties.'

'Don't forget the stocking tops.' He groaned. 'Shouldn't have mentioned them, I've really got a hard on now.'

They struggled in through the front door and made straight for the stairs, shedding coats as they climbed, followed by his shirt and her unzipped dress. They tumbled into bed, hungry for each other, all thoughts of Stella and her raunchy daddy dispelled. It was past one before their bedside lamps were switched off.

13

The Wedding and an Aubergine Balloon

The day was perfect, sunny, warm and enveloping Delia with a huge feeling of the love and happiness from her family and friends. Back at the house that morning, it was Manda who helped her to dress, with Tilda assisting.

'Lovely outfit, Delia. The colour is so you.'

'And weren't you the lucky one, Mum, to get shoes that perfectly match?'

Danny, Ray and Mike were downstairs washing up after breakfast. She could hear the banter and felt the pleasure of having them all there as it crept through her. She answered the two women automatically, directed where necessary, and generally allowed herself to be swept along in the importance of her wedding day.

Her mind, however, was ahead of these arrangements: there was a more important task to plan and implement, one that had to be carried out with deadly precision. And cunning. Manda must go after her serious indiscretion regarding Carl. Delia could not believe what she had said at the dinner table, two nights ago, when Bob had taken them all out for a stag-and-hen night as he called it. Especially as the party included his brother and sister-in-law, his three police buddies and Stella.

'To Bob and Delia, may they know true happiness.' Manda had stumbled, grabbing the tablecloth and hiccupping. And that stupid expression on her blotched and reddening face.

Tilda or Danny, Delia could not remember who, had stood up and finished the toast, 'Third time lucky, Mum.' With a big grin on their face.

Manda had recovered herself enough to say, 'Fourth you mean.'

'Third, Aunt Manda, Dad, then H and now Bob.'

'What about the nasty Carl?'

Delia's stomach had churned. *Stupid cow, how could she?* She quickly explained. 'Oh, your Aunt Manda's referring to a rather nasty *boyfriend* I had before I met your Dad.' And she had glared at her friend. No excuse, Manda, she thought. Don't care if you're drunk or sober. Subject Carl is taboo. Manda stared back, her eyes glazed with their surfeit of alcohol.

'Yeah,' she slurred. 'Nasty *poyfriend.'* And stabbed at the word with a curl of her lips.

A quick glance at the others gave Delia an uneasy feeling that she was being questioned in their minds. Best change the subject and ignore her so-called friend: soon to be ex-friend was now a distinct possibility. The party continued and everyone seemed to relax and enjoy the evening.

As far as Delia was concerned, Manda had outlived her usefulness and her value as a friend and as godmother to Danny and Tilda. She reasoned that Manda would leave everything to the twins, probably quite a considerable sum of money, *and* the valuable contents of her house in the Midlands. It was the only way...

'Mum, you're so quiet. You ok?' Delia smiled, willed herself back to the present. 'Course I am, darling. Sorry... I was miles away.' Less than one, to be exact.   Already, in her mind, at the Priory. Ceremony over, the sit-down reception finished. All of them, drinks in hand, she and Bob wandering from group to group socialising, enjoying the background music of the resident quartet, The Four Cliffs of Dover, as they waited for the restaurant staff to rearrange the tables around the room and clear the small parquet floor ready for the dancing. She imagined Bob's hand clasping hers with the pride of new ownership and exultant anticipation of what was to come when they were on their own.

'Come and sit, Mum.' Tilda again. 'Let's get your hair done.'

She allowed Tilda and Manda to arrange her hair and finally place the small, jaunty fascinator on the side of her head. Sitting by the window, she looked out to clear blue skies and the distant sea, above the rooftops beyond the railway. Gulls performed their aerial ballet, above the trees that edged the little station, before heading back out to the coastline.

'There,' said Tilda. 'What d'you think?' She held a mirror before her mother.

Delia's face widened in delight. 'Perfect, my love. Oh boy, I feel twenty-one again.'

Manda laughed. 'You'll always be young, Delia. All this husband-gathering.'

'Mm... Is that a tad of jealousy I detect?'

'God no! Couldn't be happier for you. Besides, I think you've got a goodie in Bob.

'He's lovely, Mum.' Tilda hesitated. 'Gotta be honest, I didn't much like H.'

'Oh I don't know,' said Manda. 'I thought he was quite raunchy.'

'You would say that, Aunt Manda.'

Delia considered. 'Maybe not the best man in the world, but don't let's bad-mouth him now he's gone.' She wondered what they would say about Manda when she became the dear departed. Probably canonise her... She felt good. Looked forward to the simple ceremony in the flower-decked gardens of the Priory, the reception following, and – more – to what she planned to happen afterwards. She felt a breathless excitement as she pictured Manda sprawled out on the rockery below the balcony. Would there be much blood? Would her dress ride up showing fleshy thighs, her knickers? And her eyes, open in shock at the violent impact after her fall? Or would they be closed?

Delia's heart-pace quickened, saliva flowed into her mouth causing her to draw it to the back of her throat, swallow it like a drink.

'Mum!'

She shook herself. 'Sorry, what were you saying?'

'Where've you been Mum? Your face was a complete blank just now.'

She smiled at her daughter. 'I was picturing us all at the Priory.'

'Right. I just asked you what time are the cars coming?'

Delia looked at her dainty gold watch, a pre-wedding gift from Bob. 'In about half an hour, twelve noon.'

'Great. Come on, Aunt Manda, time for us to dress and put on our slap.' She turned to the door and called downstairs. 'You guys ready? The cars are coming in twenty minutes.'

The women smiled as they heard the sudden rumble of feet on the stairs.

'Bloody hell,' said Mike. 'Twenty minutes?'

'Ok, thirty then,' conceded Tilda. 'We need to be waiting downstairs when they arrive.' She called to her brother, 'Danny – you got the champers chilling? We'll need a glass before we leave.'

'Roger that,' he replied. He was currently into copying Prince Harry.

Ten minutes later, they were all in the front

room, glasses in hands and waiting for the cars to transport them to the venue. Mike squeezed his mother-in-law's arm. 'You ok, Delia?'

She smiled at him. 'I'm fine, even better after this.' She held up her glass of bubbly. 'Santé everybody.'

'Yeah, cheers sweetie.' Manda clinked glasses with her best friend, blissfully unaware it might be one of the last times she would do so.

Delia had watched with annoyance as Manda carefully wiped the rim of her glass with a tissue, before giving Mike a chance to fill it. She had noticed a few irritating habits about her friend this week. Was Manda turning into an old maid with fussy little habits? Only yesterday Delia watched Manda run her fingers along the kitchen window sill, and resisted the urge to say, 'Dust collecting?' They used to, she remembered, have so much in common, though not anymore. Just as well with what's going to happen to you, she thought... in a few hours' time. She indulged herself, imagining the scenario; she would persuade Bob back into the room to mingle with their guests, and Manda? Manda would be led by her out onto the balcony, glass in hand, and filled not only with champagne, but with a phial of colourless liquid that she had filched from Stella and Phil's bathroom some weeks ago. She had discovered that it was a 'souvenir' Phil confiscated from one of their drug traffickers whom he and Bob had arrested months before. Perhaps there would be enough to share with Stella's glass. Kill two birds with...

Delia felt sick with panic. The day was passing quickly, too quickly. Her plan of Manda falling off the balcony was not going to happen.

'You won't get me near there,' she'd said to Delia, when invited to look at the view. 'Vertigo, big time.'

Since when did *she* suffer from it? She never showed signs of it in Portugal, but of course they had had a ground floor suite that led out onto a patio and then out to the lawned gardens. The lawn that the massive black guy used to water every morning. The man that Manda used to flirt with outrageously, and she clad only in the scantiest shorts and sleeveless pyjama tops.

'Wonder you weren't raped,' Delia had scolded her later, and Manda had smiled. 'Might have been fun. Never had it away with such a dark skinned guy. Fantastic physique too, did you notice?'

'You're impossible,' Delia remembered answering her.

Bob crept up behind her, puncturing her thoughts. 'More champers, Mrs Shackleton?'

It sounded good, Mrs Shackleton. 'Be silly not to.' She turned and grinned at her husband of thirty minutes. He grabbed two glasses off a passing waiter's tray.

'Have I told you...?'

'...lately that I love you?' she interrupted.

'That as well, but I was going to say how amazing you look in blue. Is it cornflower?'

She nodded and sipped her drink, enjoying the bubbles. She could see Manda over the other side of the room, pushing away a dish of appetisers and shaking her head at the waiter. But Delia turned her attention back to Bob, who had slipped his warm hand over her own as he caressed her new wedding ring and gently, suggestively, rubbed a finger over her palm. All thoughts of Manda and her vertigo left her. At that moment a gong quaintly sounded and the proprietor, in the role of Maître d' called out, 'Mr and Mrs Shackleton, ladies and gentlemen, lunch is served.'

They moved as a group from the reception hall into the dining room. Delia drew in her breath with pleased surprise at the decorations. Yellow and white balloons floated up from the horseshoe-shaped table arrangement, anchored by gold and white curled ribbons. There were scatterings of matching rose petals on the white damask cloths, along with bottles of wine: the whites in sparkling iced sleeves and the reds seated on round, silver trays.

At the far end of the room the quartet struck up 'Congratulations' and one of them sang it in a Mike Reid voice, grinning just like the late veteran comedian.   For a fleeting moment, Delia was reminded of H, just for a moment... Friends and family clapped them to their seats, where white-shirted, burgundy-skirted girls stood waiting to serve the food, their male counterparts in crisp white jackets and burgundy trousers ready to pour the wines.

Delia and Bob had chosen courses from several different menus, preferring to mix and match. The fish dish, from menu one, grilled fillet of fresh trout served on a bed of crushed almonds within a tempura-battered samphire appealed to both of them: chilled Chablis would be the perfect wine to accompany this course.

'It'll have to be some kind of steak dish for my police buddies,' he'd said. 'Even if they can't have chips.'

'Course they can have chips. We can give everybody the choice of two main courses, steak or chicken breast. How about,' she read. 'Medallions of Angus Fillet in a cream and pepper sauce or Breast of Chicken prosciutto asparago?'

'What's that?'

'Breast of corn-fed chicken filled with asparagus and prosciutto ham, served in a rich Neapolitan sauce of tomato and fresh basil.'

'Sounds good. I think Phil's wife, Stella would like that.'

Delia gave him a keen look. *You fancy her, don't*

you?

Bob returned to the sample menus, oblivious to her observation. 'Châteauneuf du Pape for the steaks and either more Chablis or another white, maybe some rosé as well. Are we having a pud?' he continued.

'I thought maybe a lemon sorbet between the fish and meat course, then possibly a fresh-fruit salad for dessert, or a Charlotte Russe, followed by a cheeseboard and Madeira or Port.'

'Excellent. I feel hungry already. They had phoned in their choices to the Priory and celebrated with bed and bubbly. Delia enjoyed being wickedly unmarried and hoped the lovemaking would be just as good when she had Bob's gold ring on her finger.

'You're very quiet darling, everything ok? Not regretting marrying me are you?'

'I'm fine,' she smiled. 'And no, of course I've no regrets. I was just thinking about the day we chose this feast,'

Bob grinned. 'Four-poster fun tonight eh?'

Unfortunately their four poster nuptials would be delayed by several hours past a normal bedtime. Thanks to Manda's untimely death from nut poisoning. Delia had completely forgotten her friend was allergic to nuts, and Manda had no clue as to what was on her plate. Her own fault. When Delia, a few days before, had attempted to describe the wedding feast to her, Manda had gone all dramatic on her. 'Oh, don't tell me. Let it be a surprise; you know how I love surprises,' she crowed, her arms waving about like a rebellious windmill.

The surprise turned out to be fatal. The culprits being the crushed almonds, barely visible, hidden as they were in the tempura-battered samphire and under the grilled fillet of trout.

It didn't happen immediately, the lethal reaction. All the courses had been served and enjoyed, and everyone was waiting to listen to Danny's speech, as the giver away of the bride, which would be followed by Phil's best man speech. Champagne had been poured and the top layer of the wedding cake removed, ready for the head waiter to begin cutting the bottom layer. Plates with thick, yellow and white paper serviettes, decorated with wedding-bell corners, were placed in front of each guest, along with frilled-lace favours filled with iced almonds for the ladies and almond filled boxes shaped like dinner jackets for the men.

Danny stood up first, fingering his collar and looking slightly pink in the face. He gratefully received an encouraging nod and smile from Ray, then cleared his throat. It came out as a fearsome choking sound, causing everyone to look up. But it had not come from his gullet. Two seats away from him, Manda was grappling with her throat. It was she who was making the terrible and terrifying sounds. She looked like a wild horse with bulging eyeballs, and her rapidly swelling face was turning deep purple.

Looking round in horror at her friend, Delia was uncannily reminded of a Harry Potter film, where he had cast a spell on a hateful aunt: she had inflated like a huge balloon and floated through the French windows, up to the sky. Manda, she thought, reminded her of a rapidly-inflating, purple balloon. Now her friend was suffocating through her own swelling throat and, maybe, Delia's earlier death wish. If Manda had let Delia reveal the menu to her, and she had not 'forgotten' her friend's severe allergy to nuts, this would not be happening, (or would it?).

Everything seemed to be creeping agonisingly forward in slow motion, until some of the staff abruptly motivated themselves. Others rushed towards Manda and tried to loosen her clothing; someone else pulled out their mobile phone and dialled for an ambulance. Guests jumped up from their seats, some spilling champagne, others rocking the table and tipping over their chairs. Utter chaos. Except for Delia. She just sat there, watched the scenario from a distance, as if it was some weird play or film and nothing to do with her or this special wedding day. Only Manda could take away the attention from her. It's what she did. Stole the limelight, made sure the focus of attention was on her and no-one else.

She was aware that Bob had left her side and

was trying to help revive or save the choking woman. She heard the ambulance siren as it stopped on the gravel drive outside, saw the green uniforms of two paramedics as they rushed into the room, bags in hand, one carrying an oxygen cylinder, to the dying patient. Because that was what Manda now was: dying, soon to be very dead. No more wiping imaginary specks from a wine glass, no more looking for dust on Delia's window sill, and no more blurting out Carl's name and his role in her friend's life. Perhaps Delia should worship a new god, or what that god could do to certain people: endow them with a fatal allergy to nuts. She almost forgave Manda for her previous drunken transgression but would despise her memory forever, because she had spoiled her perfect day, her wedding day, hers and Bob's. How could they possibly enjoy the rest of the afternoon and evening, the entertainment and pleasure of being with family and friends on such a special occasion? Thanks, Manda... for nothing.

14

Two weeks later, they went on their belated honeymoon, after Manda's funeral and the reading of the will. Surprisingly she had left her house and contents to her friend Delia and the sum of twenty-five thousand pounds each, to 'my two godchildren, Tilda and Danny'. There was a further sum of money, from her life insurance, thirty-five thousand pounds that the solicitor said would go towards the funeral costs, his fees, and the rest would pass to Delia. Beneath her wide-brimmed black hat, as she watched her friend's coffin disappear through the fawn coloured drapes, Delia whispered to herself 'Thank the Lord for almonds.'

She and Bob stayed the night at the Hilton in Birmingham and flew out to Portugal the following morning to begin their much delayed honeymoon, considerably richer than they would have been had there not been the drama of Manda's death.

Several times during their honeymoon in Alvor, Bob pointed out the little apartment above the souvenir shop where he had stayed: the one that belonged to Stella's father. Only he kept saying the 'Delectable Stella's daddy'. Delia wished he wouldn't, felt a stab of jealousy, felt somehow that Stella overshadowed, or even governed, their lives. She noted the way Bob had almost deferred to her at their wedding. Certainly before Manda's drama had overtaken all events. Secretly she thought there had to be ways to curb Stella's influence in their lives. One thing for sure, they were not going to live at Bob's house, especially now they had Manda's money to refurbish her own. She could spend quite lavishly, make it attractive enough, enticing enough, for Bob to prefer it to his own place, and not want to live underneath the Delectable Stella. Bitch, bitch, bitch...

She would also erase all memories of H, anything they had shared together, bought together. (The bed had already gone, long gone). Delia, most definitely, did not want to live under the Delectable Stella, or want Bob to be aware of any lingering memories of her own late spouse.

Before the wedding, she had privately vowed to kill the wretched woman if she bought them a toaster for a wedding gift. Stella went one further, she and Phil gave them a matching set of electric kettle, coffee maker and the dreaded toaster. Stella's fate was sealed... time for that afterwards, Delia thought, as they sipped their in-flight champagne, when they took up their new life together. A new life that did not include 'the Delectable', or her oh-so-boring daddy.

Pity really, she quite liked Phil: boyish, muscular

Phil that she had once seen in his cotton briefs stretching in front of his full-length kitchen window that overlooked Bob's small back garden. She had noted the healthy-looking bulge in his crotch that caused an unexpected, abrupt excitement and sent flutters beneath the dressing gown she was wearing. Even though sex with Bob was more than satisfactory. Once – later – she had actually dreamed about making love to the younger man when she and Bob were doing it. She imagined a musky smell from his body and the thrust as he penetrated her. She and Bob had climaxed together that time...

Bob asked, 'Would you like to fly on to somewhere else? We don't have to get back immediately. When all's said and done,' he grinned a schoolboy's grin, 'we don't have to get back for work or anything.'

She thought about it and admitted to herself that the little fishing village had lost its charm for her, imagining as she did, Stella around every next corner, or maybe Manda's ghost.

'I wouldn't mind... yes, I think that's a great idea. Fancy Italy? One of the lakes? I hear they're beautiful at this time of year.'

'Not the exotic east then?' He smiled again. He really was very attractive, she thought.

'No, Europe's fine. I'd get fidgety on one of those long haul flights.'

'Ok, Italy it is.' He was about to say 'Wonder if

Stella and Phil have been to Lake Como?' Instinct stopped him. 'How about Lake Garda... or Lake Como? Or Venice?'

They settled for a week in Venice and a week in Gravedona, a small town on the shore of Lake Como, a dot on the map of Italy and its lakes.

Delia was fascinated by Venice, and a little awed. Those narrow streets that criss-crossed over equally narrow bridges. Not over roads but canals where boats of all description lapped against houses and warehouses like parked cars in other city streets. The view from their hotel bedroom window, overlooking the Grand Canal, could have been straight out of a Canaletto, with craft of every description – gondolas, water taxis, private boats, and barges – all vying for space and pace. A short walk away, San Marco Square echoed with orchestral music from the luxurious street cafés, where gliding waiters in long black aprons and gleaming white shirts held their trays up high, and deftly swirled them onto whichever table they were serving. Delia watched them, fascinated and entertained. She loved the internationality of Venice, with its Babel of tongues, accents, and dialects. She was fascinated by the voices teasing her ears with their foreignness, some gushing from mouths like an oral waterfall, others spat out in guttural, north-eastern tongues. She listened to the twang of American intonations vying with the guitars and violins of street musicians. Above all, the colours of landscape, waterscape, people, and fluttering pennants, delighted her wherever she chose to turn her head.

Bob smiled, 'Happy?' He reached for her hand across the damask covered table.

She smiled back, nodded. 'Couldn't be happier.'

'Different here, isn't it?'

'Certainly is. Different and mesmerizing. Something special wherever you look.'

'Have you spotted the jewellers over there?' He pointed across the huge square, beyond the strolling tourists, towards a cloistered set of retail premises, their windows decorated with intricate filigree pieces.

Her eyes lit up. 'No, I didn't. Can we go and have a look when we finish our coffees?'

'Course we can. If you're very good I'll buy you something nice.'

'How good?' She dimpled like a teenager.

He calculated. 'As good as last night. Didn't realise what fun a four-poster bed could be.' He licked his lips, pursed them and sucked in his breath. 'Marvellous.'

She allowed him the moment before she said, 'I love silver filigree, but it doesn't come cheap. I'll have to be very good tonight. Or this afternoon. Siesta and all that. Panties-on-the chandelier good.'

'Christ woman. Too much detail, I've got a hard

on already. Stoppit...'

They finished their coffees, paid as much for them, without wincing, as a three-course pub meal back home, and strolled hand in hand towards the cloistered shops. Delia smiled inwardly: money was no object this holiday. *Thanks Manda. Pity about the almonds, but all in a good cause...*

They spent twenty minutes or so, noses pressed against several shop windows, marvelling at the intricate pieces displayed. Sometimes a shop owner ventured out to tempt them inside. The successful one caught Delia gasping at a silver galleon, amazed at its intricacy.

'You like, signora?'

She nodded. 'I like very much.'

'I have more inside. Why don't you both come in and have a look? Share a delicious grappa with me?'

She turned to her new husband. 'Come on, let's.'

Once inside this Italianate Aladdin's cave, they accepted a glass of grappa each and gazed everywhere, appreciating the jeweller's rich variety of delicately-crafted pieces.

'The galeone, signora, it means something special to you?'

'Yes, in a way. When I was a little girl, my mother used to say, ''When my ship comes home you shall have all the treasures in the world.'' We didn't have a lot of money then, and I never had the toys other children had.' *Was she making it up as she went along? It was true about Mum saying that, though, when her ship came home, but Delia couldn't exactly remember poverty.*

'And your mamma, where is she now?'

'Oh, she died when I was eighteen, both her and my father, killed in a car crash.' *Another lie. They come easy to you, don't they? They didn't want you to marry Carl, thought you were much too young. So you were. They only gave their reluctant permission for you to wed because you told them you were pregnant. You never saw them again, did you? Yes, they did die years ago, both of cancer. No car crash. What made you think of that? Crazy woman...*

'Che piccato, signora. What a pity.' His face showed sympathy as he refilled their small glasses. 'I give you nice discount on il galeone.'

'Grazie signor,' she said. 'We are here on our honeymoon.'

The elderly Italian beamed. 'Bene, bene. In that case I give you two discounts and a bottle of grappa for your wedding.'

He dropped the price of the galleon from 300 Euros to 275, then changed his mind and settled for 250. He wrapped it beautifully in an expensive looking silver foil paper, tied it with green, white and red ribbon, and gave them a similar gift-wrapped bottle of grappa. 'Have a very happy life together,' he beamed. 'Lots of bambini, eh?'

'Not at our age,' Delia laughed. 'But thanks for the compliment.'

They left the dim interior of the shop and strolled out into the sunshine again. She clutched her precious galleon, leaving Bob holding the grappa.

'Nice guy,' he remarked. 'I could get used to this drink. What's it made of?'

'The skins, pulp and seeds of grapes I think, distilled after they have been fermented for wine.'

'You're a fount of knowledge, woman. Where did you learn that?'

'Can't remember now. I think I asked an Italian restaurateur once.' She shook her head, 'No, can't tell you. Forgotten. We can always look it up on Google when we get home.'

'Ooh, we can look it up on Google. Proper little computer buff you're becoming Mrs S.'

She laughed. What a happy day...

For the next few days, they were wakened by a serenade of halyards from yachts bobbing about in the harbour, the chug of water taxis, and the cries of straw-hatted gondoliers as they greeted and passed each other on the canals. They became tourists and rode the canals by water taxi and once on a gondola. They watched Murano glass-blowing in small, out-of-the-way factories, wandered along the canal sides and through streets of souvenir shops, and gazed again at the jewellers' windows. They wined and dined in Venice's many restaurants and, at night, enjoyed the delights of their hotel bedroom with its four-poster bed. On their last day in Venice, they strolled back to the Murano glass factory where Bob bought her an exquisitely-designed glass vase.

'You can put flowers in it next to the silver galleon, decorate the front room window shelf or something.'

'I haven't bought anything for you. That makes me feel selfish and spoilt.' She clutched the well-wrapped gift in one hand and slid her other inside his own.

'Don't be silly. What do I need? Apart from you, of course: between two slices of bread would be good.'

She grinned, was about to make some pert reply, and thought too long about a witty response, which allowed him to commit an unforgivable offence.

'We must come back here.' He said. 'I bet Stella and Phil would love Venice... don't think they've been here, never mentioned it anyway. Maybe we can all come here together some time?'

Are you kidding, lover boy?

Later, as they lay in bed, he stroked her hair and her neck with one hand, caressing her body with his other hand. He pressed himself against her so she could feel his hardness beneath the bedclothes, saying her name over and over. How could she resist? But her response to his lovemaking, for once, was semi-automatic, perfunctory, even with some false whimpering of enjoyment. He failed to notice that, as he spooned into her with a final climatic thrust, and whispered 'fantastic woman' before he turned over for sleep. His hand sought hers but she slipped away from him. 'Just going to the bathroom.'

She showered Stella and their lovemaking away. As she towel-dried she made plans, at least thought through possibilities. The bitch had to go, but how?

Next day, they hired a car and drove to Lake Como, to the small town called Gravedona. It was late afternoon when they arrived, with the sun still shining above the mountains on the other side of the lake. Their hotel was only a cobbled-street width away from the water's edge and the marina where motor boats ferried people across the lake to the opposite towns. Half an hour to register, to be shown to their suite, and change into fresh clothes, before they went downstairs again and out onto the warmth of the street.

They crossed over towards the marina, leaned on the railings and watched as people disembarked: men shouldering their laptop cases, women with shopping baskets and fancy carrier bags. They smiled as they listened to the chatter of little ones. Couldn't understand the words, apart from an occasional mamma or pappa, but interpreted the happiness and naturalness of small family groups.

'Fancy a swift glass of vino?'

She smiled. 'That should go down very nicely. Where? Back in the hotel, or find a bar somewhere?'

'Find a bar. Right, left, or up the hill?'

'Long as we don't go forward,' she laughed. 'Else we'll get pretty wet.'

'Think we drove past one, not far from here, when we entered the town.' Bob indicated right. They walked, hand in hand, along the lakeside pavement, taking in several piazzas that shared space with small cars and noisy spluttering Vespas. They passed a promenade of shops, and houses that lay back behind iron gates, hidden under hanging blooms of bougainvillea. They enjoyed the breeze coming in over the lake as it teased them with its warmth. People shouted 'Ciao' to each other, kissed cheeks in greeting, shook hands with sweaters flapping over their shoulders, sunglasses perched on their heads now the sun was lower in the sky. The giant orb was gradually losing its burning whiteness as it began its orange slide behind the mountains and shimmered amazing colours over the lake.

'This looks ok,' he said. He pointed to a large wooden promontory that spread out over the lake, where several couples sat at tables under a pergola of trailing vines and waiters slid gracefully between tables with trays of glasses and small dishes of crudités and appetisers. They found an empty table and slid onto the seats. Within minutes, a waiter came to their table. 'Signore, signora,' and in a split second he changed to English, 'what can I get you?'

'How did you know we were English?' She could not resist asking him.

He rewarded her with a dazzling smile. 'Your fair hair and complexion, signora. It gives you away.'

They ordered a carafe of vino rosso which arrived with a small dish of nuts, cheese morsels, tiny salted biscuits and grapes still glistening with the water they had been washed in. They said 'Grazie' to the waiter, he told them 'Prego, don't mention it,' and she watched him disappear over the road and back into the café-bar, admiring his neat buttocks and tight trousers.

'You undressing him or something? You duplicitous woman.'

She laughed, 'Yes I suppose I was... and am. Honest though,' she added, 'I'm all yours.'

To each other, over raised glasses, they clinked and said 'Saluté'.

She smiled, relaxed, and people-watched. She liked Lago di Como and this little town called Gravedona. And she loved her husband as he placed his large warm hand over hers.

'Happy?'

She nodded, half closing her eyes as the sun began to dip behind the mountains, coating them with a warm orange glow and dropping sparkling jewels onto the rippling waters of the lake. A middle-aged man emerged from the café interior, dressed in the inevitable perched sunglasses and shouldered sweater over his impeccably white short-sleeved shirt. He had thinning grey hair and the distinct hip-swaying swagger of the male Italian. He greeted some friends who sat near to Delia and Bob and raised appreciative eyebrows at her, calling over, 'Buonasera signora... signore.'

They waved an acknowledgement back. She glowed, and Bob grinned. 'See, I'm not the only one who appreciates a beautiful woman.'

'Not jealous?'

'Hell, why should I be? Long as he admires from a distance. If he touches you... then I shall have to kill him.'

She grinned, allowed her face to relax in the moment, enjoy the atmosphere and the grey-haired Italian's appreciation. He had joined in the noisy conversation with his friends, ordered more carafes of wine and Peroni beers from the waiter, who he identified as Agostino. He sent a carafe of wine over to their table.

'Who is he?' she asked the waiter, at the same time raising her glass in polite gratitude to the grey-haired Italian.

'Signore Olmo, he owns this place.' She nodded, understanding now.

'Tell him grazie.'

'Prego, signora, I will tell him.'

'Didn't know you spoke Italian.'

She grinned at Bob. 'Only a few words. I once worked for an Italian chef. He had a small restaurant in Hampshire. La Cucina it was called, The Kitchen.' She lost herself, for a moment, in a private memory. Bob relaxed into their silence, enjoyed the warm breeze whispering in his hair.

'He taught me more swearwords than day-to-day vocabulary.'

'Did he fancy you, like Mr Elm Tree over there?'

'How d'you know what Olmo means?'

'Cos I'm an ex-copper and we get to know all sorts of facts and figures.' He neglected to tell her there was a translation in English on the menu describing Olmo's Ristorante. Why spoil the mystery?

She persuaded him to drink the major share of the second carafe. 'Else I'll waddle and sway back to the hotel and ruin my allure.'

After waving goodbye to their temporary host, they walked slowly back along the lakeside. They watched inland gulls wheel and dip and then mysteriously disappear as the sun finally dropped behind the mountains to be replaced by strings of light along the promenade, and more illuminations that spilled from homes and shops on to the pavement. People called to each other from overhead balconies, and Vespas coughed and spluttered as they wove in and out of cars and people.

'Don't know about you,' she said, 'but I'm starving.'

'Yeah, me too. Let's go see what's on offer at the hotel.'

What was on offer was Vitello di Romagna: thin slices of veal, pan-fried in butter, white wine and rosemary, served with sauté potatoes and green beans.

'That'll do,' said Bob, and ordered a bottle of Frascati and one of sparkling water. She drank more water than wine, desperate not to fall asleep at the table after the long ride from Venice, and her share of two carafes of wine at Olmo's. Dinner over, they managed a courtesy glass of grappa in the bar with the hotel owners, and excused themselves to enjoy an early night.

They managed a brief love session before falling asleep.

'You'll have to pull my nightie down afterwards, my oversexed policeman.'

'What?   The one you're not wearing?' he yawned. 'Must be the mountain air.' And promptly fell asleep.

The following morning, after a breakfast of fresh bread rolls, fruit and coffee on a large, awned terrace that overlooked the lake, they decided to explore the town. First, they went to the left, opposite to their last night's stroll. Once again, the Vespa riders were in full throttle and voice, shouting to friends, singing, and whistling at any young signorinas they passed. Cars vied for space on the narrow streets, and pedestrians took their lives in their hands in the even narrower back streets, often diving into doorways for cover.

Delia loved the side streets and the ancient wooden doors that protected even more ancient premises.

'Wonder how old their inhabitants are? Pretty old,' she surmised. Bob laughed. 'Could well be, that's if there's anyone there at all.   Might be inhabited by dusty corpses.'

'Ugh... that's gross.'

They decided to continue their journey up in the hilly part of town, away from the lake and the burning sun.   As they expected, it was mostly residential with houses hiding behind curtains of grape vines and bougainvillea. They came across an empty house, neglected enough to allow nature to take over.   Trailing vines snaked their way unchecked along the garden walls that betrayed huge cracks. Weeds grew through the cracks and spilled from darkened, half-shuttered windows where there was no glass to keep out the wild, untamed garden. Outside, steps leading to the upper floor had permitted their cement to be consumed by more weeds.

'Looks like Mother Nature's won the battle here against man's horticultural grooming.   Is she a wrecker or what?'

'Mmn... does look a bit of a wreck... but I bet it could be made beautiful again.'   She braved the crumbling steps and turned to face the lake.   She looked down to Bob.   'The view from here is incredible... and it's for sale, the house I mean, not the lake.'   She pointed to the ''In Vendita'' board. 'Bet you could pick this up for a song.'

'Probably,' he conceded, 'but it would cost a full opera to repair it. Long way from home as well.'

'Depends,' she said, 'what you mean by home. How does that song go? ''Wherever I lay my hat, that's my home''.'

'Does that mean you'd like to live here in Gravedona? In Italy?'

She shrugged, wiped the dust of neglect from her hands, and stepped carefully down the outside stairs and through the weed-invaded garden.

'Could you,' she looked at him, 'live here?'

He thought about it, played with the lobe of one ear, leaned against a vine-infested wall. 'Suppose so. I could live anywhere really, long as it was with you.'

An old lady made a great effort to exit the house next door. She wheezed 'Buongiorno' to them in a deep, gravelly voice.

'Buongiorno, signora,' they dueted.

She flashed them a toothless smile and took her

black-sheathed body down the little winding road towards the town centre, a wicker basket bumping against her swaying hips.

'How old d'you think she is?'

Delia folded her lips inwards, then licked them, and rubbed them with her teeth. 'Don't know, could be late eighties... even in her nineties.'

'They reckon folk around here live long into their nineties, even a hundred.'

'Perhaps we should think seriously about buying here,' she laughed.

They enthused each other with DIY suggestions, for healing the wounds of the little house, and retaking the garden against nature's invasion.

'It would be a lovely place for the twins and their partners to visit. Do you think your brother and sister-in-law might like it as well?'

'Too right,' he agreed. 'I bet Phil and Stella would fall in love with it as well.'

Her day was ruined.

15

Later, at dinner, he asked her if she was all right.
'You've been very quiet all afternoon. Not sickening
for anything, are you?' he paused. 'Not pregnant?'

She managed to laugh at that. 'At my age?
Bloody well hope not.'

'Could be, not unknown for fifty year olds to get
pregnant.'

'Not this one thank you. I did my duty for the
nation nearly thirty years ago.'

'I never had kids,' he mused. 'Don't know
whether I would have wanted them... or not. Never
got married, never lived with anyone long enough to
find out.'

The arrival of their food, locally caught fish from
the lake, in a tomato and basil sauce, ended the
conversation and the two subjects of her quietness,
and possible – but – jocular pregnancy. She was
relieved, annoyed really with herself for her stupid
jealousy. She had no reason to be, no justification.
Hadn't Bob chosen her? Wasn't Stella well and truly
married to Phil? There you go then: she chided, and
chastised herself for her lack of common sense. She
gave Bob a happy smile, when their eyes next met,
and was rewarded with the look of relief he

displayed.

'D'you feel ok now?'

'Yes I'm fine thank you. Probably had a little too much sun,' she lied.

He examined her face and stroked her cheek. 'Mmn, you have got quite a high colour. Maybe we'll go for a ride up in the mountains tomorrow.'

Her eyes lit up. 'Yes I'd like that. You're on.' *Especially if you don't mention the bitch.*

Maybe Mrs Ginelli, is that her name, the hotelier's wife? Maybe she'd make us a packed lunch? Though I expect we'll find some little out-of-the-way trattoria, up there in the middle of nowhere.'

'That's what we'll do then, take pot luck.'

They finished their meal and decided to stroll along the front to Olmo's, for a post-dinner drink. Bob rested his arm over her shoulders, caressing her left ear. 'This is the life, eh?'

'Definitely habit forming,' she agreed. She felt good now, all her earlier angst gone. Even if he mentions the 'delectable bitch' again, she thought, I shall not get incensed. Still, she hoped he would not. And he didn't.

Olmo's was pretty full when they arrived, with music coming from inside the ristorante. They could hear a piano and a guitar, and the soulful, but attractive voice of a woman. They managed to find a table on the lakeside, marvelling at the evening's warmth. After only a few minutes' the waiter,

Agostino, came to their table, greeting them with a cheerful, 'Buonasera signora, signore, come stai?'

'We're fine thank you.'

'What would you like to drink?'

Bob looked at her, 'Wine or grappa?'

She considered. 'Wine, I think, maybe a grappa later. Yes, can I have a white wine please?'

'Ok, let's both have white. Frascati?'

'I'm fine with house white if you just want a small carafe.'

'Nah,' he said. 'We're on our honeymoon, let's have Frascati, or fizz if you like?'

'We have a good Prosecco, signore, if you would prefer il vino frizzante.'

'Brilliant, we'll have one of those.'

He returned bearing a tray with the foil-topped bottle in a wine cooler, wrapped in a spotless white cloth, two glasses and a small dish of appetisers. One minute later, they were saluting each other, unaware of the attention of others. Then people at the tables around them called out 'Bravo' and began applauding. Next, the guitarist emerged from the restaurant interior, crossed swiftly over the narrow cobbled street, deftly avoiding cars and Vespas, until he reached their table. To their surprise and delight, he serenaded them with an old Italian song, Bella Notte. She looked at Bob, a huge grin illuminating her face. 'How did they know?' she whispered.

He shrugged his shoulders, 'Don't know. Maybe

the waiter overheard me when I suggested the fizz. You don't mind?'

'Mind?   I'm delighted.   Couldn't feel more spoiled... or loved,' she added.

They clinked glassed, saluted the singing guitarist, and nodded their gratitude to the people at adjoining tables.   Presently, they were joined by Signore Olmo, who offered his congratulations, and gracefully accepted a glass of fizz after Agostino had fetched another glass.

'So,' he said, 'you are enjoying your Italian honeymoon?'

'Very much,' said Delia.

'Oh yes,' answered her husband.   'We spent a few days in Venice then drove up here.'

'Ah yes, Venezia, a lovely city.   Very crowded now, I think.'

Delia liked the way he pushed his hair back without dislodging his sunglasses, but noted his restlessness.   Eyes everywhere, keeping tabs on all aspects of his establishment: typical businessman, she thought.   His fingers drummed a tattoo on his knee and, she could tell, he only half-listened to the conversation.

Bob picked up the bottle, 'Can I give you a top up?' he asked.

'No, no, thank you signore.   I have a long evening to get through... and a busy bar tonight, with the music.   But please,' he paused as he stood up.

'Allow me to send you out some grappa or another liqueur maybe?'

'Grappa sounds good, thank you.' Bob stood up and shook hands with the patron. 'Have a good evening, and don't work too hard.'

Olmo shrugged and smiled. 'I have good staff, I am just the sopraintendente, the overseer. Buonasera signore, signora.'

And to you too, she thought. Now it was her turn to silently admit to an illicit attraction: she hoped Bob did not notice. Tough luck, she forgot he had been a policeman.

'Do I detect a certain fascination for him?'

'No,' she said. 'No: well, maybe admiration from a distance. I'm not averse to appreciating the male sex. Anyway,' she quickly added, 'they can't measure up to you. Bet they're nowhere near as good as you in bed.'

He grinned, tilted his glass towards her in salute. 'Ok, maybe you're right... I still think you could be a loose woman if I cut you enough slack.'

'Never.'

'Yeah, right.'

Agostino arrived with two generous measures of grappa in balloon glasses. 'From signore Olmo,' he said. 'Salute.' He placed them on small, tissue coasters and set down yet another dish of appetisers: nuts, cheese morsels, and washed grapes.

'Wow. I should soon put on weight here, the

amount of appetisers they give you, let alone the generous-sized portions they serve for dinner.'

'Nothing wrong with a bit of extra flesh, woman. More for me to cuddle at night.'

'You're biased, Bob Shackleton. But I love you for it.' She blew him a kiss across the table, sat back in her chair to enjoy the music, the grappa, and the soft breeze that teased her hair and tantalized her bare arms and shoulders.

'He put one finger to his lips, sucked it, and pointed it in her direction. 'Likewise, woman. I'll show you how much later. Not too later either. I don't want you falling asleep on me tonight.'

'I won't,' she promised.

16

She kept her promise. It must have been close on one o'clock, when they finally put out the light. 'That was a session and a half,' she gasped. 'Must be the fizz and the grappa mix.'

'You were very relaxed tonight, dear lady. Very compliant too. I didn't hurt you at all, did I?' he added. He leaned over her naked body, running his fingers gently over her nipples and kissing her shoulder.

'No, of course you didn't. I love what you do to me. I'd willingly do it all over again, except I am really and truly shaggered. Now... get off me, you brute, let me go for a quick wash before we settle down.'

'Nice choice of word, you hussy.' He lifted himself off her and rolled to his side of the bed. 'I'll have a quick shower and race you back here.'

'You're on.' She slipped out of bed and ran naked to the small bathroom. She was back in the room, washed and sweet smelling, while he finished his shower, and well snuggled under the bedclothes by the time he returned.

'Move over,' he said. 'Make room for your lord and master, or your lover if you prefer.'

'Either or both will do. Come and cuddle me.'

'Just a cuddle?'

'Yeah, just a cuddle, I'm ready for sleep now. Buonanotte signore Shackleton.'

He kissed her behind her ear, whispered, 'Buonanotte, Signora Shackleton. Dormi bene.'

'Where did you learn that?'

'From the old lady up the hill today.' He lied.

She laughed. 'No you didn't.'

'Correct. If you must know, I heard Agostino say it to a customer so I asked him what it meant. He told me it was Italian for sleep well.'

She didn't hear him. Instead he listened to her gentle breathing as she slipped into sleep. He repeated the *dormi bene* in a whisper, turned over and slept himself.

At breakfast, on the sunlit terrace, she reminded him of their promised trip into the mountains. 'It's the perfect day for a drive in the hills. Look at the sunshine out there already.'

This time it was coming in from behind the town and over the lake beyond the terrace restaurant.

'Like jewels isn't it?' she pointed to the water as it shimmered and rippled in the early morning sun. Bob nodded, his mouth full of fresh-baked roll and melting butter. He swallowed. 'Looks great. Can't wait to see what it looks like from the mountain road. Signore Ginelli tells me there's a viewing point up there that gives you a spectacular scene of miles of lake and those opposite mountains. Only he said kilometres, not miles.'

'Of course.'

They smiled thanks at his wife, their hostess, as she brought them more coffee and freshly-squeezed orange juice that she called succo d'arancia. 'You have enough panini, bread rolls?'

'Yes plenty thank you.'

She left them while she served the other guests. Later she wished them 'Buongiorno, and enjoy your day in the montagne.' Adding, 'They are very beautiful.'

They did, enjoy the day, and the breath-taking scenery. They drove round and round the narrow road and bends, seeing something different at almost every curve. They found the viewing point and Bob turned the car into its narrow lay-by, so they could get out and admire the lake below, and the distant mountains beyond. They saw red-tiled roof tops and flower-filled gardens, small allotment sized vegetable patches and grape vines hanging over pergola like structures. As they peered down, at the small town where they were staying, a fresh breeze caught their hair and conveyed a scent of pines and alpine flowers, but the warmth of the sun kept any chill away. Like any tourist, Delia wanted to take masses of photos. Bob was not one to discourage her. Instead he smiled. 'Can you take one of me leaning against the railing overlooking the lake?'

'Course. Then you can take one of me. Pity there's no-one here to take a snap of us both. Can't do selfies with this camera.'

'Not to worry, maybe when we stop for lunch later on, someone will oblige.'

They spent a further ten minutes taking shots and generally admiring the views, before climbing back into the car and continuing on up into the hills.

'Proper little tourists, aren't we?' she laughed.

'The views are stunning though. Doesn't it make you want to stop every now and then to capture them?'

'Absolutely. Oh look...' She pointed away from the lakes below to a waterfall cascading down in front of them. 'My God, look at those colours. Amazing... like a rainbow on the ground.'

'Wonder if it's got a pot of gold?' he laughed.

She laughed too. 'I doubt it, but we should get a shot of those colours in the water. D'you think they'll come out?'

'Give it a try.'

They squeezed the car into the mountain, hoping another vehicle would not come along. Delia shuddered, looking down towards the tiny town below and aware of the drop if they went over the precarious edge. They both got out on the left hand driver's side, one to take the shot of the waterfall and one to stand in front of it.

'I'll take one of you first,' Bob said. 'See if those rainbow colours come out.'

She stood with her back to the cascading waters, and felt the spray, cool against the hot morning sun.

'Ok,' he said. He looked into the camera at the shot he had just taken. 'Yep. It's come out perfectly. Look at this.' She walked towards him, peered into the viewfinder.

'Wow, that's terrific. Your turn,' she took the camera from him, told him where to stand and focussed the camera on him. 'That's great, smile or say cheese, or sex, or something.'

'Sex,' he grinned as she clicked.

'Perfect, let's get back in the car in case another vehicle comes along. They'll never pass us here.'

Ten minutes on, they found a small restaurant and bar. The stone-built place nestled into the mountainside and had a wooden, terraced area on the other side of the road that seemed to hang over the rocky edge. The tables, four of them, had floral cloths with pegs as anchors against the breeze. There were three seats against the restaurant wall, one occupied by an old man in his alpine hat and leather trousers. His myopic eyes ignored them but his ears betrayed their presence to him and he lifted his face in their direction.

'Buongiorno signore,' Delia thought it right to greet him.

'Buongiorno signora,' the old man growled back,

his voice thick from years of smoking home-grown tobacco, or maybe he smoked the dried vine leaves? She remembered her Italian chef friend telling her about smoking his grandfather's vine leaves when he was only seven, and almost burning down the loft above his Nonno's house. She was fascinated with this old man's ancient and wrinkled face; wished she spoke more Italian to hold a lengthy conversation. Bob touched her arm and nodded his head in the direction of the beaded curtained entrance.

'Shall we go in?' he whispered. He mumbled an embarrassed Buongiorno to the old man and held open the curtain to let her in. It was cool and quite dark inside, away from the sun. The floors were tiled marble, as was the front of the bar servery. Beer taps gleamed and they could hear the ceiling-high refrigerator humming.

'Looks impressive,' said Bob. 'All that marble would cost a fortune back home.'

'Yes, but Carrara marble is quarried not a million miles away from here, so it's probably cheaper than laminate.'

'Mmn, all relative, I suppose. Wonder where the owner is? Don't think it's the old boy outside, do you?'

She grinned, 'I doubt it.'

A woman emerged from a back room, 'Buongiorno, signore et signora.'

Bob nodded at her. 'Do you do food here,

signora?'

'Si, yes signore. You would like the menu?'

'Please. And can we sit outside? Over the road?'

'Certo, signore.   Certainly.   Would you like something to drink?'

'Yes please, a carafe of red would be good.'

'Please,' she indicated the doorway. 'I will bring it to you.'

They thanked her, took the menus and crossed over the small roadway to the wooden terrace. They were shaded from the sun by a curtain of vines that had bunches of grapes dangling from them, some green and others a rich, purple colour. Delia sighed, brushed her hair back from her face. 'This is the life...'

He smiled at her. 'Happy?'

She returned the smile. 'What do you think?'

He nodded. 'Definitely happy.' They examined the short menu of Trattoria Pinocchio, smiled at the little puppet logo with his long nose. On offer was zuppa Minestrone, followed by spezzatino di vitello, o pollo farcito con prosciutto e formaggio 'Any ideas what it all means?' Bob asked.

'I think so,' she said. ' Minestrone's obviously the soup of the day, spezzatino is a kind of veal stew and pollo farcito' (she pronounced it farcheeto) 'is chicken breast stuffed with ham and cheese. Both of these are served with sauté potatoes and salad. – "il tutto servito con patate sauté e insalata". Mmn...

think I'll go for the chicken. How about you?'

'Yeah, that sounds good. Yep, I'll have the same.'

They admired the view over the shimmering lake, and the tiny houses and township at least two thousand feet below. The waitress arrived with a carafe of red wine that had beads of water glistening on the glass.

'Chilled?' he questioned.

'Si signore, here we serve our new red wine chilled. It is very good, Multo bene.'

'Ok, I'll take your word for it.'

She poured them each a glass. He sipped his, nodded. 'Yes you're right; it is good.'

'And you are ready to order?'

'Yes, we'll both have the chicken, pollo farcheeto. Is that how you say it?'

'Certo, signore. Pollo farcito con patate sauté e insalata?'

'Yes please, grazie,' he said as an afterthought.

'Prego, signore.'

Bob thought what a lovely sexy voice she had, deep and velvety. But he kept the thought to himself, didn't think his new wife would share his sentiments, somehow.

'This is weird,' she said as she tasted the wine.

'Is it ok for you? I can change it for white if you'd prefer.'

'No, this is fine... just different.'

Conversation dipped as they sipped the wine and took in the stunning view. A light breeze teased the grapevines above their heads and the sun, flinking through the leaves, left speckles on their arms and faces.

Presently, the woman appeared bearing a large tray with cutlery, checked napkins, and two large plates covered with metal lids. They smelled a delicious aroma as she approached their table.

'Wow, that smells good,' said Bob, licking his lips and inhaling deeply.

Smiling, their hostess placed the two plates in front of them, handed them napkins and cutlery and wished them 'buon appetito.' She stopped briefly by the old man sunning himself. They heard her speaking but only recognised 'Papa'.

'Wonder how old he is?' said Bob.

'Older than God, by the looks of him.'

He laughed. 'That old?' And began to eat his food. 'This wine actually goes well with the food, don't you think?'

'Mmn.' She nodded and chewed appreciatively on her stuffed chicken as she speared salad leaves onto her fork. She took another sip. 'Mind you, it soon gets warm in this heat, more like the room temperature red we're used to imbibing.'

They continued eating and drinking in silence. The only sound that disturbed the silence, apart from unseen birds in the surrounding pine trees, was the old man's gurgling cough.

'Bet that took 70 or more years of smoking to develop,' Bob laughed.

The old man coughed again and brought up phlegm that he hawked up, next to his chair. The action marked the end of Delia's enjoyment of her meal. She carefully put down her knife and fork, took a last gulp of wine and said, 'Can we go?'

Bob looked up from his plate. 'What?'

'That old man,' she whispered and inclined her head in his direction. 'He just spat out a mouthful of phlegm... on the floor... by his chair.' She shuddered and pulled a prune face.

'Better that than swallowing it, I suppose.'

'Ugh... Anyway he's put me off my food.'

'Don't be silly.'

'I'm not being silly.' A note of hysteria crept into her voice. She made to stand up.

'Ok, ok. Just let me finish mine. I won't be long.'

She looked at him, saw him trying to hurry his food and regretted her stupidity. Bob was right, the old man had only done what thousands of men do. Just a shame he had to do it as she was taking in a mouthful of chicken. 'It's ok,' she said. 'You don't have to hurry. I really have had sufficient to eat. Maybe I'll have a coffee in a minute. Would you like one?'

He swallowed his mouthful, grinned. 'I'd sooner have a grappa.'

'If you do, I'll have to drive. Don't fancy my chances on this mountain road.'

'No, it's ok. I'll have a coffee too... leave the grappa until we get back to Gravedona.'

The old man hawked again, spat again. Is he doing it deliberately, she thought? Disgusting. He reminded her of Gerald. Gerald in his last days with his badly infected chest only he emptied his mouth into one of the large white handkerchiefs. Best not think about that...

The woman returned with her big tray, began to load their plates and cutlery, their now empty glasses and the finished carafe. 'Was it good for you, signora?'

'Yes... it was fine... lovely... multo bene. I am,' she patted her stomach, 'full.'

'Ah, si. You would like some gelato perhaps, or caffé?'

'Coffee would be good. Espresso for me. You Bob? What would you like?'

'A regular black. Don't know how to say it in Italian.'

'And a caffé nero for the signore.'

'Prego, signora.' She disappeared in through the curtained door of the restaurant, returning presently with a smaller tray on which rested two cups, a dish of sugar sachets and a small dish of sugared almonds.   The old man, Delia noted, had fallen asleep: his head drooped on one side and dribble oozed from his part open mouth.   She wished he would never waken again, at least while they were there.   She twisted her chair round to face the lake below, allowed the sun to warm her face and the gentle wind to tease it.   She forgot the old man.

She cleansed her mind of negative thoughts, bit into the sugared almond that accompanied her coffee.   Memories of Manda came floating back.   Poor Manda, dying and flying like a balloon.   All because of her silly allergy to nuts.   Poor Manda... rich Delia.

'How many miles away are you?'   Bob grinned.

She shook herself back to the present, felt remorseful, knowing she had upset Bob by making a drama out of the old man's behaviour and leaving the rest of her meal.   Why get so uptight?   She forced a smile.   'Nowhere in particular, flitting like a butterfly really, from one thought to another.'

'Talking of 'nother, do you want some more coffee?'

'Love one.'

He wandered over towards the curtained doorway as the woman came out.   'You would like something, signore?'

'Yes please, can we have two more coffees?'

'The same as before?'

He nodded.   'That would be fine.'   He returned to their table.   Slid into his seat just as the old man appeared to wake up and cough again. Please don't hawk again, he thought. Leastwise don't let *her indoors here* hear it. And smiled at his own pun. One glance at Delia's scowl told him she had heard. He shrugged his shoulders. Too bad, nothing he could do about it...

She also chose to ignore it and smiled sweetly at her new husband, already deciding she must stop thinking like a terminator. Ok, so Manda's death had been unfortunate, but also fortunate for them. They were enjoying an extended honeymoon, thanks to Manda's bequest and H's generous life insurance, plus Bob's generous police severance. Two dead and a dead career have given them this opportunity to travel, to enjoy the delights of Italian food and Italian mountain views. Yet still she continued thinking about perpetuating more 'departures': Stella's and the old man's. Silently and inwardly she remonstrated with herself. It had to stop: no more killings, no more death wishes. Once more, she took in the glorious vista, drank in the beauty of the mountains and enjoyed the sun's warmth. And the love... when she looked at Bob, at his face as he regarded her.

'Better now?'

She smiled. 'Yes, I'm fine. Don't know why I reacted so stupidly.' She was grateful for his understanding and his warm, returning smile. Had it been H he would have accused her of being menopausal or something. This man was giving her so much love. Loving her, not Stella.

Later, at dinner, Signora Ginelli asked if they had enjoyed their day. 'It was lovely,' replied Delia. 'We drove miles through the mountains, saw waterfalls...'

Their hostess looked puzzled. Delia demonstrated with her hand and fingers waving in a downward movement. 'Waterfall?'

'Ah... cascata... yes... waterfall. Very beautiful up there. Did you find somewhere for mangiare… to eat?'

'Yes, we stopped at a little trattoria. It was called Trattoria Pinocchio, after the little puppet.'

Signora Ginelli beamed. 'Yes, that is the trattoria of mia sorella, my sister. She lives there with my Papa. Did you see him perhaps?'

Delia swallowed, 'Erm, yes we did. He sat in the sunshine wearing his little Alpini hat.'

'Ah yes,' she laughed. 'Papa loves his cappello alpino. We bought it, my sister and I, l'anno scorso, last year. I think he would wear it all the time, and at night, how you say... a letto?'

Delia made a guess, 'In bed?'

'Si, in bed.' She excused herself after serving them their main course and went to other tables. Later they could hear her talking to her husband in the kitchen, something about la nostra coppia inglese and guessed it probably meant our English couple and was telling him about them visiting her sister's place. It made them feel good, as if they belonged.

The days passed and they repeated the pleasurable strolls around the small town; went several times to Olmo's restaurant, drove again up into the hills and took the ferry across to the other side of the lake, exploring more small towns and villages. Once they found an enormous garden centre that specialised in statuary.

'It's like walking through a wonderland,' she said. 'Maybe we could take something back as a souvenir.'

'What, on the plane?'

'Oh yes, I forgot that. Getting so used to driving around, I forgot about flying home. Silly me.'

After walking some more, they came across a life-sized statue of David, complete with slingshot and minus the modesty of a well-placed fig leaf.

'Not very well blessed, was he?'

'Not as good as me?'

She laughed, 'Vain man. But no, nowhere near as generously proportioned as you. Still,' she added. 'He wouldn't exactly have had an erection, going off to meet Goliath would he? Quite the opposite, I'd have thought.'

'True, not really the best time to feel sexy.'

They continued their wandering, went inside the

covered shopping arcade, appreciating the cool of the air-conditioning against the hot sun outside. Bob bought her a miniature statue of David. 'You can put him on your bedside table, remind you of this lovely holiday.'

'More like remind me how well blessed you are compared to him...'

'You're impossible, woman. Come on, let's get back to the boat, the hotel... I fancy a siesta... or something.'

They also returned, several times, to the little house on the hill. Even met the vendor/estate agent once, who gladly showed them round the interior. Delia carefully avoided the spiders' webs and ignored the mess left by some trespassing pigeons. She was not deterred, she really had fallen in love with the place and pictured it fully restored. Marble or tiled floors swept clean of dust and dead leaves, the fresh smell of white painted stone walls. She pictured long-handled copper pots and pans, hanging above a large kitchen stove, and a scrubbed wooden table surrounded by locally made chairs. She imagined, when they went outside again, a garden with a small vegetable plot hidden behind a screen of grape vines, a pergola beside the house dripping with bougainvillaea, and – yes – a full-sized David's statue somewhere out there beside wrought-iron garden furniture. A space for them to sit and admire the view over the lake.

'We must buy it,' she whispered.

'Yeah, but not yet,' he soothed.   'Let's think about it when we're home again.'

They accepted pamphlets and photos of this and other properties in the area that were 'in Vendita' and with that she had to be content. She also chose to ignore the damp patches under the agent's armpits and his slightly malodorous smell wafting her way.

Soon it was time to say goodbye to Gravedona, to their hosts, Nicola and Eva Ginelli. Delia persuaded Bob to take her for a last drink at Olmo's, the evening before they were going to drive back to Venice and catch the plane home.

'Want to say arrivederci to your 'lover' do you? Wanton woman.'

'Not my lover, don't be daft, you're my lover.'

'I'm your lawfully-wedded husband and by rights I should spank you.'

'Oo… yes please.'

Signore Olmo greeted them, sat with them, and bought them drinks. When it was time for them to return to the hotel, he shook hands with Bob and kissed hers, lingering she thought, as he looked up and gave her, she swore, a lecherous look.

They walked back hand-in-hand beside the lake. 'That Olmo, he's a typical Italian,' said Bob.

'What d'you mean?'

'All that hand slobbering and looks to undress you.'

She laughed. 'You're jealous Mr Shackleton.'

'No I'm not... why should I be? It's me that physically undresses you... and the rest.'

They spent the last hours of the night enjoying 'the rest'.

17

Delia gave a last look up the hill towards their little house. 'Piccola casa' was how the vendor described it. She liked that phrase, little house, enjoyed the musicality of it as it rolled off her tongue, piccola casa, whispered it several times under her breath as they drove away from the little town, 'cittadina' as the Italians would say.

They stopped once, en route, for lunch at a little roadside trattoria with its vine-covered terrace; no dribbling, spitting old man though, she noted with gratitude. By early evening they had reached Venice, returned the hire car and were sitting in the Marco Polo Club VIP lounge at the airport sipping Prosecco and watching the planes outside.

'Happy?' he said.

'Yes... and no. Happy with what we've had but sad now it's over.'

'Yeah, I know what you mean.'

Half an hour later, the good mood was dispersed. Their flight was delayed and going through the final security check chaotic with queue-dodgers coming from every direction it seemed.

'Don't know why we couldn't fly to Heathrow,' she grumbled.

'Because the car's at Birmingham remember? We had to sort out Manda's affairs, remember?'

She huffed her annoyance and sulked. When they eventually boarded the plane and took off, Bob tried to show her the night time view as they flew over Venice. She missed most of the twinkling lights with her peevishness, putting him in mind of a cranky teenager. What do I know about her, he silently questioned, even allowing a modicum of regret to creep into his mind. He wondered if she might be bipolar. But wisely thought not to go there. He gave up trying to placate her, feigned sleep, and left her to digest her own bad mood.

Half an hour later she caressed his arm. 'The cabin staff are on their way. Did we order a meal?'

He blinked himself awake, not realising at first that he had actually dropped off. 'Erm... yes... er. Oh, I know,' he brightened. 'Champagne and caviar.'

She laughed, her bad mood forgotten. 'Idiot. What did you order?

'Not a full meal, thought we'd eat out in Brum later. Er... just cheese and ham hot Paninis and Prosecco.'

'That'll do me.'

They touched down at Birmingham International a little after nine. An hour later they were driving through to Harbourne, to Manda's house, now theirs.

'Smells a bit musty.' Delia wrinkled her nose as

they stepped inside the hallway.

'So would you, if you'd been shut up for weeks.'

'Point taken.'

The hall opened up into a large L-shaped lounge, comfortably furnished with two biscuit-coloured, leather settees on a large shag-pile rug. It led directly through to a modern, well-fitted kitchen.

'Nice place, he remarked.

'Oh, she had taste, did friend Manda... if nothing else.'

He glanced at her. 'Do I detect a note of... something?'

'Not really. Manda was Manda. Very much her own person. She was a good friend.' Apart from her drunkenness and mentioning Carl, she thought.

'I presume we'll stay here tonight? Too late to drive down to Kent anyway.'

'Suppose so, after all it's ours now,' she swept her arms around the room. 'Until we sell it, or rent it out, or something. Maybe someone in the TV world might like it.'

'That's a thought,' he agreed. 'Come on, let's take a look upstairs.'

They were pleasantly surprised at the master bedroom, with its discreet, built-in furniture and a generous king-sized bed.

'Wonder why she had a king bed?'

'Oh, knowing my friend, she probably had a houseguest or two. Not together,' she added. 'She wasn't kinky, raunchy maybe but not three-in-a-bed quirky.'

The smaller room had been Manda's office, with floor to ceiling shelving, a large computer desk and a foldaway sofa bed. Bob approved. 'Shouldn't be too much trouble to sell, if that's what you decide to do.'

'Hope not.   Anyway, we'll think about that later.'

When they went downstairs again, they found several cards for Balti and Chinese takeaway places in the kitchen, pinned to a notice board.

'Fancy a Chinese?' she asked. 'Only there's no food in the house, except for a couple of tins.'

'Fine, I'll order them. I see there's a nice wine rack next to the fridge. D'you want to stick a couple of whites in the freezer? They'll be chilled enough time the food arrives.'

'Ok. Then I'll pop upstairs and change the bed linen.' She didn't fancy sleeping on her friend's remains, or smell her perfume on the pillows. By the time she had found the fresh duvet cover and pillowcases, the food had been delivered. Bob shouted up its arrival to her.

'Good timing,' she said. 'Bed's all done. How's the wine?'

'Ready and waiting.'

She was pleasantly surprised to find the table laid with plates and cutlery, shining glasses and lighted candles. 'You have been busy, Mr S.'

'Come and sit.' He placed a napkin on her lap, poured a generous glass of wine and said, 'Buon appetito signora.'

She smiled. 'Prego, Tesoro.' They clinked glasses. 'Yes... it was a good holiday wasn't it?'

He nodded, caressed her with his eyes. She thought how attractive he was and how 'sex in the city' would be good tonight. 'Let's eat,' she said.

Next morning, they stopped off at an estate agent, filled in forms, gave the man Manda's house keys and were able to set off quite quickly for the drive home. It transpired Manda had used this same agent, when she bought the house, so he was familiar with its outlay.

'I'll take a look round it this afternoon,' he promised, 'and let you know how much you should aim to sell it for.'

'That's great.' Bob answered for the both of them, and they shook hands and said their goodbyes to him.

'Glad we've decided to sell,' she said, when they were in the car. 'I can't imagine renting it out: all the aggravation of employing an agent, or interviewing prospective tenants.'

'Quite agree, especially considering the 400-mile round trip if we did it ourselves.'

Heavy traffic and a drizzling rain deterred any conversation, leaving Bob free to curse and swear at some of the idiot driving. Delia lay back and partially reclined her seat. Her mind drifted back to Italy, to Venice, and Lake Como. She thought about the 'piccola casa', the little house, on the hill, how they could renovate it, restore it, give the garden a makeover. If it happened... if… she wouldn't want to share it, not let it out as a holiday cottage. Maybe the twins and their partners, but not to anyone else... not the Delectable and her husband, or Stella's lecherous father. Bob turned the car into a motorway service station. 'Gotta have a break... traffic's awful, so is the rain.'

'Let me drive for a while,' she offered. 'I'll drive till we reach the Dartford Crossing if you like.'

'Ok, but I still need a break, coffee and a Danish, and a visit to the gents'.'

They parked up and ran through the driving rain, dodging oncoming cars seeking a space nearer the entrance. 'Bet some greedy swine takes a disabled space.'

'Yeah, there's always one.' She shook the rain from her hair, brushed spots off her shoulders. 'That's better.' She looked around. 'Where d'you want to sit?'

'We'll go into Starbucks. Arm-and-a-leg job I know, but it's fairly decent coffee and their pastries aren't bad either.'

'I'll meet you in there, just going to get a newspaper. Anything you want?'

'Boiled sweets or something. Keep our mouths moist on the journey.'

'Ok. See you in a minute.'

Half an hour later they were back on the road again, Delia driving and Bob perusing the Daily Mail. The rain had all but stopped, but the wet road meant lorries splattered the windscreen with mud. She frequently squirted them but he warned her that they might run out of window washer.

'What am I supposed to do then? Drive with dirty windows?' She sounded irritated.

'D'you want me to take over?'

'If you wish. We should be coming to another service station soon. Just pull in and we'll change seats.'

'Have you done any on the puzzle page?'

'No, thought I'd leave you the pleasure.'

Her irritation ceased, particularly as they passed a sign telling them the next service station was three miles away. Two miles on, she crept into the inside lane, tolerated slow-moving lorries and the odd towed caravan until she gratefully turned off the motorway, found a parking space, and switched off the ignition. She got out and stretched, relieved their mammoth journey from Lake Como, Venice, and Birmingham was nearly at an end. It would be good to be home. Bob joined her in a stretch. 'Not long now, sweetheart. We'll be home in less than two hours.'

'Good.   It's been two solid days of travel. Enough, don't you think?'

'I do.   Can't wait to carry you over the threshold.'

'You've already done that,' she laughed.

'Have I? Don't remember. Never mind, I'll do it again.'

18
After the honeymoon

Next morning, Delia slipped quietly out of bed and padded downstairs, leaving Bob asleep. It was good to be home, despite the wonderful honeymoon. Good to be able to wander half-naked from room to room, along the hallway and down the stairs.

She opened the door to her front room, saw people hurrying over to the railway station. A glance at the regulator wall-clock told her it was eight-thirty, still rush hour and time for the next train to London via Herne Bay, Whitstable and Faversham... yes... Faversham.

Pulling the newspaper from the letterbox, she carried it through to the kitchen. Time for coffee. She would let Bob sleep for a while longer. Maybe take him up a tray of tea and toast, maybe go back to bed herself. No... She was restless, had things to do. Unpack the cases. They hadn't bothered yesterday. Too tired to do anything except chill out in front of the television with another takeaway and a bottle of rosé, and later fall into bed.

There was, she supposed, a mountain of washing, and more clothes to shake out and hang up in their new wardrobes that Bob had purchased before the wedding. There'd be souvenirs to unwrap, including the silver filigree galleon, David's statue, and the beautiful Murano-glass vase.

She smiled, remembering Venice and San Marco Square. The sights and sounds, and tantalising smells of delicious foods, as they sauntered through the crowds and passed so many restaurants. And the little man in the jeweller's shop who gave them grappa, as he carefully and lovingly wrapped the galleon. One day, she thought, they would go back. One day.

Taking her coffee out to the garden, she felt the sun warm her face, barely listened to the screeching gulls as they performed their aerial ballet above her. The garden was in full bloom and she gratefully breathed in the sweet floral aroma. Yes... it was good to be home. Walking back indoors she decided to go for a walk, when she'd finished her coffee, down along the coastal promenade. Let the sea-breeze blow away the last fuzziness of the flight and the long drive home from Manda's house in Birmingham.

Ten minutes later, dressed but not showered (she'd do that after her stroll), she left the house and her sleeping husband and walked over the railway bridge towards the beach. Surprisingly, the streets and the promenade were deserted. Everyone gone to work? Or *everyone's gone to the moon* like the old song said.

Gulls wheeled and dived, and she watched as

waves dashed against the sea wall, showing their strength and power in full tide. Rather than turn left towards Minnis Bay, she decided to walk towards Westgate and Margate. Wrong decision... here the coastal path was narrower and the waves seemed determined to dash over it, leaving their spray halfway up the cliff face. Delia got soaked by more than one mischievous upsurge, swore as her inadequate jacket absorbed the spray. Her feet almost slipped from under her on green, slimy seaweed. The path here, and the lower cliff walls, were permanently discoloured with the slippery mess.

She rounded the next bend and was relieved to see the path had widened out again. Room here for five or six to walk abreast. A sound surprised her, until she remembered the wild dovecote. Up there, in the ruins of an old coastguard cottage, set in the cliffs more years ago than most people's memory. Unreachable now without climbing gear, though she supposed those lower scars had once been steps carved out of the cliff, now eroded. Some twenty feet above her, she could see broken wooden railings with stairs behind them, leading to the old ruined cottage. It was now home to a motley collection of cross-bred pigeons and doves who had mated throughout countless generations, defying any human invasion with their sinister cooing and aggressive, staring eyes. Some flapped their wings at her approach, like an ululation of native shields warning an enemy of their menacing presence.

'Don't worry,' she muttered. 'I won't disturb you.' And regretted, once more, walking in this direction rather than go to the sandy beach at Minnis Bay.

She had almost reached Westgate. Time, she thought, to leave the wet promenade and climb the steps where the cliffs indented into a natural passage, and walk into the village. Maybe she could pop into Angelo's deli for some freshly-baked rolls and walk back through the streets to home. No good. She had no purse on her, no loose money in her pockets, not so much as a penny. She caught a glimpse of herself in a shop window. God, what a mess. Hair tangled from wind and sea spray, damp spotted clothes and soaked feet, when she looked down at them...

'Hello Delia.' The voice made her jump. Stella. It would be. 'What's happened? You look like a drowned rat.'

Delia forced a smile. 'Hi Stella. Just been walking along the lower path. Didn't realise it was high tide... got soaked, as you can see.'

'Mmn. Erm, I'm just about to catch the train to London. Old Bailey session today. Why don't you come with me and get off at Birchington? You don't want to walk around in those wet clothes.'

Delia smiled again, a rueful one this time. 'No money, came out without my purse.'

'Don't worry, I'll pay your fare. It's only one stop, won't exactly cost a fortune,' she laughed.

Delia hesitated, reluctant to tolerate this woman's company even for a five-minute journey. Her damp shoes and clothes forced her to accept Stella's offer. She was acutely conscious, as they got on the train, of Stella's impeccable appearance against her own dishevelled one. Oh well...

'So... how was the honeymoon? Went to Portugal didn't you? Back to Alvor?'

'Yes, for a few days, then we flew to Venice, spent a week there, then drove to Lake Como.'

'Excellent... where did you stay on the Lake?'

'Oh, here and there,' she lied, reluctant to tell Stella about Gravedona and the little ruined house they were thinking of buying and repairing; didn't even want to make even the most nonchalant conversation with her. If she'd been on her own in the carriage, she would have casually planned Stella's demise. *Difficult to do that when your victim is sitting next to you, isn't it?* There was no time for more revelations as the train had swished into Birchington. The two women said hasty goodbyes with casual promises to meet up soon, perhaps for dinner as Stella suggested.

As Delia walked over the road from the station, she saw old Mrs Casey from next door but one come struggling out of her garden gate. She tutted to herself, the old biddy was the last person she wanted to bump into looking this bedraggled, (apart from Stella of course). Didn't like meeting her at the best of times, miserable old crow that she was. But wet and a mess like she must look now, she did not relish a confrontation with Mary bloody Casey. The crabby woman was one of those types, Delia thought, who were happy being miserable at best, and positively unbearable when she was in a cantankerous mood, which was much of the time. Delia failed to see why ninety years of age was any justification for bad-mouthing people or for carping on about the 'good old days' when men were gentlemen, not the sweaty t-shirted yobs of today, and women were respected as the gentle sex. As for children's behaviour nowadays? It didn't bear thinking about; rude, ill-mannered and no respect for their elders. She watched the hunched form draw nearer and winced when Mary said, 'Good morning, Delia. What the devil have you been up to? Such a mess you look.'

'Oh, hello Mrs Casey.' *If you must know,* she thought, *I got splashed, down on the front, not that it's any of your bloody business.* Instead, she attempted a smile and said, 'I've been walking on the promenade and got soaked by a couple of high waves.'

'So why are you coming over from the station then?'

God, that woman misses nothing. Bet she was curtain twitching all the time, waiting to see who got on and off the train.

'I walked as far as Westgate, got the train back 'cos I started to get cold.' Not that it's anything to do with you, another thought.

'Now I've caught you,' the old woman said. *Yeah, like a female spider catching a fly.* 'I wonder could you pop to the shop and get me a pint of milk, I ran out last night and don't have even a drop for my breakfast cuppa.'

She felt like saying, they don't have pints anymore, it's half litres. What was the point? It would only prolong the time she wasted with the old crow. She forced another smile, 'Sure Mrs Casey. You go back indoors and I'll bring it to you.'

Five minutes later, she knocked on the old woman's door.

'It's open, come in.'

Delia turned the ancient, rusted door-knob and let herself in to a gloomy hallway. It was like, she thought, going back in time to the Victorian era; dark-flocked wallpaper adorned the walls, and her feet slapped on a cold, tiled, red and black floor. Mrs Casey was in the kitchen at the back of the house. She was standing at a gas stove that had probably been fashionable back in the nineteen fifties, and certainly cleaner then than it was now. Delia wrinkled her nose, trying not to breathe in the stale kitchen smells. She watched as the old lady lifted a heavy, brown kettle from the stove and poured water into a brown, china teapot that had a badly chipped spout.

'Put it down there,' she indicated the table where a large cup and saucer rested. Delia placed the milk next to it and prepared to leave. 'Aren't you going to stay for a cuppa?' It was said with ill grace, Delia thought.

'No thanks, Mrs C. I'd best get back and change out of these wet clothes.'

'And smarten yourself up for that new husband of yours no doubt,' she muttered. 'Though I don't know what was wrong with your other one. Poor Mr Fontaine, such a lovely man.'

And so dead, thought Delia. She excused herself and almost fled through the hallway and out of the front door. *What a hateful woman, one that this world could well do without...*

She walked past Dez and Jess's house and let herself in to her own, shedding shoes and jacket as she went through to the kitchen. She was surprised to see Bob seated at the table, the newspaper spread out before him as he drank his coffee. She smelled toast and felt hunger rumbles in her stomach.

'Hello,' he said, a huge grin spread over his face. 'Where have you been? Did you get caught in a shower or something?'

'No,' she laughed and bent down to kiss him. 'I got soaked by sea spray. The tide's in and I was too close to the edge.'

'Hold on, I'll get a towel from the shower room.'

She liked that, the shower room, better than the old downstairs loo now they'd had it converted. He stood up, went through the back of the kitchen and returned with a bath sheet. He rubbed her hair dry, then kissed her. 'That better?'

She nodded.

'Will I get you some toast? And there's plenty of coffee left, I've only just made it.' He pointed to the cafetière. 'Help yourself while I put some toast in for you.'

'Bread,' she said.

'What?'

'You put bread in and toast comes out.'

'All right, Mrs Clever-Bugger. Bread in, toast out.'

She didn't bother to tell him about old Mrs Casey, or meeting Stella, or coming back from Westgate by train. No particular reason, apart from not wanting to include either of them in conversation on their first morning back from honeymoon. Ten minutes later he said, 'I'm just popping to the newsagents. Anything you want?'

'No, thank you... what you getting?'

'Computer Monthly, comes out today.'

'You can always have it delivered.'

'Yes, I know, but I chop and change which magazine I read. Don't particularly want the same one every month.'

'Ok. I'd better go and change. Best take your key with you, in case I'm still upstairs.'

'Will do.' He kissed her and was gone.

She fetched her clothes from upstairs and came back down to shower. By the time she had finished showering and dressing Bob still had not returned from the shop. She shrugged and wondered what was keeping him. She began to clear away the breakfast things and plan the rest of her day. Presently, she heard his key in the door, felt a sudden gust that followed him in until he shut the door behind him.

'Bit breezy out there now.' He tossed the magazine onto the kitchen table. 'You didn't tell me you went into old Mrs Casey's.'

She busied herself at the sink. 'No, didn't think to. She wanted some milk.'

'She just collared me as I was coming in here, kept going on about dear Mr Fontaine. Doesn't she know he's dead? She made me feel like a right outsider, daft old biddy.'

'She's mad as a hatter. Don't worry about her. Didn't upset you did she?'

'No, course not. Just went on and on about dear Mr Fontaine who used to come and change her light bulbs and any other job she wanted done.'

'What? What is she on about? H never went into her place as far as I know. She's probably just fantasising... or mischief making. Don't take any notice of her,' she added.

'Oh yeah,' he said. 'There was something else... she said you came off the train. Is that right?'

She was nettled now. 'What is this? Some kind of inquisition?'

Bob laughed. 'Hey... cool down. I didn't take any notice of her anyway. She just seems a bit lonely... wants to talk to whoever will listen to her.'

Delia decided it was time to change the subject. Mrs Busybody Casey could go to hell... and stay there. 'Right,' she said. 'I'm going upstairs to unpack our luggage and get the first wash ready.'

'D'you want a hand?'

She relaxed and smiled. 'No I'm fine. Anything you've got planned for today?'

'Not really,' he paused. Might go over to Westgate, start packing up the things I shall need over here. Get the flat ready for new tenants. I presume.' He paused. 'We *are* going to use this house as our permanent home... unless you'd like to move?'

'Erm... I hadn't thought of moving anywhere else. Are you ok with living here?'

'Absolutely fine. It's a great house, plenty of room for us and enough spare rooms for the family to stay and any overnight guests, whatever.'

'That's ok then,' she smiled again. She was happy with this man and with their decision to stay in the house. 'There's lots we can do to make it ours, don't you think?'

'For sure.' He flicked his way through the computer magazine. 'Perhaps I'll have another coffee and read a bit of this. Then I'll go over to Westgate. Do you want to come with me?'

'No. Best to let you decide what's coming here and what you're going to leave there. Are you letting the place furnished or unfurnished?'

'Furnished, I think... else I won't know what to do with everything.'

She continued upstairs and left him browsing through his magazine. 'Let me know when you're off,' she said. 'If I'm still upstairs.'

'Will do, sweetheart.'

She tipped both suitcases out onto the unmade bed, and decided the sheets could go in the wash as well. She made two piles of washing, whites and coloureds, and shook out clean or unused clothes and put them on hangers, ready to go into the wardrobes. A sudden noise from out back made her move to the window. Two doors away, she could see the old lady throwing bread up into the air to attract the seagulls. *Stupid woman, it's people like you that encourage the bloody creatures away from the beach. Then they mess all over paths and roads. You wouldn't do it if you had to clear up the shit. But you can't even keep your own place clean, let alone the town... you really ought to go... or be locked up in an old people's home or something.*

Delia moved away from the window, shook her

head, bit her lip in annoyance, and continued her sorting.

Bob called upstairs. 'I'm just off... be back around lunchtime, unless you want to meet me somewhere?'

She leaned over the banister, noticed a small bald patch on the top of his head. *Haven't seen that before...* 'Where?'

'Fancy the Blue Elephant in Margate?'

'Ok, that'll be good. What time?'

'I'll ring you on my mobile when I've finished at the flat. Meet you over there.' And he was gone with a cheerful whistle and a gusty bang of the front door. Delia smiled and went back to sorting their washing...

19

Half an hour later, the first batch of washing in the machine and the next wash in the laundry basket, ready to go, she thought coffee might be good. She looked out into the garden through the utility room window.   Autumn is a-coming in, she thought, noting a few scattered, golden leaves on the grass. She went back through to the kitchen to put the kettle. Instant will do, she decided, and in two or three minutes she was seated at the table scanning the newspaper, wondering whether to do the daily Sudoku or maybe the crossword. She was so lost in her own little world and almost fell out of her chair when the doorbell rang. Postman? Jess next door? Only one way to find out, she said to herself, go to the door. She could not identify the figure through the frosted glass. Someone not very tall... Right, it was the old girl, Mrs Casey.

'Hello Mrs C. What can I do for you?'

'The elderly woman sniffed, wiped her nose on a not-too-clean sleeve. Delia mentally shuddered.

'Is your husband in?'

'Erm, no. Afraid not.'

'Where is he then?'

She was so tempted to say none of your bloody

business but good manners forced her to explain. 'He's gone into Westgate and then he's going on to Margate. Won't be back till after lunch... Can I help?'

'Um... don't know. Are you any good at changing light bulbs?'

Delia smiled, despite her initial annoyance. 'I expect so. D'you want me to come round now?'

'Yes please. It's the one on the upstairs landing... I can't see a darned thing in the hallway without it. Times like this,' she added, 'when I miss my Charlie. Never had to do anything like that myself. He could lend his hand to anything, could Charlie. Your new husband handy like?'

'Don't know really,' she confessed. 'We've only just got married.'

'Yeah, well, he slept here before you got married, didn't he?'

Delia blinked in shock. She wondered what that had to do with DIY skills, or whether it was any business of the old biddy anyway. She said nothing. Except, 'Right, let me get my shoes on and I'll come and see what I can do for you.' She followed the shuffling old lady back to her house, waited patiently while she fumbled with the key, turn the ancient doorknob and let them both in. The hall smelled musty and gloomily refused to let the sunshine in from outside. She bumped into an old-fashioned hallstand. Funny, she thought, I don't remember that being there this morning when I got her milk. She walked carefully around it, noted worn brown spots on its ancient mirror.

'Do you want a cup of tea before we go upstairs? I'm gasping for one.'

Delia suspected that was a dig as she hadn't offered the old dear a drink, hadn't even asked her inside, come to think of it. Ah well... She didn't relish drinking out of one of Mrs Casey's cups and shook her head, forcing a smile at the same time. 'I haven't got long,' she lied. 'I'm meeting Bob in Margate later.'

The old lady sniffed but didn't, to Delia's relief, wipe her nose on her sleeve again. It already looked shiny enough, like a snail trail, to have been used more than once for the purpose.

'We'll have to go in the front room,' she said, 'it's where I keep the spare bulbs, in the sideboard.' She opened the door and led the way in. Daylight bravely filtered in, through heavy drapes and grubby net curtains. The room was cluttered with solid furniture and a vast amount of china and glass ornaments that filled shelves, the mantelpiece, and inside a small, corner display cabinet. Delia estimated a modest fortune in the original but dust-ridden Victorian knickknacks. The coating of dust, of course, was worth nothing. On the mantelpiece, she saw a photograph of a young man in uniform.

'Is that your son?

'Course not,' the old woman snorted. 'Never

had kids. That's my Charlie. In the War he was, out east. Came home in August 1945. He never slept in our marriage bed for months. Always under it, waiting for the bombs to drop I reckon... Shell shock they called it then. Got a different name for it now, not even a word... PT somethin' or other.'

'PTSD, stands for Post-Traumatic Stress Disorder.'

'Well, that's what he had, my Charlie... I was a virgin for the first month after we got married you know. He had to get himself right before he could service me, so to speak.' She let out a laugh that reminded Delia of the cackle of a pantomime witch. She even looked like one with that hooked nose, Delia thought.

Mrs Casey shuffled over to the drawer beneath Charlie's photo. It opened stiffly, crammed full as it was with goodness knows what. But she found the spare light bulbs and handed one to Delia. The small box was grubby and old and marked 60 watt. *Not exactly energy saving.*

'There's steps upstairs on the landing so's you can reach the light fitment.'

'Fine. Are you coming up with me?'

'I'll follow you.' Said the old lady. 'You'll be quicker than me anyway. Not so good on my pins anymore.'

It was difficult for Delia to pierce the gloom of the upstairs hallway. No doors were open on the

landing. 'Can I open a couple of doors up here?
Can't see much without a light.'

'Open them all up, if you want. Can't have you
standing on a step ladder in the dark, can we?'

She opened three out of four doors, one of which
was a bathroom, complete with fittings last seen in
the Ark she thought. *Looks like the last time they were
cleaned too. How can anyone live like this? Yuk...*

'See all right now?' The old woman puffed her
way up the last stair.

'Just about.' She stood on the small stepladder
under the dangling light fitment. 'Can you pass me
up the bulb?'

'Here you are,' she struggled it, with gnarled
arthritic fingers, out of its grubby cardboard case and
lifted it up to Delia, who had managed to extricate
the old one from its socket. She handed the old one
down to Mrs Casey and prepared to fit the new bulb,
slightly startled when the light came straight on.
'D'you mind flicking the switch off, please? I don't
want to get electrocuted.'

'Oh, my Charlie used to put it straight in
whether the switch was on or off.' She moved over
to the wall with ill grace, muttering under her breath,
and lifted up the old brass lever. *Yes, and I'm not your
Charlie.* Delia fiddled with the bulb, eventually
getting into place. 'Right, now you can switch on.'

The old lady flicked the switch, illuminating the
small space with a bright light. 'That's better.'

Yes, and thank you wouldn't go amiss. The old woman began to descend the stairs, leaving Delia to get off the ladder and make her own way down. Anger made her catch up with the old biddy faster than she anticipated. Some other emotion willed her to shove and shove hard. She watched in fascination as her elderly neighbour rolled and tumbled down the stairs, her head rattling as it hit the banister rods, her long shabby dress riding up beneath her and a look of pure horror on her wrinkled face...

The look was still there when she made contact with the tiled floor down below and lay there, still as could be, her neck twisted at an odd angle and a trickle of blood oozing from her mouth and one exposed ear. Delia, staring down at her, walked backwards to the top again, put the stepladder back in place under the hanging light. She took out the new bulb and set it on the worn carpet next to the old one. She pulled a large tissue from her pocket, wiped both bulbs, and rubbed the stepladder and the banister rails on both sides. She gazed down at the staring face below. Mary Casey, ninety three years old, would not reach ninety four. Mary Casey was well and truly dead. Poor old thing. Fell down did she? All the way to the bottom did she? Looks like it. *Well... I can't stay here... things to do indoors: washing, getting ready to meet Bob. Lovely! Lunch out. Gotta go.*

She stepped over the inert and twisted body, and

felt her way along the hall till she reached the front door. A cautious look outside reassured her there was absolutely no-one about. If Jess and Dez were home, she guessed they would be in the back, Jess in the kitchen cooking and baking, and Dez probably down in the windowless cellar that was his den, where he kept his prized coin collection. Still, she crept furtively past their house, silently praying they did not see her. She was relieved when she unlocked her own front door and slid inside unseen from anyone she hoped. The phone started to ring as she heeled the front door shut behind her. Quickly, she picked up the receiver, 'Hello?'

20

'It's me. You ok? You sound out of breath. Not been beach running again?'

She managed to laugh. 'No I've been up and down the stairs a couple of times.' She didn't say whose. 'Sorting the washing. Have you finished at the flat?'

'Sort of. Had enough for one day, plus the car's full up with bits and pieces. I'll do some more tomorrow... You ready to come out for lunch now?'

'Sure am. I'll just put on a bit of slap. Be with you in fifteen minutes or thereabouts.'

'Right then, lovely girl. See you at the Blue Elephant. Bye for now.' He sent a kiss down the phone and rang off. She ran upstairs and applied a small amount of make-up, pulled a brush through her hair and rushed downstairs again. All the stair climbing had given her an appetite. Pity about the old girl falling down hers. Not that *she* knew anything about it. How would she? Expect she'd hear about it on the local news... or read about it in the Thanet Journal. That came out in two days' time, so maybe it would, maybe it wouldn't, be reported in time to be included in this week's edition. Friday 13th, that would be the date. A good date to report a death by misadventure. She liked that, death by misadventure.

Delia shut the front door, unlocked her car, climbed in and started the engine. She carefully reversed out onto the service road and then onto the main road. She smiled, nodded to herself. Life was good, and so would lunch with Bob be...

Only it wouldn't, and wasn't. Who should be there with Bob, when she arrived at the Blue Elephant? Stella, the Delectable Stella. What the hell was she doing there, here? She should be in London. Hadn't she said goodbye to her on the train? Bob got up to greet her and kiss her.

'Hi darling, look who I found at the house.'

'How come... I thought you were in London today?'

'I was. Wrong day,' Stella laughed. 'Stupid me, I got all the way to the Old Bailey, only to be told my case wasn't coming up until Friday. Don't know how I managed that mix up. Anyway,' she continued. 'I decided to catch the very next train home, and arrived just as Bob was letting himself in. We had a coffee together, then I gave him a hand sorting things.'

'Yes,' said Bob. Delia most definitely did not like the smile he gave to the Delectable. Did not like it all: same as she did not appreciate Stella's 'helping hand'. 'I thought she deserved lunch on us as she had worked so hard with me.'

Delia tried, and hoped she had not failed, to give her sweetest smile. 'Great. Good that you could join us. Now, what's for lunch, I'm starving.' *After doing two loads of washing, changing a light bulb in a dirty house, and helping one old crone to fly.*

'There's steak and ale pie on the specials, or sea bass.'

'Oh, not for me, I'll just have the ham salad,' said Stella.

You would, thought Delia. Can't afford to put on an extra gram or three can you? 'That's boring, can't we tempt you to something more interesting?' *Maybe a nice dish of arsenic served up with deadly nightshade?*

Stella gave a noble sigh. 'The sea bass is tempting,' *It would be, it's the dearest thing on the menu.* 'But,' she continued. 'Phil and I have entertained so much while you two were away I swear I've put on inches around the waist.'

Delia shrugged. 'Your choice. I think I'll have the sea bass. What does it come with, darling?' She held his hand over the table, knew he would try to pull it away in front of the Delectable and gripped it tighter so he couldn't.

'Erm, new potatoes and veg of the day, or hand-cut chips and peas or salad.'

'I'll have the chips and peas *and* a side salad.'

'Sounds good to me. Think I'll have the same.'

He turned to his soon to be ex-neighbour. 'Sure you won't change your mind, Stella?'

She waggled her head from side to side. 'Mmn, I'm tempted... but... no, I'll stick to the salad.'

'Right then.' Bob stood up. 'I'll go up to the bar and order. What about drinks?'

'White wine for me please, darling.' Said Delia

'A small white wine for me too,' said Stella. 'And a glass of ordinary tap water please.'

'Might as well get a bottle then,' he said. 'As we're all drinking white. Won't put us over the limit if we all drink the same amount. Pinot Grigio ok with you two ladies?'

'Fine by me.'

'Yes, me too,' said Stella. She turned to Delia. 'I see you've recovered from your splash this morning.'

Delia's smile did not quite reach her eyes: more like a straightening of her lips. 'Of course.' She dismissed the subject as of no consequence. 'A pity about your day... such a mix up. How come you made that howler?'

Stella grinned. 'God only knows. Should've remembered. Friday the thirteenth of all days. Must be going senile or something.'

Or something... like going towards the end of your life. Except I haven't quite worked out how or when. Mustn't leave it too long, else you might have another day off to help Bob with his sorting out. We can't have too many of those days, can we?

'Which planet are you on?'

Stella's laugh brought Delia back to the present. 'Sorry, I was miles away. Back in Italy, I think.'

'Yes, Bob told me about your wonderful sojourn there. And he mentioned you were thinking of buying a second home there, an old cottage needing a face lift. How exciting. I've never been to the lakes,' she added. 'Spent most of our holidays in Portugal these past few years. At Daddy's apartment. Boring really, I suppose. Maybe we should go further afield.'

Did Delia detect a hint in that? Was she angling for a share in their secret hideaway? *Think again, Delectable; dream on.* Bob's return with a bottle, three glasses and a glass of 'just tap water' interrupted the conversation.

'Food's ordered. Shouldn't be long according to the barmaid.' He looked around the room. 'She says they're not very busy today. Must admit... there doesn't seem to be too many about.'

He sat down and poured them each a glass from the chilled bottle then slid it into a bottle sheath to keep it cool. 'Nifty, eh? This bottle cooler. Wonder where they get them from?'

Delia shrugged. 'Probably from their wine merchant. Maybe we can get one, from that nice catering shop in Canterbury?'

'Good thinking, woman.' He raised his glass, 'Cheers, ladies. Good to be home, although,' he added. 'We had a fab time in Italy... and Portugal of course.'

Speak for yourself, about Portugal, thought Delia. Delectable's daddy around every corner, or the bitch herself. Poor Phil. Reckon there's three in their marriage. Not going to be three in ours, that's for sure. *You'll have to go, dear girl. Not room in this town for both of us. Not room in the world, come to think of it.*

Presently the waitress brought over their food and asked them, 'Is there anything else I can get you?' Followed by, 'enjoy your meal guys'. They did. The sea bass was cooked to perfection, as were the chunky chips, and the salad was beautifully dressed, although Stella picked daintily at hers. Delia hoped she'd find a caterpillar in her lettuce. Serve Stella right if she did.

Under the table, Delia could feel Bob playing footsies with her. She liked that, and almost managed to reach up between his knees to his crotch. He'd like that, she surmised.

Stella seemed to guess what was going on.

'Why don't you two get a room?' She said, sounding cross...

Jealous bitch, thought Delia. *Well he's mine now and if I want to toe his crotch, that's my business.*

Bob had the grace to offer a laughing apology. She didn't. They ate the rest of the meal in silence with a few polite smiles across the table and feet under their own chairs. Stella continued to pick daintily at her salad. Delia thought the Delectable should consider becoming an actress, maybe here in Margate, a pantomime dame with a face full of ridiculous makeup. It gave her a sinister idea... not the method of Stella's departure, but certainly how she could look when her body was discovered. Delia's mind went into overdrive as she tried to imagine where Stella's body could end up. On the tide line might be an idea, with gentle waves of a receding tide washing around her, teasing her body to join them as they moved away from the beach towards the open sea. That pantomime face grinning up at the wheeling gulls whose appetites for flesh were constant.

'Hey,' said Bob. 'Where were you?'

She shook her thoughts away. 'Sorry,' she laughed. 'I was miles away. Back in Italy, I think.'

'Renovating that adorable cottage, I suppose,' added Stella.

Delia was sure she detected a sneer in Stella's voice.

'Something like that.' She took a sip of wine and cleared her mouth of food. 'Mmn, that was lovely. Thank you, darling.' She blew a kiss at her man. *Her man.*

His plate was already emptied. 'Pudding, anyone?'

Stella still played around with the odd lettuce

leaf, and some remaining tomato wedges. 'Oh, not for me, I'm full.'

What? On two leaves of lettuce and a slice of ham? Delia thought, as she set down her own knife and fork. 'Don't know. What about you darling? You want a pud?'

'Yeah, why not? Saves you having to cook tonight. 'Bob caught the waitress's eye and she sauntered over to clear their plates. 'All done? Everything all right?' she asked, eyeing Stella's remaining salad.

'Fine, my love. Can you bring us a dessert menu over?'

'We don't have a written one, but I can tell you what's on offer today,' she paused, balanced the plates against an ample bust. 'Right... we've got banoffee pie with cream or ice-cream, and apple crumble and custard. Or you can have that with cream or ice-cream... strawberry cheesecake... '

'I know,' Bob grinned. 'With cream or ice-cream?'

'You got it,' she grinned back. 'And ice-cream... or cheese and crackers.'

'Ladies?'

'Nothing for me,' was Stella's predictable answer.

'Just ice-cream for me. What flavours do you have?' asked Delia.

The waitress considered. 'Erm, vanilla,

strawberry, mint choc chip, rum and raisin: have them with cream if you like.'

Delia pondered.   'Ah, I'll settle for rum and raisin, and no cream, thank you.'

'Same for me,' said Bob.   'And three coffees to follow.' He turned to Stella. 'I presume you'll join us for coffee?'

'No, actually I won't. I'd better get back, Phil's home early tonight. Don't worry about a lift, I'll walk home along the front. Get a bit of sea breeze and walk my lunch off.'

'You sure?'

'Absolutely. Thanks for the meal. See you both soon.' She blew a kiss and quickly left the table.

The waitress still hovered. 'So that's it then, two R&R followed by two coffees.' She looked at Stella's disappearing figure, weaving through the tables towards the entrance, and shook her head. Delia could imagine her thinking 'strange woman' and half smiled in agreement.

It was gone three by the time they drew up outside the house, surprised to see an ambulance outside old Mrs Casey's house and a police car. At least, Bob was surprised. Delia guessed why they were there, but was slightly perturbed with their presence so soon after the old woman's 'accident'. Had anyone seen her, after all, when she left the woman's house? Had anyone heard the old dear fall? Jess and Dez's house was attached to the old lady's but not on the staircase side. Who could have heard the fall, if anyone?

'Wonder what's going on there?'

'Don't know,' she replied. 'Maybe Mrs Casey's been taken poorly.'

'Not with the force there. Gotta be more serious than that. Mind if I go and take a look?'

'Ever the policeman,' she replied, and struggled to sound amused, trying to keep the trepidation out of her voice. 'What about unloading your car?'

'Oh, I can do that later. No hurry. You go in,' he said and added. 'I'll just go and see what's going on.'

She locked her car and went inside. She could see what was happening through the lounge window but would have a better view through the front bedroom window, so she ran upstairs and rushed through to the front room. The paramedics were bringing an empty stretcher through to the ambulance. She could see them load it into the ambulance and stayed at the window, watching Bob talk to two uniformed police and their next door neighbour. His face looked serious and several times he glanced towards their house. Why? She began to feel an uncomfortable knot in her stomach and regurgitated a foul tasting combination of fish and ice-cream which she spat out into a tissue, not wanting to swallow it again.

One of the police looked up to the window

where she was standing and, instinctively, she drew back. Could he see her? No, he couldn't possibly; not through the nets. She was going to have to be very cool and clever, if someone had spotted her coming from the old girl's property earlier. Someone like Dez? Who else could it be? Why was he there? Was it him who called the police? So many questions, for which, as yet, she had no answers

She watched Bob walk back towards the house, then stop, as an unmarked car drew into the service road and parked up behind the squad car. Two plain clothed detectives climbed out. One she recognised as Phil, the other she had not seen before. Bob shook hands with both men, and chatted with them, while a uniformed policeman placed blue and white tape round the old lady's property. A few minutes later, another car drew up. A plastic-suited man climbed out, closely followed by a female counterpart. Between them, they carried two heavy-looking bags. All four ducked under the now-fastened blue tape. All four disappeared into the house. Bob and Dez remained outside and chatted to the uniformed policeman on the doorstep for a few more minutes. Delia could hardly bear the suspense and, if she was honest with herself, the fear of possible discovery.

21

After what seemed a lifetime, Bob returned to their house.

'What's happened? Why are the police there?' Her voice, she was sure, was almost at screaming pitch.

He looked at her for a long time before answering. 'It would seem that the poor woman has been... has fallen down the stairs. Looks like she broke her neck in the fall.'

'Oh my God, is she dead?'

'What do you think?' His lip curled. 'After a fall, down a whole flight of stairs?'

She was about to rebuke him for his sarcasm. Thought better of it. Her mind raced. Did he suspect her? Had Denzil Black said anything about her being there? Why hadn't they taken the body away? Why bring detectives out? It was all she could do to remain calm. Must try to bluff it out, she told herself...

Bob scuppered that idea with his next words. 'Did you go round there this morning?'

'Round where?'

He sighed. 'To Mrs Casey's. Dez says he thought he saw you coming out of her place earlier on.'

'Me?   Well you know I did, I told you she wanted me to fetch her some milk.'

'I mean later on, when I went to Westgate. Dez says he saw you.'

'He must be mistaken. Anyway how could he see me? He's always downstairs in that cellar of his, playing with his coin collection.'

Bob looked at her: a serious look, and an accusing one if she thought about it. 'He was in his front room this morning. Changing a light bulb would you believe. You can see an awful lot up a ladder.'

She did not like the look of accusation he gave her. *Come on Delia, bluff your way out of this. It's only Dez's word against yours... isn't it?*

'So you believe him? His word against mine? I'm your wife... doesn't that count for something, anything?'

He examined her face, unsure what to say next. 'Why would he lie?'

'I... I don't know. Maybe he saw someone who looked like me. You know where I was, here, doing the washing, sorting our holiday clothes. Why would I be round there?'

'You were there, early this morning, weren't you? Getting her milk, you said.'

'Yes, I know. I already told you that. Anyway, that was before you went off to Westgate.'   She paused. 'Perhaps I should have come with you, left the damned washing to do itself. Then they would have had to find someone else to blame.'

She was agitated, that was for sure: walking backwards and forwards through the kitchen and the adjoining hallway, massaging her hands as if she was washing them. Washing away the guilt? What was he to think? This was the woman he loved, the woman who had just been on the most wonderful honeymoon with him.

Bob the man wanted desperately for Dez to be wrong, to be mistaken, that it was someone else he saw coming out of Mrs Casey's house. The policeman in him told him this woman was a disturbing enigma: a woman who had mood swings, whose eyes flickered alarmingly from warmth to ice-cold in seconds. A woman who aroused suspicious instincts. How well did he really know her? He knew she was passionate, especially in bed. Oh yes. He was also painfully aware of her jealousy: towards Phil's wife, Stella, for one. He also remembered her sudden anger towards her friend Manda, the late Manda, over some bloke she used to know. Manda had said he was her first husband. Delia had denied this, and forced Manda to climb down and admit he had been an early boyfriend. Truth or lie? He had no-one to corroborate this now. Manda was dead, conveniently, and Delia's children did not seem to know anyone of that name. Perhaps... he could get a copy of her marriage certificate to Gerald, find out what surname she used?

'Well?' She was staring at him, challenging him. 'What's going to happen?'

He shrugged, kept his voice low and soothing. 'I really don't know at the moment. Forensics are in there. They'll find evidence whether there was anyone in there with Mrs Casey. For the next few hours, it's up to them.'

She felt his distance and it frightened her. But she was also sure they would find no evidence of her being in there. Hadn't she wiped all the surfaces clean of her fingerprints? She forced herself to relax, to smile, and show Bob that she was still the loving Delia he had married: the woman who had shared those wonderful days in Portugal and Italy with him. She went to take his hand and was shocked when she felt him stiffen and make to pull away.

'Bob,' she pleaded. 'It's me, not some murderess who pushes old ladies down the stairs. She must have fallen when she tried to change the light bulb.'

He let her take hold of his hand but felt sick inside. He must keep her sweet. He knew now for sure that she was guilty. How else would she have known about the light bulb? He hadn't mentioned what was upstairs, had he? It was best to withhold that piece of info, but how to keep her from knowing what he knew, or suspecting what he suspected? That was the challenge. He desperately needed to confer with Phil and Ken Yallop, the other detective, and hoped an opportunity would arise...

The remainder of the afternoon and early evening were taken up with emptying his car and finding places to put things. It was times like this he wished they had a garage to dump everything in. He certainly did not feel like finding permanent places for his possessions. Not anymore.

Delia helped him, suggested where to put things, and carried clothes and shoes upstairs, in between bringing in baskets of dried washing from the garden. She made admiring noises over some of his precious items, his police certificates and his old family photos.

'We can make a collage of them if you like. They'd look good on the walls of the back room, when we make it into an office for both of us.'

He nodded agreement, a pretence really. How could he possibly think of this house as a permanent home now? The walls seemed to close in on him and he wished he was still in his Westgate home, surrounded by police buddies and friends, not with this possibly mad woman who was stifling him.

It was on his final visit to the car that he saw the two detectives coming out of the old girl's house. Phil had his mobile to his ear. Ken saw him and waved him over.

'There was definitely someone else upstairs. Forensics have found depressions of other feet on the carpet and strange fingerprints on the ceiling light fitting.'

Bob nodded. 'Now what?'

'Well,' said Ken. 'Gotta be considered a murder case now, or at least a suspicious fatality.' He examined the ex-copper's face. 'You ok?'

'Kind of. You heard,' he said and paused. 'Who the next door neighbour saw coming out of there this morning?'

The detective shuffled about on the pavement, looking down at his feet. 'Yeah, I did. Your new bride, I believe,' he said and stared at Bob. Eventually he added, 'You know we'll have to question her?'

'Of course... look... do me a favour. Let me find an excuse to be out when you come round. I really don't want to be there.'

The other man nodded. 'I understand mate. Phil's on the blower now ringing the station as to procedure. Awkward when it's one of your own so to speak.'

'Thanks I appreciate that.'

Phil closed his mobile down and moved towards them. 'Bob,' he said.

'Hi Phil... What next?'

'Well... she's not being arrested, but we've instructions to bring her in, and get her to answer a few questions, informally so to speak. That ok with you?'

'Of course. Erm... I've just asked Ken here if you'll give me chance to get out of the house before you approach her. Best if I'm not there... no drama.'

'Yeah that's fine by me. We'll give you up to half an hour then go and see her. Tell you what, I'll drive over the road there,' he indicated the station car park. 'Then I can see you leave the house.'

'Great, thanks Phil... And you, Ken.' He walked slowly back towards the house, thinking up an excuse to leave her there on her own. From the corner of his eyes, he saw Dez and Jess's front-room curtains twitch, but purposely avoided looking full-face at them. They'd know soon enough. He felt sick inside; could not believe what was happening so soon after their marriage. Delia opened the front door.

'What's happening? I saw you talking to those two. What have they found?'

'I don't know, love,' he lied. 'Forensics are still examining the house and Mary's body.'

She stared at him. Could she believe what he said?

'Shall we have a cuppa? Tell you what,' he said. 'How about I pop round to the baker's and get one of their nice walnut cakes? Perhaps we can invite the boys in for a cuppa?'

She brightened. 'Ok, I'll put the kettle on.'

He shut the front door behind him but left it on the latch. He walked over to the station car park entrance, waved to the two detectives and gave them the thumbs up. He pointed to his watch, to indicate that now was a good time, and was relieved when they climbed out of the car and made their way across the road to the house. Unbeknown to Delia, he had picked his car keys off the hallway side-table in case it was necessary for him to keep away from the premises for longer than a five-minute gap, and continued to the baker's.

Ten minutes later, the house and the station car park were back in view. The unmarked car had gone, and, so he saw, was Delia's car. The relief was like a ten-ton weight being lifted off him. He let himself in to the now empty house, and put the wrapped cake down on the kitchen table, next to four mugs and the teapot. The silence was therapeutic, until the doorbell rang. Now what? Or who?

The 'who' was Denzel. 'Hello mate, what can I do for you?'

His next door neighbour looked embarrassed. 'Er... I've just come round... erm... to apologise really. I feel really bad if I've put Delia on the spot, so to speak. All I said was, I'd seen her come out of Mrs Casey's house and perhaps she might know something. Maybe I should've kept my mouth shut. Jess is always telling me to mind my own business.'

Bob stopped him before he could gabble on anymore. 'It's ok Dez. You did the right thing.' He soothed. 'I'm sure it'll all work out.'

'Yes, well, me and my big feet. Hope she'll be all right, your missus. I saw those two detectives knock on your door and she drove off soon after. Followed them, it looked like. Although, having said that, I'm sure one of them was in her car with her.'

Bob got rid of him as politely and quickly as was decent. He really did need a cup of tea now. Maybe something stronger. It wouldn't too be long, he thought, before he got a phone call from the station...

22

Delia looked round the bare walls and sniffed disapprovingly at the shining paint that was streaked in parts: through condensation, she supposed. It was a colourless room with a neutral surfaced table, four straight-backed chairs and not much else, apart from the wishy-washy cream paint on the walls. Not to her taste. Still, neither her being here was what she wanted. She wandered around the room, which took little effort as it was only about ten or eleven feet square. Just about dining-room size if you didn't want a sideboard in the room: maybe a small side table, a Pembroke, like she had at home, only the leaves at the end had been removed. She couldn't remember when: way back in Gerald's days she thought, long before H for sure.

A large, rectangular mirror hung on one wall. She looked at her reflection, relieved to find some make-up still in place and her hair fairly tidy, but she still patted it. She wandered back to the table, wished she had a book or a magazine to scan through; wondered how long she'd be left here before they came back to 'have a wee chat' as one of them had put it. Not Phil, the other one. She thought he said his name was Yallop, Ken Yallop.

She remembered going to school once with a boy of that name, only he was Maurice Yallop. Not really going to school with him, he had been in Saskia's class, two years up from hers. She wondered if this was the same Yallop. No he couldn't be if his name was Ken. Also he was younger than her. Maybe he was related? To Maurice Yallop...

She didn't have long to wait: the door opened and the detective called Yallop entered followed by a no-nonsense looking female in a black suit with a pale-blue blouse underneath. The sort of clothes that Stella wore to work. She had thick, untidy hair, bordering on auburn, little make-up and a brown mole on the corner of her upper lip. Delia wondered, did she lick it a lot? Knew *she* would if it was on *her* mouth. She almost did it now... in sympathy.

The woman detective carried a buff folder, an A4-sized writing pad and several pens. Detective Yallop apologised for keeping her waiting, addressing her as Mrs Shackleton, and introduced his female counterpart as DS Forbes, elongating it in explanation to Detective Sergeant. As if she didn't know! They joined her at the table, sitting opposite her, which made her feel outnumbered, and slightly intimidated. She knew she would have to apply cunning to show her innocence, even though they called this an 'informal interview'. She wished Bob was here with her, on her side both physically and emotionally.

The woman, DS Forbes, gave her a brief smile that did not quite reach her eyes and opened the A4 writing pad. She wrote today's date on the top, looked at her watch and said 'fifteen forty five', then looked at DI Yallop as if cuing him to begin.

'Ok Delia, d'you mind me calling you Delia, or would you prefer Mrs Shackleton?'

Privately she thought it rude of him, to address her by her first name, but best to humour him. 'Delia's fine,' she smiled. 'After all, it's the name I've had for longer than Mrs Shackleton. I'm still getting used to that one.'

He managed a thin smile, adopting what she suspected was his soothing tone. 'This is just an informal enquiry, regarding what you may or may not know of Mrs Casey's unfortunate death. We were given to understand that you visited the old lady this morning.'

'Yes, I did, but that was early. I met her in the street, I had just been out for a walk along the sea front and, when I got back, she asked if I could go to the shop and get her some milk. I left her making herself a pot of tea. She seemed perfectly all right to me.'

'What time would that have been?'

'I don't know exactly, around half past eight I suppose.'

DI Yallop stared at her and she heard DS Forbes scratching her pen over the writing pad. She looked up, when she finished writing, and also stared at Delia. *Disconcerting.*

'And was that the last time you visited the address?'

She barely hesitated. 'Yes. Bob went out after breakfast, to his house in Westgate. He wanted to sort through his belongings, decide what to leave and what to bring over to our home in Birchington. Meantime,' she added. 'I had piles of washing to do... after our honeymoon in Italy. We didn't get back till late last night from Birmingham. It took me all morning, several machine loads. Then I joined Bob for lunch at the Blue Elephant in Margate. Stella was there as well, Phil's wife.'

'The Delectable Stella,' he said and grinned.

'Yes... the very same.'

Both he and DS Forbes noticed the scowl that appeared on Delia's face but kept bland faces. 'Why Birmingham? Wouldn't Gatwick have been more convenient for you?'

'I suppose it would have been, but a very dear friend of mine died... at our wedding too. We had to go up there, to sort out her affairs, before we were able to start our honeymoon.'

'Yes, I heard about that. Tragic. And what a day for it to happen, on your wedding day.'

'It was pretty awful,' she agreed. She fidgeted in her chair.

'Would you like a cup of tea or coffee, Delia?'

This from DS Forbes.

'Oh, yes please.   Coffee, almost black and no sugar.'

As if by magic a uniformed policeman appeared at the door and took their order of three coffees. How did he do that? She wondered. *Maybe they've got a bell under the table their side.* She wanted to look but didn't think it would be a good idea. Best to appear as relaxed as possible.

DI Yallop continued with his questions. 'So you didn't see the postman, or Mr Black outside this morning?'

'No. As I said, I was doing the washing. Our machine is in the utility room at the back of the house. I went out into the garden from time to time, that's also in the back, to hang the washing out. I didn't see anyone.'

He stared at her again. 'Wonder why Mr Black thought he saw you coming out of Mrs Casey's later on: about eleven he thought?'

'I... I really don't know. Maybe he mistook me for someone else.'

For a few moments no-one spoke. She felt edgy and tried desperately not to fiddle with her hands. The door opened and the uniformed policeman entered carrying a tray with three mugs and a plate of biscuits.

'Which one's nearly black with no sugar Eddie?'

'This one,' and he handed it to Delia. 'I presume

it's for you, ma'am. These two like milk and two spoonfuls.'

'Biscuit?' offered the woman detective.

'Delia smiled. 'No thanks. I'm still full up from lunch. We had sea bream followed by ice-cream.'

'Very nice,' said DI Yallop. 'Beats the canteen Shepherd's Pie we had. Right Irene?'

Irene gave one of her brief smiles and licked the mole at the side of her lip. 'Certainly does.' And immediately looked down at the writing pad, making a drum major's twirl of her pen.

So, she does lick it. Why not have it cut out... Why am I here?

DI Yallop brushed crumbs from his mouth and drained his mug. He too licked his lips. 'Right then, shall we continue?'

'I don't know what else you want me to say, really I don't. I never went upstairs.'

He paused, gave her a keen look. 'I never asked you if you did. What made you say that?'

'I... I don't know. I thought you said she fell downstairs.'

'I don't think so, Mrs Shackleton. Irene, could you read through the notes so far?'

The woman detective read in a monotone. Delia felt sick: he was right, DI Yallop. Nowhere had he mentioned Mrs Casey falling down the stairs. She hadn't missed him suddenly calling her Mrs Shackleton either. What was that all about?

'I expect Bob told me about her accident. The ambulance was there, so we guessed something must have happened to her. Bob saw his police friends there and went to talk to them. That's right,' she brightened. 'It was Bob who told me she was at the bottom of the stairs. Poor old thing, she must have fallen.'

Again there was silence, apart from DS Forbes' whispering pen across the page. It put Delia in mind of a quotation she had once heard, 'The moving finger writes, and having writ moves on...' Was it from Omar Kayam?

When she finished writing, the two detectives looked at each other. 'Would you excuse us for a minute?' They stood up and made to leave the room 'Won't be long,' and he smiled at Delia.

She sat and stared at their empty chairs, at the tray of mugs and the plate of untouched biscuits. What next? Her fingers drummed nervously, impatiently on the plain wooden table. She raised and lowered her heels, making a tapping sound. It was the only noise to break the silence, except for her giving an occasional sigh or sniff. She stood up, walked over to the mirror, adjusted her hair, brushed an imaginary crumb from her lips and thought about the woman detective's mole on the side of her mouth, suddenly glad that *she* didn't have one on hers. She walked around the small room before sitting again, sighing again and tapping her heels, her fingers, even began rocking her body a little. Her mind asked the question again. What next?

23

'What d'you think?' Ken Yallop stared down into the room they had just vacated through the two-way mirror. DS Forbes was by his side.

'I don't know... there's something strange about her.'

He watched her prowling round the small room below. Noted the body language and her staring eyes as they ranged the walls. 'Can't quite put my finger on it. I think she's lying... about not being in the old girl's house when the neighbour says he saw her. Could be a tricky one, her word against his, unless forensics come up with anything.'

'Mmn... Can't very well take her fingerprints or anything: she's come in for an informal chat.'

'What about her coffee mug? There's probably prints on that, and her saliva.'

'Well said, Irene. Wait a minute... what's she doing?'

They both peered down into the room.

'Cheeky bugger,' said Irene. 'She's wiping her prints off the mug. We'd better get down there.'

'No, wait a minute, look what she's doing now, fiddling with our mugs. Daft cow's putting her prints all over them.' He picked up the folder and writing pad. 'Come on, let's go. See if we can catch her in the act.'

By the time they had gone down the steps of the surveillance room and reached the door to the interview room, Delia was sitting demurely on her chair, the tray of cups and biscuit-plate over their side of the table. She scrunched a tissue in her hand.

'Would you like me to get rid of that for you?' DS Forbes said in a casual voice.

'No, no it's fine. Just had a bit of a sniffle, that's all. I'd better keep hold of it, in case I need it again.'

Both detectives guessed it was what she had used to wipe her prints off the mug.

'I can soon get you another tissue,' offered DI Yallop.

'No thank you. I'll be ok with this one. Anyway,' she continued. 'Can I go soon? I've still got lots of clearing away to do at home.'

'Yes, of course,' DS Forbes this time. 'I'd just like to read these notes back to you, make sure they're correct. Then you can go... and thank you for your help.'

She proceeded to read. Peering up over the page every now and then to make sure she had Delia's attention.

'Right then, Mrs Shackleton, Delia. Do you agree with what I've written?'

'Well, it seems to be all right. Don't see how it helps you. But there you are, you're the police and I am just a lowly citizen,' she forced a laugh, stood up and scraped back the chair. 'Oh, sorry about that, didn't mean to make a noise. Bit heavy these chairs.'

DI Forbes held out his hand. 'Once again, thank you so much for coming in. We'll be in touch when we find out anything more. Sorry,' he added, 'for such an unfortunate home-coming from your honeymoon.'

He prevented the smile from reaching his eyes. They remained steely blue and penetrating, questioning, making Delia feel uncomfortable and anxious to get out of that claustrophobic room. It irked her that she had to follow them, as she had no idea whereabouts in the police station this room was situated. The five minutes it took to be shown to her parked car seemed like a lifetime's journey, and she was extremely relieved to watch the woman detective walk back into the station. She let out a long sigh, put the key into the ignition, switched on, and locked herself in. Only then did she feel slightly secure. In fifteen minutes she'd be home, safe, with Bob.

There was little traffic about now and a glance at the dashboard clock told her it was gone six o'clock. How long had they kept her there, in that awful room? Questioning her, trying to trip her up she was sure. She smiled to herself, she'd given them as good they got; and managed a little throaty chuckle. Slowly and carefully, she drove through Margate and negotiated the roundabout where lights from the Blue Elephant spilled out over the flowerbeds that decorated the small, stone built circle. She briefly saw people standing by the pub window. Office and shop workers enjoying Happy Hour, while she had struggled to drink a cup of cheap instant coffee. They were free from their toil and daily cares as they drank their beer or sipped their Chardonnay; ate dry roasted peanuts or crunched on flavoured crisps and chatted happily. She had been offered tired looking biscuits, had had to choose her words carefully. No spontaneous conversation for her, no easy laughter with friends and colleagues. Each sentence designed in her head to indicate her innocence, both in vocabulary and voice inflection.

She practised it now as she drove along, past the Blue Elephant, past that small parade of shops where Caius Whatshisname lived above the florists. Was he still there? Had his painting made him famous? Of course it had, and no, he didn't live there anymore. She remembered now, reading about him being hung in the New Turner Gallery along by the harbour. Funny expression that, being hung. Not funny really, more like gruesome. Except they don't do hanging anymore. Not in this country anyway. Supposing, she said to herself, supposing they do find you guilty. What are you likely to get? Ten years? Or will a good lawyer get the charge commuted to manslaughter, or accidental death. I mean, she continued chatting to herself. You could always say you tripped on the worn stair carpet and accidently fell onto her and down she went...

Her mind went on to 'good lawyer' and... Stella. Oh no. Not her. But she was a solicitor, she couldn't defend her in court. It would have to be a barrister. The man with the wig and a well-modulated, commanding voice like you see in TV series. Martin Shaw, as Judge John Deed, would definitely let her off such a charge. Anyone but Stella, the Delectable. She knew that Bob would say straightaway, 'You must let Stella find you a good lawyer' and she would have to agree. Be forced to, in case she lost him...

She drew up outside the house, made a noisy pull on the brake, switched off and sat there for a minute. She saw there were no lights on next door, not in the front room. No of course not, Jess and Denzil would be in the back, sitting in the kitchen having their tea, as he called it. Not dinner, they had dinner at lunchtime and tea at dinnertime. Why hadn't he been in the back or down in his den this morning? She wouldn't have had all this aggravation if it hadn't have been for him. Him changing a light bulb indeed... ironic that, changing a light bulb. It's what has got her into this mess, changing the old crow's light bulb. Now how to get out of it?

A light went on in her own front room. Bob

opened the front door, came out to the car wearing an anxious expression. He opened the car door and peered in. 'You ok?'

She nodded, tired now, felt drained. 'Yes, I'm all right. Glad it's over. Not the nicest way to spend an afternoon.'

'Come indoors. D'you want a cuppa, or something stronger?' He even managed a smile for her and she was glad about that.

'Something stronger would be good.' She climbed out of the car.

'Here, give me the keys, I'll lock it for you. Go indoors, put your feet up. I'll pour you some wine when I come in.'

'Thank you darling, you're an angel.'

He grinned, despite his anxiety and suspicion. 'Not yet, I hope.'

'No, not yet.' She kissed him and went indoors, kicking off her shoes in the small, front hallway as she moved through to the lounge. Bob had switched on a table lamp by the settee and it gave the room a warm, cosy glow. She sank back, put her feet up and waited patiently for him to spoil her with a generous glass of Chardonnay or Pinot Grigio, whatever came first. He kissed the top of her head on his way through to the kitchen. 'Won't be a minute.'

He neglected to tell her about the phone call he had received from Ken Yallop.

'Can't do much for a while Bob. Not till

forensics have given us their info, and you know what they can be like at dragging their heels. Be different if we were the Met, aye?'

'Yeah, I know what you mean.'

'For the time being, it's Delia's word against his, your next door neighbour. No-one else seems to have seen her, and she does admit to being in there this morning, but earlier.' He paused. 'Anyway, we've sent her home, she'll be with you in ten or fifteen minutes, ok?'

'Yeah, thanks Ken. I owe you. Oh,' he added. 'I'll see if I can dig up anything this end.' He winced at the inappropriate words. 'Don't know what, but there might be something that'll help us.' By including himself, he realised, he still felt part of the team. Yes, there was a certain amount of guilt as well, disloyalty towards his new bride, but if Mary Casey's death was not an accident, then it had to be treated as suspicious. And Delia was first in the queue for that suspicion to be in her direction.

He took a tray through to the front room with a freshly opened bottle of Pinot Grigio and two glasses. There was also a dish with small cheesy biscuits and another with a freshly opened packet of cashews.

'Thought you might be hungry as well as thirsty,' he said as he put the tray down on a small table and set it in front of her.

She smiled. 'Reminds me of Gravedona and Olmo's.'

'Well, we don't want to come down to earth too soon, do we?' He poured two generous measures, passed her a glass, and sat down next to her. 'Nuts or cheesy bics?'

'Can I be greedy and have some of each?'

'Course you can,' and he pushed the dishes closer to her. They clinked glasses, said 'Saluté' and both took generous and relieved gulps of the pale liquid.

'Do you want to talk about it?' He hoped his voice sounded casual enough.

'Later... do you mind? I just want to relax for a while.'

'Of course.' They sat in a comfortable silence until he said, 'Do you want to go over the road for a pub meal? I don't suppose for one moment you want to cook. Or I can go and get a Chinese?'

'You're right, I hadn't thought about dinner. Don't fancy going over to the 'View' though, one pub meal is enough for one day... Maybe we'll have a Chinese a bit later. Does that suit you?'

'Yep, that's fine by me. You ready for a top up?' He replenished their glasses. 'Shall I put the telly on, or do you just want to sit?'

She was beginning to be irritated by these inane questions, his trying to be natural, normal. Was he trying too hard to be nice? She must stay on her guard. 'Put it on if you like. We'll have missed the national news but we might still catch the local.' As soon as she said it she regretted it. What if today's episode had reached the Thanet Newsroom? What if they had a photo of her? Too late now, Bob had switched on and was turning the sound up. Better to sit back and look as if you're relaxed, she thought. Her stomach did the churning while her mind ran as breathless as a marathon runner's lungs might if he was on his last legs. She willed herself to listen as Ellie Clarkson read through the news from Dover, Folkestone, and Maidstone. Two High Street robberies in Maidstone, a lorry full of immigrants crashing on the A20 out of Dover, and a man severely beaten outside a Folkestone nightclub: police are appealing for witnesses.

'Nothing about Mrs Casey then,' declared Bob. He sounded relieved, she thought. She shrugged, said nothing and continued staring at the flickering screen.

'News has just come in about a death in Birchington,' Ellie looked up from her studio computer. 'Ninety-three-year old Mrs Mary Casey of Station Lane, Birchington was, this morning, found dead at the bottom of her stairs. It appears her neck was broken. There will be a police investigation as foul play has not been ruled out. Kent police are appealing for witnesses because it was reported a person was seen leaving the elderly person's house shortly before her body was discovered. Calls can be made to... '

Delia froze, her glass halfway to her lips. She knew Bob was staring at her. What was he looking for? Signs of her guilt? *Think again, darling man. It's his word against mine: him, Denzil, nosey Denzil. Should've been playing with his coins or taking his manky dog for a walk, then I wouldn't have all this aggravation: wouldn't even be considered a suspect.*

Anger flared in her mind, and in her nostrils. She had never liked him, not really. Always thought he was a bit of an old woman. *Don't know how she puts up with him, Jess. She's not a bad soul. But neither of them are really my type, good enough as neighbours. Leastwise she is...*

'So... How were they towards you, down at the station?'

'Fine. Polite. Gave me a cup of coffee, cheapo stuff and stale biscuits. Can't complain. They weren't rude or anything.'

'Did they bully you?'

'No,' she smiled. 'They were quite gentle I suppose. I didn't feel intimidated anyway. The woman detective, Irene Forbes I think her name is, took notes of what I said. Not that I said much. She was a bit officious but that's her job isn't it? They're not running a charm school after all.'

'True. What's he like? Ken Yallop?'

'Quite nice. Polite... Did he take your job?'

'It would seem that way. Ironic really, they give me the push and, six months later, fill the post.'

She stared at him. 'Does it bother you?'

He thought about it. 'I must admit, when I saw him with Phil today, I did feel a bit peeved. But, if he's just been promoted to DI he won't be getting what I was paid. Not for a couple of years at least. So I guess they're saving some money from putting me out to grass. Who knows,' he added grinning. 'He might even need a place to live, and take my old flat. At least I'd get some money back off him and the force for sacking me.'

The evening was ending peaceably enough, she thought. They watched TV with plates of Chinese takeaway on their laps and glasses of wine on little side tables next to them. Not really the way she liked to dine but it was fine for tonight. It also meant she didn't have to talk too much, discuss the Mary Casey business. Bob did once make her feel uncomfortable. After a half hour's silence, he suddenly asked, 'Who was Carl?'

'Carl? Carl who?'

'I don't know, you tell me. Manda mentioned him a couple of nights before we married. You remember? At dinner. I was sure she said your husband.'

'What made you suddenly think of that?' She was rattled and hedged a reply.

'Oh... erm... the name cropped up on the radio while you were out,' he lied. 'You know how your mind works, one thought leading to another.' He let it ride for a while, emptied his glass and poured them both another. He dared to ask again. 'So, who was he?'

Her eyes barely met his. She fidgeted on the settee, and put down her half-finished plate. That made him feel slightly ashamed, but he could tell she did not like the question. She took a generous gulp of her wine, swallowed, it and pulled a face as if she was sucking a lemon.

'His name was Carl Fletcher. He was no good. *And* a bully... End of.'

'What happened to him, after you split from him?'

'I don't know.' Her voice rose, sounding slightly hysterical. He told himself to tread carefully, but he was sure that something was not quite as it should be. He was rewarded by her next words, yet sorry she uttered them. 'I moved away from Hampshire. I met Gerald and we got married. I did hear, 'she hesitated. 'I did hear that Carl was involved with a bad set. Got stabbed or something.'

'Stabbed? Fatally?'

'So I was told later. I was away at my sister's at the time.'

'I didn't know you had a sister. I thought you said you were an only child?'

She hesitated. 'Well she wasn't really my sister, we just called each other that. We were close friends, went to school together, later worked together. Years ago. We lost touch, haven't heard from her for ages.'

He knew now, something was very wrong. Why did she say sister, then change it to friend? When they were making their guest list she had denied having family. He decided to let the matter rest... for now. He also promised himself to do a bit of delving in a very discreet way. Best keep her sweet... for a while.

24

They did not make love that night. Instead, Bob encouraged her to have more wine. He took the plates out to the kitchen, shouted through that he would wash up and bring another bottle. When he went back into the front room her face had a slight flush to it and her eyes were flickering. He persuaded her to drink one more glass. 'One for the stairs,' he grinned. The grin was a struggle. It worked though. She relaxed, even laughed a little before the yawning started.

'Come on, sweetheart. Let's go to bed. Been a bit of a day today, hasn't it? One way or another.' He said he would take the glasses and bottle through to the kitchen. 'You go on up. See you in bed.'

She did not argue, gave a cavernous yawn instead and struggled off the settee. 'All right darling. See you in a little while.'

He heard her stumbling up the stairs as he rinsed the glasses and put the bottle back in the fridge. He listened when the toilet flushed and pictured her going into the bathroom next door; hoped she wouldn't gag when she brushed her teeth. Perhaps, if he hung about down here for ten minutes or so, she'd fall into bed and go to sleep immediately.

There was something he wanted to look up on the computer, more than one thing. Best to do it while Delia was out of the way.

After a while, all was silent upstairs. He took a chance and crept up to their bedroom to check on her. Yes, soundo, well away with the fairies she was, and snoring as well. Time to get back down there, go online and click on the genealogy site. Now he had Carl's surname he could check whether the late Mr Fletcher had ever been married and to whom.

Three hours later Bob had compiled a disturbing history of one, Cordelia Fletcher (née Webster), then Cordelia Manning, Cordelia Fontaine and now Mrs Shackleton. According to records, she had married Gerald Manning as a widow, and Harry Fontaine the same. Now him. He'd make damned sure there wouldn't be a widow named Cordelia Shackleton...

He also came across three children who shared a mother called Cordelia: a Maria Fletcher who died in her first year, followed three years later by twins Matilda and Daniel Manning, Tilda and Danny. Now he needed to discover how the little girl called Maria died, wondering if it had been a suspicious death.

He leaned back in the chair, looked out onto the beginnings of daybreak, stretched and yawned. God, he felt tired now, tasted a stale mouth and rubbed his hands over a stubbled chin. Was it worth going to bed? He shook his head in the quiet room. Might as well go and have a shower, put on fresh clothes and maybe go for a walk on the beach. But if he went upstairs to shower and dress, then he'd wake Delia. He could of course shower downstairs, but then he'd have no clean clothes to change into. Decisions, decisions as they say... Perhaps he'd just go for a walk to clear his head, think over the night's discoveries, maybe ring Phil and appraise him of these new facts. Damned if he was going to ring Ken Yallop. Let him hear of them through Phil. He switched off both the computer and printer, stuffed the printout into his trouser pocket and walked towards the hallway to fetch a jacket.

She stood there in the doorway, silent. He hoped she could not see the fright she gave him. Christ!

'Hello sweetheart, up already?'

She answered his question with a question. 'Have you been up all night?' She was not smiling. He knew to tread very carefully.

'No, I came up to bed, fell asleep on top of the duvet, and woke up about half an hour ago. Decided to come down and make coffee. You ready for one?' he added. He hoped his smile and the glib answer fooled her.

'Why are you in here then?' She glanced over to the computer.

He prayed he had deleted everything and emptied the recycle bin before he switched off, knew she was computer-literate enough now to search for recent activity. 'Oh I just came in to see if there were any emails.'

'And were there?'

He didn't like the tone of her voice, detected an aggression there. 'Er... no. I don't know. I didn't switch on in the end, decided I needed a coffee more. We had a fair amount to drink last night, didn't we?' He hoped the change of subject might calm her suspicions.

She stared at him for a few seconds more then let her face relax into a loving smile. 'Yes, we did... I'll go and put the kettle on.'

He followed her slowly through to the kitchen, conscious of his scruffy appearance, grimly aware of the cat-and-mouse game they were playing. He needed to get out of the house, phone Phil and pass on this information to him, the details he had printed out that were now secreted in his pocket, burning a hole in there if he thought about it. First, he had to keep Delia sweet, knowing or guessing that she suspected him, that she was aware of his own misgivings. He had to draw on his years of experience as a detective, get her relaxed enough to trust him again, like stroking a rabbit before you cuffed him dead. It was not going to be easy. Now he was sure, in his own mind, of her deviousness, he had to put on the act of appearing that nothing was wrong.

'Coffee's ready. Do you want some toast with it?' She dangled the wrapped bread.

'Yes please.'

'One or two?'

'Pardon?'

'One slice or two?'

'Oh... two please.' He forced a smile and took one of the coffees from the table. 'I'll go for a swift walk after. Get my head cleared before going back to the flat.'

'D'you want me to come with you?'

He was about to say no, thinking she was referring to the walk, then figured out she meant going to Westgate with him. 'There's not much to clear, but two of us would get the job done quicker. Yeah, I'd like that.' Another smile. He was getting good at this. Maybe he should join the local amateur dramatics society... maybe not.

'I meant shall I come for a walk with you, but going to Westgate might be better: give me time to have a shower.' She busied herself with the toast and butter. 'Jam or marmalade?'

'Marmalade please, sweetheart.' He drank the coffee black and unsweetened; allowed it to burn his mouth, punishment against the lies and deceit, except he wasn't the guilty party.

'By the way,' she said. 'If Stella is there, and if we decide to go out to lunch again... can we please go on our own?'

'Of course. Don't suppose she will be around though. Didn't she say she had to go back to the courts today? I think she also said something about visiting her father this weekend. Anyway, doesn't matter if she is, we'll go off on our own.' Anything, he thought, to keep his wife relaxed and happy. He forced himself to eat the toast slowly, not to cram it all into his mouth and rush off out.

After what seemed a lifetime, he managed to be casual. 'Right. Swift walk down the front and I'll come back for my shower.' He brushed her cheek with his lips and when she turned her face to his he said, 'I don't think you want to smell my stale breath. I'll kiss you properly when I get back.'

'You might do more than that, once you've showered and brushed your teeth. We can always go back to bed for an hour or two.' She gave him a coquettish look and grinned.

'Shame on you, woman. Thought you'd had enough of my body on honeymoon.' He shrugged on his jacket and squeezed his arms to his sides to make sure his mobile was in one of the pockets. Yes. One problem less.

'Don't be long.' She said it with a smile but it sounded to him almost like a command. Christ, how paranoid can you get?

'See you later.' And he was out of the door, walking quickly to the railway bridge and on towards the beach. He waited until he was down on the promenade before fishing out his phone. The tide was out and the walkway was deserted. Even the gulls cooperated and had flown off somewhere else to do their screeching and sky diving. He walked backwards in case she had decided to follow him. There was no way he wanted her to creep up on him.

Phil answered the phone after only two rings. 'Hiya Bob. You ok?'

'Kind of mate. Listen, I won't waste time, I've got some info for you regarding Delia. I need you to investigate it further.'

'Ok. Fire away.'

Bob read out the facts he had gleaned from the computer, suggested where his young ex-sidekick could investigate more.

'Forensics have given us more fingerprints, not those that match the old lady's. Ken and Irene are going to compare them with the ones they lifted off the mugs yesterday, after Delia had touched them. Doesn't look good, mate.'

'I know,' said Bob. 'I gotta be very careful for the next couple of days. I've got a bad feeling she could have been involved with more than one death. Oh yes... 'He added. 'Don't phone me back, or if you do wait till I let you know it's safe for me to talk. If it's not I'll make some excuse to ring off, say it's a wrong number or something.'

'Got that. Stay safe, Bob, and,' he paused. 'I'm

sorry about this.'

'Not your fault. Speak soon.' And he rang off. He felt better for talking to his friend, sure now that things would start rolling.

He walked back with a certain reluctance, suddenly aware of the heavy clouds that had crept into the sky. The rain hit him like a shock wave, spitting into his face, soaking through his jacket and trousers and drenching his hair. In a way he found it strangely cleansing, washing away the torment of her and what she might have done.

To be widowed three times, to have lost a baby... and Manda... and Mrs Casey, added up to a lot of 'what ifs' in his mind. Ok, so there were all extenuating circumstances, apart from Carl Fletcher who was stabbed to death. Gerald Manning died of pneumonia, a natural death; Harry Fontaine from a brain tumour, considered again death by natural causes, he supposed. Manda had a severe nut allergy that Delia swore she knew nothing about. True or not true? She certainly hadn't rushed forward, he recalled, to help Manda as she choked to death. He couldn't say about the little baby, Maria Fletcher. Maybe when he sent for her death certificate (or got the boys at the station to) he would find out what caused her demise.

He shivered, mentally, from these thoughts, and physically, because he was bloody soaking wet. So much for an early morning walk. By the time he reached the house he was freezing cold as well. He felt in his pockets for the front door key, found the piece of paper with all the names on it. It was easy to screw it up into a ball, turn it into an unrecognisable piece of papier maché and toss it away before Delia could even begin to discover what it was.

She must have been watching for him. 'My God, look at you,' she said. 'What happened? Did you fall into the sea or something?'

'Or something,' he said, shaking himself off in the hallway and removing his wet shoes. 'It's raining a hurricane out there, and my luck to get caught in it when I was nearly at Minnis Bay.'

'Couldn't you have sheltered somewhere?'

'I said nearly at Minnis Bay. I was still under the cliffs when it tipped out of the sky.' He made for the stairs. 'I'll go and have my shower, change out of these wet rags. Any chance of a coffee please, sweetheart?'

'Of course. Go and have your shower and I'll make some fresh in the cafetiere. It'll be ready by the time you're out.'

He warmed up under the hot cascade, felt his body tingle with pleasure. Five minutes later he was dried, dressed and on his way downstairs. He had tossed his wet clothes into the laundry basket after first removing and flushing the screwed-up ball down the lavatory.

'Coffee smells good,' he said as he entered the

kitchen. 'And you look good.' He kissed her and lightly brushed her cheek with his fingers. He felt a moment's remorse, regret for what might have been and what was surely to be. *Keep her sweet...*

25

They decided against a trip to his Westgate apartment. Went back to bed instead, made love and slept the rest of the morning away, waking at around twelve-thirty.

'I'd better go over the road and get something for lunch. Anything you fancy?' she asked.

'Apart from you on toast?'

'You've had the toast… and me. So think again.'

'Erm... erm... how about something simple, like a pizza?'

'That all? Are you sure?'

'It's fine. Quite enjoy a pizza every now and then.'

'Ok, pizza it is then. I'll buy a basic cheese and tomato and add my own toppings. Lots of chopped-up veg and some salami and chorizo.'

He licked his lips. 'Can't wait.' He also couldn't wait for her to leave the house, convinced that Phil would ring soon. Hoping so. Wondering what he had found out.

'Right, I'm off. See you in a bit.' She gave him a swift peck and ran downstairs. He heard the front door slam and breathed more easily. If his friend didn't ring within the next five minutes, he would ring him. He dressed quickly, felt his chin stubble, decided against a shave, and went downstairs. The phone started to ring when he was halfway down. He skipped the remaining steps, rushed into the hall and picked up the receiver.

'Hello?'

'Bob?' It was Tilda.

'Hi sweetie. Your Mum's just popped to the shops. She won't be long.'

'That's ok. Actually,' she hesitated. 'I need to talk to you as well. One of my old school friends rang me last night. Told me the old lady two doors down from you had died. She also said something about Mum being taken in for questioning.'

'How would she know that?'

'So it's true then. Fern's related to your next door neighbours, Denzil and Jessica Black. That's how she knew about Mum... Is Mum all right?'

'Yes, she's fine. It was just an informal chat. Seems Dez saw your Mum coming out of the old girl's house. She says she wasn't. She'd been in there earlier but not when he said. Her word against his, I suppose.'

'You don't sound very convinced, Bob.'

'Oh I am, I am.' He knew it sounded anything but convincing, but her next remark sent him reeling.

'Have you ever noticed how Mum can turn? Like a chameleon?'

'What?'

'She kind of acts... odd... every now and then. Turns against people very easily. She used to do that with our friends when we were young.' He noted how she was rushing the words as if she wanted to run away from them. 'We were allowed to bring friends home. So she could vet them, but if she didn't like them, they were never invited a second time.'

His mind raced as he caught up with her words. He thought about baby Maria, Carl's baby. And Manda. Delia's resentment towards Stella and the old girl too. 'How do you mean?' He could imagine Tilda, at the other end of the line, pausing while she couched carefully chosen words.

'There was one friend I had, when I was at Art College. Damien. He was a bit of a hippie and Mum disliked him on sight: you could tell. She was kind of... frosty towards him, very polite but in a distant, controlled way.'

'What happened to him? Did she send him packing?' he tried to laugh, didn't quite make it.

'Damien died... of poisoning.'

Bob went cold and into police mode. 'Poisoning? How?'

'He ate poisonous mushrooms. Went out into the woods near to our house one morning. I'm sure Mum told him where they were, even pointed them out in a fungi book she used to have, only they weren't the same ones in the woods. Renal failure, that's what they said he died from.'

He hoped Delia wouldn't come back while her daughter was on the phone, not while he was finding out these valuable pieces of the jigsaw that was beginning to take shape. He also wanted to keep Tilda ignorant of what was going on this end, both his discoveries and what was happening (he hoped) at the station. Time enough for her to find out later, if all these two-plus-twos added up to five. 'Terrible way to die, poor lad.'

'He wasn't the only one.'

'What?'

'There was Danny's first boyfriend, the one he was going with when Mum first found out Danny was gay. Tim his name was, Tim - um - Cadwallader. He fell onto the line at Highbury tube station, just as the train was coming in. Got crushed to bits...'

Bob went cold as he remembered his architect/designer who worked on the Westgate house. How he told him he had lost a son on the London Underground. He had forgotten the man's name, but Cadwallader did ring a bell.

'Danny was heartbroken,' Tilda continued. 'Until he met Ray. Mum made a weird remark at the time. Least I thought so.'

'What did she say then?'

'Something about... I don't know, it was weird. She reckoned Tim could have been pushed by a woman in a burka.'

'Why would she say that? How would she know? Where was she at the time?'

'There, at the house. Birchington, said she'd been shopping in Faversham that morning.'

He thought about it. Odd, very odd. Maybe he would get Phil or Ken Yallop to do some research. 'When did this accident happen?'

'Oh, ages ago. Let me think. Must be seven or eight years ago. Might be more.'

It tallied. He heard the front door being opened. 'Ah, sounds like your mother's back. Shall I put her on?'

'Yes, but don't let on what we've been talking about.'

He could hear the panic in her voice. 'Course not.' He shouted out to Delia, 'Your daughter's on the phone.'

Delia came through to the kitchen carrying two or three plastic bags. 'What does she want?' she mouthed, as she set them down on the table.

He shrugged. 'Just a chat,' he whispered and handed her the phone.

'Hello darling, how are you?' Then, 'Yes, we're both fine. Think we need another holiday though,' she said, and laughed. 'To get over this one. It's been a bit non-stop here, as well, since we got back.'

Bob motioned to her: did she want him to unpack the shopping. She shook her head, mouthed that she would do it. 'Listen, sweetheart, can I call you back? We're both starving and I've got to prepare a quick lunch, before Bob eats me instead of food.' She nodded her head at the phone. 'Yes, I'll ring you in about half an hour. That all right?'

She listened and nodded. 'Ok, speak in a while. Love you lots. Bye.'

To Bob she said, 'Sorry about that. I've bought some fresh pizza bases from the baker's. They've just started making them. Got veg from the greengrocer and salami in the butcher's.'

He let her prattle on, watched as she unpacked the bags and began chopping and slicing to top the pizzas. A sudden thought flicked across his mind. *Keep your distance Robert, while she's wielding that bloody great knife.* He dismissed it, smiled and nodded in what he hoped were the right places. Asked her if she'd like a glass of wine while she was preparing their lunch.

'Good thinking, Batman. A glass of white would go down well.'

'Coming up ma'am.' He felt he was getting good at this sweet talking, keeping her easy. He bloody hoped so. Seen enough murderers in his time to know how devious they could be. He knew it might sound sexist (if he said it out loud), but he felt easier with male killers than he did with their female counterparts. He supposed it was built into his psyche, his male psyche. Whoever thought up the idea that men and women were equal must have been out of their tiny minds. Oh, he wasn't against equal opportunity. God forbid, there were plenty of good female police, plenty of brilliant women doctors, and so on. But he still maintained, and he would voice this in any discussion, female killers could be very dodgy people. He maintained this train of thought while Delia chatted and put the pizzas in the oven, and kept himself at a distance from her chef's knife.

'Right,' she said. 'Ten minutes and we can eat. Did you mention a glass of something?'

'Certainly did, ma'am. Sorry, I was busy watching you doing your stuff. Good to watch a master or mistress at their skills. One wine coming up.' He walked over to the fridge, fished out the bottle from its door shelf, grabbed two glasses from the draining board and began to pour. He handed her one and she smiled.

'What did Tilda have to say to you? Was she on the phone long before I got back?'

'No. Only a few minutes. She asked me did I, did we, enjoy the holiday. I told her about going on to Italy from Portugal. She thought that was good, very adventurous of us.'

'Did you tell her about the cottage we want to buy?'

'No, I didn't get round to that. Like I said, she only rang a few minutes before you came in.'

She took a sip of wine. 'Mmn, lovely.' She peered into the oven. 'They'll be ready in two minutes. D'you want to get the cutlery?'

'Sure.'

He wondered if Phil would ring soon. Hoped so, but also hoped now it would be after lunch. He was starving. Thought over all that had happened this morning... and yesterday. A house in Italy? He didn't think so. *One step at a time, Robert. Eat first...*

He also called to mind something else the old girl had said to him when he went to the newsagents yesterday. She talked about 'dear Mr Fontaine' but in addition she made some remark about windows being wide open in all seasons. He struggled to remember what her exact words were. Delia put down a plate in front of him. 'There you go, one almost home-made pizza.'

'Lovely, thanks sweetie. Smells good. Lots of toppings too.'

'Onions, peppers, mushrooms, chillies, and salami.'

His stomach churned with hunger and his mind did a bit of churning too. Mushrooms? What had Tilda said about mushrooms? He dismissed it, told himself to stop being paranoid, just eat. Then it entered his mind what Mrs Casey had said about windows. 'She's a rum one, your missus. Used to open the bedroom window in the midst of winter.' Strange thing to say, he thought. Should he mention it to Delia?   Looking across at her now, a halo of innocence, eating the same pizza he was eating, the same toppings, including mushrooms, best if he kept quiet about it. But it nagged at him and one thought led to another and another, as theories do.   The discovery he had made last night about her husband, Gerald, father of her twins; how he died from pneumonia at Christmastime, wintertime. Did she have their bedroom window open that winter?

'Penny for them.'

'What?   Oh, I was just thinking about Italy, Gravedona.'

She smiled, relaxed. 'It was lovely there wasn't it? Can't wait to go again.' She continued eating and lost herself in the memory.

Keep her sweet, you're fighting for survival remember... A vibration in his shirt pocket alerted him. Mobile. Phil.

'Hello?' He heard Phil's voice down his phone. Phil told him the news was not good. Bob mouthed across to Delia that he would take the call in the front room. Mercifully the house phone rang at the same time.   Probably Tilda ringing back.   A blessing; meant Delia would be occupied with that and not listen to his one-sided conversation with Phil.   He handed the house phone to her and walked through to the lounge.

'So what's new?'

'Fingerprints.   Ones from upstairs in the old

girl's house match your wife's. It's serious, Bob. We'll have to bring her in.'

'Really... when?'

'Soon as.'

'D'you want me to be... chauffeur?' he tried to disguise the reality in case she was listening to his side of the conversation. She was. She had come in from the kitchen and leaned against the doorway, her phone dangling, lifeless, and switched off. 'Chauffeur? What or who?'

He mouthed to her 'give me five minutes' and said to his buddy. 'No mate, not me. Maybe someone else?'

'Is she there?'

'Yes.'

'Nearby?'

'Absolutely.'

'Ok, Bob. Understood. We'll send a car out. Be ready.'

He switched off the phone. 'That was Phil, trying to arrange a boys' night out.' His laugh sounded hollow even to him, hoped it didn't to her. 'Wants to draw straws for driver.' He pointed to the phone in her hand. 'Tilda?'

'Yes... I told her I'd ring back.'

He had reservations about her expression. It was tense, suspicious. She reminded him of a cornered wild cat or stray dog, ready to attack, not willing to be caught. What could he say or do to relax her? Suggest more unpacking after they had eaten? Find places to put things? Not that they'd be homed for long. His eyes took in the room, the small inner hallway beyond and he smelled the pizzas cooking coming through from the kitchen. His mind wandered backward and forward. Nothing stays the same. Last night he had waited for her return from the station, in this room, looking out of that window. Watched when she drew up and knew life would possibly, probably, never be like it was only those few days ago when they were still in Italy, walking by the lake and admiring the golden, sun-drenched mountains across from the shimmering waters of Lago di Como.

'If only' came to mind. For a short while out there he had known a happiness not felt before in months, weeks, days. Now it all had to come to an end. He knew without doubt that this woman he had grown to love was a murderer, a woman – strangely – who had lovingly raised two children. And just as easily killed more than that many... children and adults. He looked at her and knew she was regarding him, a puzzled, troubled look on her face.

'What is it Bob? Why are you staring at me?'

He shook his head, blinked. 'Was I? Sorry,' he tried to make his voice sound natural, a trace of humour in it. 'I was day dreaming again. Shall we go and eat?'

'Why? Why do you want me in the back room?'

There was panic in her voice, cunning in her question. She gripped the hard plastic phone like a weapon, her back to the window. She did not see the blue and yellow-striped squad car pull up outside, nor set eyes on four burly, uniformed police climb out, spring out, with purpose. He held her gaze, desperately wanting to prevent her turning round too soon.

The front door was unlocked. He had told Phil it would be, thankful to his old buddy for suggesting he do so. Delia turned around when she heard the door burst open, stared with bulging eyes when she saw four uniforms rush in, surround her, grab her arms. She let out a primeval scream that echoed around the room, through the house, assailing his ears with its rage and its fear. The look on her face that she directed towards him was one of pure evil, distorted, ugly, and full of hatred. This the face that had so recently shown him love, passion, humour. Not anymore. He could not imagine that venomous expression ever changing back to one of tenderness.

In seconds she was handcuffed, but still fought and kicked with animal ferocity, her teeth bared in snarling rage.

'Watch she doesn't... ' but Bob was too late with the warning. She drew blood from one of the policeman's cheeks as she sank her teeth into his flesh. His reaction was expected but still shocked her husband as the policeman gave her a vicious backhander and called her a fucking bitch. He covered his wound with the other hand, blood trickling through his fingers as he pushed her towards his companions.

'Here, come into the kitchen, I'll get something to cleanse it,' Bob told him.

The policeman followed him while the other three bundled her outside to the squad car, telling her she was arrested and anything she said... But her screeching drowned their words.

'Sorry about that, Bob, not the sort of reaction normally permitted, but that bloody hurt. Christ mate, she's like an animal. Ever do that to you?' He was still holding his face, trying to stop too much blood escaping, trying to hold the torn flesh together.

'No, no she hasn't. It's like... she's turned pure evil. Christ...' he was speechless. He led the officer into the kitchen, and pulled down a first aid box from on top of one of the cupboards.

'Sit down, I'll get some water and wash that.' He made a face. 'Think you'll need stitches in that. Tetanus jab as well unless you're up to date.'

He cleaned it as best as he could and gently place strips of plaster across the wound to keep the pieces of skin together. He could see the marks where she had sunk her teeth into the man's face. The sight of them made him shudder and killed any love he might once have had for her.

'Thanks sir, gotta go, better get Lady Hannibal to the nick. Reckon you've had a lucky escape.' As an afterthought he said, 'D'you want to come along?'

'No thanks, Gerry,' he suddenly remembered the man's name. 'I'll get in touch later. Better do a bit of ringing around first. Oh, can you tell Phil I'll be in touch soonest? Tell him I'll arrange for a solicitor for her, but not too quickly. Get yourself to A&E as soon as,' he added and let the man out. She was still screaming in the car but he could not look at her. He went in and quickly shut the door, ran through to the downstairs lavatory and vomited up the remains of his breakfast toast: thankful it wasn't the Pizza with mushrooms... He doubted he would ever eat mushrooms again, probably not pizzas either. He thought about Tilda's ex-boyfriend, the late ex-boyfriend who ate poisonous mushrooms and died of renal failure. He felt better when it was all up, but could have done without the foul taste the vomit left behind.

The phone rang, the landline. He went out into the hall but the receiver was not on its cradle. Of course, she had held it. Where was it? He found it, too late to answer the call, on the floor by the settee through in the lounge. When he looked at the small screen he recognised Tilda's number. Now what? What could he say to his new stepdaughter? How to tell her that her mother had turned into a screaming, attacking animal?

The phone rang again, same number. He pressed the green icon. 'Hi Tilda.'

26
Two months later

Strange to say Bob was enjoying the meal, appreciating comfortable surroundings, the fine cuisine and more, this mixed company. Tilda and Mike sat opposite Danny and Ray. Phil and Stella the other side of Irene Forbes and Ken Yallop. Bob took the top place and faced them all. He was relieved the trial was over and the verdict given. Imagined they all were. It had been a tremendous strain on all of them, especially Delia's son and daughter, and it showed in their stretched tight faces, the first time he recognised them as twins. He hoped this evening together would bring closure to the weeks of pain they had suffered, not only the twins and their partners, but his police buddies and Stella. They had all, in their way, shared the ordeal.

He lifted his glass, 'To all of you.' There was nothing else he could say that would be appropriate, fitting.

'To us all,' they said together.

The arrival of the first course signalled a change of conversation as they informed the waiter which dish they had ordered. When they were all served Bob said, 'buon appetito' and immediately wished he had said 'cheers' instead. No-one said 'grazie stesso per te' (same to you). He covered his embarrassment by remarking on the dish. 'Soup's good.'

They sipped and chewed their way through their first courses, washed them down with glasses of wine and each one of them struggled, he could tell, with thinking up neutral conversation.

'When are you two off?' he asked Tilda and Mike.

'Next week: we fly out Tuesday.'

'Where you off to?' asked Stella. 'Somewhere exotic?'

'We're going to Oz, Mike's got cousins out there. Thought we'd pay them a visit.' Tilda told her.

'Great, have you been there before?'

'I haven't, Mike went over there a few years ago, before we met. Bob's having the dogs for us, bless him.'

He grinned at his stepdaughter. It was good to feel happy enough to do so. 'They'll keep me fit, all that running on the beach.'

Everyone relaxed, conversation became normal, about holidays and dogs and who was going where and when. Danny and Ray were going up to Shropshire to stay with Ray's parents and pick up their baby son, Alfie, who had been staying with them. Phil and Stella were returning to Alvor. Irene and Ken had not yet planned their holidays. Ken was into golf and said he fancied a couple of weeks in Tenerife, heard they had good golf courses there.

Irene said nothing. She gave Bob a look of kindness. 'Any plans, Bob?'

He sighed, hadn't meant to. He didn't want pity, now he had found peace. He was back in his own apartment and, with the twins consent, the Birchington house was on the market. So was old Mrs Casey's, but hers was proving difficult to sell it being in such a disgusting state inside and being the scene of a murder. He thought he had a better chance selling his one: his and the twins. They had agreed to split the monies three ways. Incarcerated or not, Delia was still alive and Bob agreed to ensure she had any extras she was allowed inside.

'Not really,' he replied. 'Not yet. Besides, I'll be dog-sitting for six weeks. That'll give me a fair while to plan where I want to go next.'

More food arrived and more wine was ordered. An evening to enjoy and get slightly pissed, he thought. There would be time to go over Delia's trial and the verdict when he was on his own, when he was with the dotty Dalmatians, and taking the odd coffee with Ossie, the ex-lag and his part-time gardener.

Delia would never come out. The judge had decreed she should serve an indefinite time in a psychiatric establishment, not prison. In prison she could constitute a danger to others and would be more carefully monitored in a hospital. She had sat quietly throughout the trial, until the verdict was given and her sentence decided. Then she had sprung up, despite being handcuffed to a tough-looking prison warder, and given that blood-curdling scream again. They could only stem the flow of obscenities that spewed from her mouth, by removing her to the cells below and injecting a powerful drug into her veins. The venom had been directed at him and to her children, but lastly to Stella's name. She hated Stella more than anyone, blamed her for her arrest for some bizarre reason.

Time, he hoped, would heal their wounds, but not hers. She, he could never, would never, forgive. Not just for all the murders but for Gerry Sinclair's wound, when she bit him, that turned to septicaemia. Gerry died before the trial began, leaving a young wife and two babies. He had not deserved that, had not deserved to be the ultimate sacrifice. Bob would make sure, with his now sizable bank balance that Gerry's two kids would want for nothing.

'Anyone for dessert?'

He looked up.

'You still with us, Bob?' Phil laughed.

'Sure am. Who said dessert?'

'I did,' said Ray.

He should have guessed it was Danny's partner by the lisp. The waiters came over to clear their plates and handed menus round. He was back in the room again, enjoying the company and the normality. Bring it on!

27
The Now of Delia

Inmate number 36U. She liked the numbers, all multiples and divisible of three. Her special number, her lucky number. Maybe it meant she would soon be released: only serve a token sentence. She hadn't, after all, held any bad feeling towards her victims. Not really. Anyway who, out of all of them, was she actually responsible for killing? Carl was stabbed by someone else, Gerald died from pneumonia, Damien from poisonous mushrooms that he had picked and cooked himself. Danny's friend Tim had been pushed off the railway platform, but not by her. She was several passengers away from him. And H? H had a brain tumour and went walkabout at night time. Walked himself over the cliff edge. As for old Mrs Casey, silly old biddy. Fancy wanting a light bulb replaced. Upstairs too. She should have slept downstairs like most old dears do. Should've lived in a bungalow instead of keeping on that great big house.

She wondered what the U stood for, 36U. Unsurpassed? Unique? Ultimate? Unusual. Yes, that could be it, she was unusual. Maybe it meant none of these. She shrugged her shoulders, little did she care. It actually meant 'unpredictable' as far as the staff were concerned. They liked to label the inmates: found it easier to cope with the mood changes.

Seconds later, Delia wriggled an itch out of the material her dress was made of. It was grey in colour, loose fitting, and extremely unfashionable. Perhaps that was what the U stood for.

She smiled at her reflection in the window. It was dark outside and with the coming of the darkness came her mirrored likeness. There was no mirror in the room, the cell, and the three metres by two metre enclosure that was hers. By day she could see out, beyond the bars, to the grounds below, lawned and pleasantly cultivated with shrubs and seasonal flowers.

By night, she could gaze at herself, talk to her reflection, and discuss the day just past, the people she had encountered. She didn't like the one they called Head Nurse, stern bitch, hard as nails. Delia could not imagine her ever smiling, had probably never done so all her life. Born po faced...

She didn't like the one who brought her meal tray. Ugh! If you could call the disgusting contents meals. Cold, elastic toast, thinly spread with some kind of margarine and cheap, basics jam. That was breakfast, served with weak tea or flavourless coffee.

'One slice or two?' she had been asked, that first morning of her incarceration.

'Pardon?'

'One slice or two? Toast, idiot. D'you want one or two?'

'What else is there?'

'Truffles and bleeding red wine,' came the cackling answer. 'What d'you expect, stupid cow.'

She filed that insult away for a future retaliation. Stupid cow indeed. No-one had ever called her that. Had they? Maybe Carl, her first husband, coarse, common Carl. He was worthy of such a remark. But he was already dead, this bitch wasn't... maybe later... Could easily stab her with the knife and fork they brought round with lunch (they called it dinner in here), or tea. This last meal of the day being something boring like beans on toast or dried-up scrambled egg on toast. The lack of imagination on the part of the chef was astounding. Toast for breakfast, toast for dinner, no... tea. Hadn't he or she heard of fresh vegetables and fresh meat? Or pepper and salt for that matter. Everything here was bland, tasteless, and unpalatable.

She missed the wine; a glass of Montepulciano (a large glass) would have enhanced the taste of the grey, disgusting mess they served as stew. She had almost gagged the first time she tasted it. Lumpy, only part-cooked potatoes, carrots past their sell-by date, slimy onions, and the toughest, gristly meat she had ever had the misfortune to chew upon.

After her first week of incarceration, she was made to join her fellow patients – or inmates as they called them here – in the dining canteen. It was a large, plain oblong room with two rows of tables, each seating ten people. Ten tables, one hundred diners, consisting of the oddest looking individuals Delia had ever had the misfortune to set eyes upon. They were divided between the two rows, men on one side and women on the other. She imagined a sign over the entrance 'Abandon hope, all ye who enter here'. Was that hopelessness she viewed in most of their faces? Hopelessness or cunning? Their eyes were lowered or averted. Some had their eyes staring at some unidentified spot on an imaginary horizon. Blank, unseeing eyes.

The smell of food was almost unbearable as was the sight of it... and the noise of those eating it, slurping it, belching in between slapping lumps of the uneatable over toothless gums. Running noses added to her revulsion and nausea crept up into her throat and into her mouth. She stared at the unpalatable contents of her plate, and played her fork in and out of the lumps making rivulets of the cooling mess.

'Don't yer wannit?'

She turned to the woman sitting next to her, noted the badly cut hair as if it had been chopped with garden shears. She managed not to flinch at the sight of old razor scars sliced across the woman's arms, now pale with age, and the face, picked with sores. Slate-blue eyes stared hungrily at her plate.

'Well? D'you wannit or not?'

'Um, no, not really.'

'Gissit then. Swap plates.'

She allowed the creature to take her plate and replace it with her own, licked-clean one. Delia retched and barely managed to swallow back her ill-digested breakfast toast as she watched her fellow diner suck up the food greedily from the plate, then tilt it to her lips to slurp the watery gravy, some of which dribbled down her chin. This she wiped away on the skirt of her dress.

Delia could see it was not the first evidence of food or something that shone like a snail trail on the skirt hem. It reminded her of someone, that silvery track. Oh yes, Mrs Casey, the stupid woman who had caused her to be here among these sub-human creatures that ate so noisily, so messily. Momentarily, she forgot her present disgust and directed a memory of hate towards her late neighbour. *May you rot in hell, you evil, foul bitch.*

A sudden clattering of cutlery advised her the meal was over. She went to stand up.

'Siddown, silly cow. Yer got pudding to come yet. Pass yer plate up.'

Delia then saw hands to her left grabbing plates and cutlery and passing them to the end of the table, where they were collected by a woman with a trolley. There were two square bowls on each of the trolley shelves. Cutlery was clanged noisily into one bowl and plates stacked carefully in the other. There was no slop bowl, there were no slops, only cleaned plates. As the trolley was rattled away to the end of the room, where it disappeared through swing doors, another appeared at the table in the form of a tall metal box on wheels. The side opened and the smell of cooked suet and custard escaped from it.

A wodge of the pudding was spooned into each dish and covered with thin, runny custard. These were passed along each side of the table until everyone was served. Even before the last person was given their dish, the first ones had shovelled the pudding into their mouths, licked their lips and spoons then belched noisily. Ten tables were thus served, and a hundred mouths were fed. Except for one. Hers.

The suet pudding was just that. No fruit, no jam or syrup, just a lump of squeezed-together suet and flour with not a hint of sweetness. And the custard? A yellow, watery liquid was the only way Delia could describe it, if anyone had bothered to ask. One mouthful was sufficient to start her gagging again. Once more, her self-harming neighbour with the dreadful haircut exchanged dishes with her and greedily gorged the contents of a second dessert dish.

Delia was relieved when the order came to vacate the room. She filed out with the others, uncertain of where she should go on that first day of mixing with this doubtful humanity.

'P's to the library, M's to the workroom, U's to the garden or kitchen to help with the washing up.'

Delia looked blank, caught the eye of the woman barking the orders.

'You,' she pointed at Delia. 'U's to the garden. 36U, that's you Shackleton.'

She shook her head, bewildered. Was the woman addressing her as you or U? If U, what did it mean? What was the U for? She did not think the woman would enlighten her, instead she followed several others who were headed for the gardens. They looked a frightening bunch and she was relieved to see a formidable-looking male nurse apparently take charge. She privately hoped none of these creatures would be given shears or secateurs to use... Or garden forks for that matter. She imagined they were all capable of using such instruments as weapons of destruction. How safe was she, the only sane one among a cluster of mad ones?

28

On the third day of her visit to the canteen, Delia stabbed one of her fellow diners: her neighbour with the self-harming scars. With a fork... on the back of her hand, between the middle and forefinger. She missed the digit bones and the knuckle bones by fractions, pinning the thin fleshy piece to the table.

The stabbed woman screamed as blood spurted out around the prong that imprisoned her to the table. Her fellow diners shouted anything from 'Fucking hell' to 'Oh my fucking God'. Others screamed at Delia, and stood up, moving threateningly towards her. The nurses moved quicker; more than usual were on dinner duty it seemed. If not there to begin with, the number quickly grew as if they came out of the woodwork. Two of them grabbed her arms and pinned them round her back, tying her wrists with plastic ties. Another two rushed to the injured woman and released her hand by pulling out the fork. One of them carried some sterile dressing and quickly wrapped it around the wound, saying 'Hush Tina, it's ok, ok.'

The other two dragged Delia none-too-gently from the room, away from the baying crowd and along the corridor where they threw her into a padded cell, first cutting through her plastic handcuffs.

'Cool off in there, bitch,' said one.

'Go fuck yourself, you evil cow,' said the other.

She fell onto a padded mat away from the door that clunked shut behind her. Her breath came in short sharp gasps and she tried to calm herself by breathing in through her mouth and out through her nostrils. She could feel her heart beat and her temples throb. Tears sprung to her eyes and fell unchecked onto her cheeks.

'Not my fault,' she sobbed to the silent walls. 'She spat phlegm into my stew because I wouldn't give it to her. She had all mine yesterday and the day before. I was starving today, starving...'

Delia glanced around the bare walls, noted there were no windows and wondered where the light was coming from. She looked up at the ceiling and saw a bare bulb encased in some kind of metal cage. It was well out of her reach even if she stood on tiptoe. There was no furniture, only the thick, padded mat, the sort found in gymnasiums. The walls were padded too, in a patchwork of tough plastic shapes, stitched together, she guessed, with unbreakable thread. Or maybe glued together. Didn't matter, they had still put her in a padded cell. She did not deserve that. *She* should be in here, not her; the one who had gobbed that foul phlegm onto her plate.

A lidded bucket stood in one corner: next to it there was a chest-high basin with a single tap. 'Am I supposed to drink from that?' She spoke to the walls again. 'How? By putting my tongue under the faucet? Why no cup? Surely I'm allowed a cup?'

Her stomach gurgled. She'd had nothing to eat since breakfast, thanks to that evil cow spitting on her food. She'd not even managed one mouthful before – what's her name? – Tina, that's it, before Tina tried to drag her plate away from her. When Delia held onto it, Tina had hawked up a globule of phlegm which landed in the middle of her stew.

'There you go bitch,' she had cackled. 'Now eat it.'

Delia remembered the black rage that had swept over her: the near blindness as she turned away from her plate and looked into the face of that greedy cow leering at her. Something had snapped inside her, the elasticity of reason. She took the fork, raised it above her head and plunged it into Tina's hand where it rested on the table. She'd felt the vibration as the prongs bit into the table.

Now she was here, hungry, frightened and very alone. She missed the twins, Danny and Tilda, and worried who would fetch them from school. She worried about Gerald and his pneumonia. And H. Who would lead him away from the dangerous cliff's edge? Make him mouth-watering meals soaked in delicious red Burgundy? The cottage in Gravedona: did she and Robert purchase it before they left Italy?

So many anxieties, so much drama, and cruelty shown to her. Finally, Delia slept... in the padded room, on the gymnasium mat. No darkness, not with the encased light bulb overhead. She slept in timeless sleep, knowing neither night nor day in that man-made cocoon. Sometime during her sleep, she covered her face with the skirt of her dress, maybe to shut out the light or give warmth to her face.

While she slept, two nurses looked at her through a peephole, quietly unlocked the door, and crept cautiously towards her inert body. They injected something into one bare leg. Delia hardly flinched, did not waken, and slept a drug-induced sleep for another twenty-four hours.

She awoke when the warm dampness spread between her legs. Sat up quickly, horrified. She had wet herself. Unbelievable. She had never done that in all her adult life. The shame matched the discomfort and she was helpless. She crept towards the door, banged on it and cried out. 'Please, someone, anyone. I've wet myself, I need clean clothes. Please let me out.' She sobbed while she waited. Her nose ran and she salivated like a teething baby.

Eventually a voice boomed at her from somewhere: she could not work out from where.

'Get away from the door, Shackleton. Go and stand by the bucket.'

She obeyed the voice stood unsteadily and held onto the small basin. Her mouth was dry as a desert and had a bitter taste. She could smell the urine and was mortified. The door opened and two male nurses entered. One of them carried what looked like a gun.

'This is a stun gun, a taser,' he said. 'Any trouble and I pull the trigger. Understand?'

She nodded. Her voice when she spoke was scarcely above a whisper. 'I've wet myself, I'm sorry. Please... can I have some clean clothes?'

They did not sneer at her. In fact, she swore they both had a look of almost sympathy.

'Stay there,' said the one with the gun. 'Nurse Johnson here will fetch you some.'

The one he called Nurse Johnson slipped back out of the door, shutting it behind him. A few minutes later, he was back with a change of clothes. He threw them to her. 'Now, strip off and change yourself.'

'What? While you're here?'

'We're nurses,' he sneered. 'Not bloody rapists. Now take your wet things off and put on the clean clothes.'

She began to peel off the wet things, starting with her knickers. She put the clean pair on before she stripped off the damp and slightly smelly dress.

Neither man looked straight at her, instead they gazed at the ceiling but kept her fully in their view. *I'm not going to hurt you two. Didn't really mean to hurt her. Not really. It just kind of happened.*

When she was fully changed, she stood up. 'What shall I do with these?'

'Bundle them up and throw them over to us.'

She obeyed, then saw they were preparing to vacate the room.

'Please,' she said. 'I'm very hungry. Can I have something to eat? I've not eaten since breakfast. What time is it anyway?'

'You've lost a day, Shackleton. It's nearly lunchtime... we'll bring you something soon.'

'Can't I come out of here?'

'Fraid not. You're on punishment.'

'Well... how long do I have to stay here?' A note of hysteria crept into her voice. 'It's lonely in here... and... scary.'

The one with the gun grinned. 'We can always give you a jab to send you back to sleep. It'll make the time pass.'

She shook her head. 'Is that what happened? My mouth tastes foul, bitter. I'll behave,' she added. 'I won't attack anyone. Promise.'

'That's what they all say. You're in here for at least another day, then maybe we'll transfer you back to your room. If you behave yourself, that is.'

'Oh I will, I will.'

'You can start by sitting down on the mat. We'll bring you something to eat shortly.' With that they both withdrew and she heard a key turn in the lock.

Once more she was alone, no furniture, no view, but at least she was dry. She stood up, turned on the tap inside the small basin and rinsed her face. She looked round. No towel, so she wiped her face on her dress sleeve. What about if she wanted to use the bucket? Where was the toilet roll? She lifted the lid from the temporary toilet. It was clean inside, unused *and* there was a few sheets of toilet paper in there. That was a relief. No more wetting herself either. She vowed to be on her best behaviour so they wouldn't drug her again. She wished she had a toothbrush and some nice mint-flavoured toothpaste. Licking her tongue round her mouth, she was acutely aware the bitterness remained, accompanied now by plaque and a general feeling of stale, unclean teeth. She leaned over the basin again, turned on the tap and tried cleaning her teeth with her forefinger. She then rinsed her mouth, swirling the cold water round and round before spitting it out.

'I wish I had a book to read,' she spoke to the padded walls again. 'Like on Desert Island Discs. They're allowed to choose any book they wish for, as well as getting the Bible and the complete works of Shakespeare. I'd settle for a Mills and Boon at the moment.'

She tried doing an anagram word game in her

head. Had to be a word of at least nine letters, then see how many words she could make from those nine.   She allowed herself three letter words upwards. Not two letters, wouldn't be fair. She chose the word envelopes; began with words beginning with 'e'. Eel, elves, elope, the 'n' nee, nose, novel. She sighed, bored, did not want to finish the game, but was so lost in it she did not hear the door open until the one called Nurse Johnson entered the cell and placed a tray on the floor. His sidekick stood in the doorway, stun gun at the ready. *Stupid man. I'm not going to attack you.*

'Dinner, Shackleton,' he said, and not unkindly she noticed. She was grateful. 'Enjoy,' he added.

She had the good grace to thank him and to add his title, Nurse Johnson. That'll prove I'm not like the others, she thought.

For once, the food smelled good. She was surprised and delighted to see a plate of fish, chips and peas under the metal cover. She guessed this had come from the staff canteen, an unforeseen luxury. Not, she supposed, justified by her previous behaviour, but maybe they were forgiving her. Unexpected in this grim place, but appreciated, especially with this flavoursome meal in front of her.

Her stomach hurt with its emptiness, but Delia knew better than to wolf down the food; difficult anyway without cutlery. She did her best to pick daintily at the chips, splitting a few open to use as spoons to scoop up the peas. The battered fish was easy to break apart into mouth-sized portions and she savoured every mouthful. A wedge of lemon, she thought, would have been a good accompaniment, and perhaps some tartare sauce. But, hey, beggars can't be choosers, so she relished and enjoyed what she had been given. It was when she pushed the plate to one side that she noticed a plastic knife and fork. She grinned, replete, once more in a good humour. *Please let me out soon, I shall be so good you won't even know I'm here. Or there, wherever 'there' is.*

On cue the door was opened again. Nurse Johnson almost managed to smile at her. Almost. 'Finished?'

She nodded. 'Yes, thank you. It was delicious.'

'Would you like a pudding?'

She nodded again. 'Yes please. What is it?' She suddenly remembered the suet stodge.

'Treacle sponge and custard.'

She took a chance, hoping that it too was from the staff canteen.

'Mug of tea with it?'

'That would be lovely, thank you very much.' It was almost like hotel room service. Well nearly.

He took the tray and left her seated on the mat, returning in a few short minutes with a dish of sweet-smelling dessert and a mug of steaming tea. These he placed near the door. 'I'll be back later,' he said, and left her without another word. She was aware that during both his visits, the first with the dinner plate and then with the dessert and tea, he had not been accompanied by the gun-toting other nurse.

She was released from the padded cell after a further three days, then taken to the shower block where she spent a blissful five minutes under a steaming hot shower. The women nurses accompanying her handed her a fresh set of clothes after she dried herself. And a brush for her hair.

'Where do I go now?' she asked.

'Back to your room. You'll have all your meals there from now on.' The nurse who answered her looked as if she had never smiled in her life. Her mouth was set in a grim straight line and her eyes had no crows' feet around them, indicating the lack of humour, happiness, and amusement in her life.

Delia ruminated, chewed on her lips. 'Will I be allowed into the garden?'

The woman nodded. 'You'll have supervised exercise periods, either walking in the grounds or in the gym if it's bad weather.'

'You won't be allowed to mix with the other patients, not after what you did.' It was the other nurse who spoke. Again with a folded expression forbidding any humour.

Delia did not bother to answer. Privately, she

was relieved to be kept away from the others. At least in her room she could read, borrow books from the library. Maybe they would let her have a radio, even a small television, some writing paper. It wouldn't be anything like the solitary confinement of that dreadful padded room.

29

Midsummer, her favourite time of year, when the roses were especially sweet smelling and needed her constant attention. The bees loved every minute of the warm weather, drunk as they were with lavender pollen from nearby bushes. Pungent rosemary, thyme, oregano and mint floated their perfume from the herb garden and numerous other flowers provided a riot of colour in their beds around the lawns.

Delia picked her way carefully along the brick inlaid path. She was not so steady nowadays and frequently relied on a walking stick. Arthritis, the doctor had diagnosed, but she secretly knew better. It was the foreign bugs that were constantly invading Britain's shores, bringing with them a crippling virus that attacked your bones. There was no cure yet, but one of the big drug firms would soon, she thought. Someone from Pfizer or the Wellcome Foundation sitting patiently at their laboratory bench, surrounded by test tubes and things, they would find a cure, have their eureka moment. Then the invader from across the ocean would be destroyed forever.

Nurse Johnson led her to a seat close to the rose bushes.

'This ok for you, Delia?' (They no longer used a surname to address her as it confused and upset her).

She nodded and rewarded him with a grateful smile. 'Perfect, young man,' she said, though he was no longer young she thought. His hair was turning quite grey, but then, she supposed, we are all getting older. 'I'll rest for ten minutes before I help Seymour with the dead heading.'

Nurse Johnson gave her one of his rare smiles. 'I'll come back for you when it's time for tea.'

They trusted her now, especially here in the garden. She and old Ted Seymour had formed a tenuous friendship during her early weeks of being allowed to walk in the grounds and between the flower beds. He was suspicious at first. He didn't take kindly to strangers, but he gradually let her into his private world when he discovered she knew the names of all the flowers. He liked the way she touched them with gentle, appreciative hands.

The garden, for so long, had been his domain. Here he nurtured the seedlings, and under his care they prospered and grew into beautiful flowers. The ones he had to prick out were respectfully buried on the compost heap, where years before he had buried those children. No, that wasn't right, the little kids were hidden under dead leaves in the forest, but he liked to think of them as being under his watchful eye.

The woman, Delia, had become his assistant in

all things horticultural. (He didn't tell her about the children).   In spring she helped him with the planting, with tidying the floral borders. He made sure she folded and tied the dead daffodils, leaving them in their plots for another month untouched. Only then would he begin to replace them with primulas, violets and the sweet-faced pansies, so like the faces of those little children... only he didn't tell her that. She might not approve of his loving them and leaving them asleep in their secret places in the forest.

Spring bounced into summer, blossom flowered the trees in April and blossom blew away in the frisky breezes of May. Ted picked the first rose of summer for her: the 'yellow rose of Texas' he called it.

'Make your room smell nice,' he said.   Then blushed when she thanked him so prettily. For the remainder of summer she weeded for him, in between the beds of riotous colours.   And dead headed the roses. She had this pleasant way of gently prising off the dying rose petals from their stems, then scattering them like confetti onto the smaller plants and the earth that nurtured them.

Ted had a kettle and two mugs in his shed, a concession to his being the resident gardener. It was old and battered, almost as old as the number of years he'd been incarcerated here in the hospital, but it still boiled the water for tea. The kitchen staff kept him supplied with tea bags, milk and sugar, even the occasional packet of digestives, in exchange for the excellent herbs he grew for them.

After spring had turned to summer that first year, Seymour had invited Delia to join him for a cuppa in his private domain, the garden shed. At first she was in awe of the place. How neat he kept it with tools dangling on their hooks around the wooden walls, and cleaned flower pots stacked in sizes under the work bench. He had an old, stuffed armchair in there that had seen better days but it suited him fine. The first day she took tea with him he gracefully offered her the chair.

'Thank you Seymour, but I'm quite happy sitting outside in the sunshine.'

'Aw right, suits me,' and he had followed her to one of the garden seats, his pocket stuffed with a packet of digestives and a crumpled piece of tissue for his dripping nose. 'It's Ted,' he said when they were seated.

'Pardon?'

'Ted, my name's Ted. You can call me that if you like.'

'Ok,' she smiled. 'Ted... '

The friendship did not last. Her friendships never did. After two or three years, she was not sure how many, could have been more, and as she got to know him, little things began to irritate her. His constant sniffing and the need to wipe away drips from his nostrils slightly disgusted her: the way he would mumble something indistinct and turn away as he said it, that was irritating too. She tired of always having to ask him to repeat himself, of having to follow him around like some obedient sheep dog. That was not Delia's way. She liked to be in charge. Huh! Impossible in this God-forsaken place, run as it was by bullying nursing staff. Why she had to extend this obedience to a man like Ted Seymour was beyond her.

'Why do you always leave the grass cuttings after you've mown the lawn?' she asked him one day.

'Why not?' was his taciturn reply.

'It looks such a mess, cloggy.' She picked up a handful of damp cuttings to prove her point. 'I mean, this is horrible. Must stifle the new grass coming through.'

He looked at her under his white furry eyebrows. 'Always done it like that,' he said. 'Kind of fertilises the lawn. Leastwise that's what I think. Anyways, I'm in charge here. I'm the gardener so's I'll do what I thinks.'

She gave him a 'hmph' as she limped away from him. She was doing that a lot lately, limping. Her hips hurt her more and more. The foreign bugs, bringing their crippling virus had not been destroyed or controlled, that was obvious. For the first time in weeks, months, maybe years, she refused the tea he offered.

'No thanks. I'm going back indoors. My hip hurts,' she said by way of explanation.

'Arthritis,' he said. 'Bugger of a complaint once it starts.'

'I haven't got arthritis. It's a bug, a virus. Brought in by one of those damned ferries over the Channel.'

'Suit yourself.' And he shambled off towards his shed. Delia broke off the friendship after that, no longer helped him though she still continued her dead-heading. Only when she was accompanied by Nurse Johnson and her two walking sticks. He had suggested to her that she might have a hip replacement but she shuddered at that, became severely distressed.

'No, no, no,' she almost sobbed. 'I don't want that.'

'It's all right,' he soothed. 'You don't have to. No-one's going to make you.'

And she had calmed down.

She began to have her afternoon mug of tea back in her room. Sometimes, if he felt generous, with a digestive donated by Nurse Johnson. Ted Seymour became a thing of the past. Now she was into reading. The librarian had noticed her making notes one day, from a book of creative writing.

'You can borrow it if you like, Delia. It's an old Open University book. Plenty of activities in it. You might become a famous writer one day,' she grinned. 'Our own answer to J K Rowling.'

'Who's he?'

'She. You know, the creator of the Harry Potter books.'

'Oh of course. Yes... J K Rowling.' She kept a serious look on her face. 'I don't think I want to be famous. Quite like the idea of doing a bit of writing though. Thank you.' And she had taken the blue-covered book back to her room and some lined sheets of writing paper, eager now to begin.

Somewhat surprisingly, Delia enjoyed reading the BBB (Big Blue Book) as the librarian described the old creative writing tome. She readily took up the challenges of the activities in each chapter. She began writing short pieces of perhaps a hundred or two hundred words, gradually increasing these to short story lengths of 750 to 2000 words.

The librarian was impressed. 'D'you know, Delia, these short stories are good... very good. I think you could get them published, in a women's magazine.'

'No... They're not that good. Are they?'

'Tell you what I'll do, I'll type them out and staple them together, make a little booklet of them. We can pass them round the hospital, get the opinion of some of the staff and the inmates. Those that read, of course,' and she laughed as she said it.

'If you're sure.'   Delia sounded uncertain but was secretly flattered by the librarian's praise and enthusiasm.   The writing had taken away the inevitable boredom of her incarceration, though she barely remembered why she was here.   Her memories of past relations and relatives were confused and confusing, sometimes giving her severe headaches and agitating her.   That was when Nurse Johnson would soothe her, give her a tiny little injection that sent her to sleep.   When she awoke, she remembered nothing of the distress, and was only aware of the bitter taste in her mouth that she had to scrub away with huge blobs of toothpaste on her toothbrush and not rinse it off her teeth.   That way, she enjoyed the mint freshness instead of that dreadful bitter taste.

Next day the librarian handed Delia the typed stories in the form of an A5-sized booklet.   She had entitled it 'The Crystal and Other Stories by Delia Webster'.   She had even put a copyright on the inside cover pages and a numbered list of where the stories began.

'Why have you called me that?' she asked.

'What? Delia Webster?'

'Yes, Webster.'

'I found out it was your birth name. Is that ok?'

'Yes... yes. Thank you, I like that.' She examined the booklet, re-read one of the stories she had written, a feeling of pride and pleasure coating her shoulders. 'D'you think they'll like them? These stories? I mean anyone who reads them?'

'I certainly do. I'm handing some out to the staff today to gauge their reaction. Then I'll make copies available in the library for anyone who wants to borrow them. Well done, Delia. Now off you go, time for lun... dinner.' She dismissed her then, as was her duty. Must not appear too friendly to the inmates was the dictum put out by Head Nurse.

Delia returned to her room, clutching a copy of 'The Crystal and Other Stories' by Delia Webster. After her dinner of corned beef, beetroot and mashed potatoes, followed by a small cube of cheese and crackers, she settled down to read her very own book.

Nancy, one of the trusties, arrived to collect her tray. 'What you got there, Deelie?'

Delia sighed, she so hated that woman using that name for her.

'It's a collection of my short stories.'

'What d'you mean, *your* short stories?'

'What I mean. They're mine. I wrote them and the librarian has typed them out for me, made them into a little book.'

'Blimey! Let's have a look then.'

Delia clutched the pages to her chest. 'I've only got this one copy. If you want to read them, you'll have to see the librarian.'

Nancy cackled and shook her untidy head. 'No

use me going there, can't read. Or write come to that. Still, be nice to hear them stories. Fancy you writing them. Clever old soul, aint you.'

Delia looked at her. 'Really? You can't read or write?'

Nancy nodded. 'True. Never went much to school, always having to look after my old lady or my younger brothers and sisters while she dropped the next one. Thirteen she 'ad altogether.'

'I'll read you one if you like. Come back later when you get rid of the trolley.'

'Ok.' Nancy smiled, showing broken, stained teeth with a few gaps in between. 'That'd be great. See yer later.' And she was gone, rattling the trolley along the corridor, singing 'Once upon a time there was a little white bull... '

Delia moved onto her bed, took her pillow to the other end so the light from the window aided her vision of the type-written lines. She began to read. 'Poppy Field Grave' was the title of this particular story...

True to her word, Delia read a story each day to Nancy after she had dispensed with the trolley. Nancy showed her appreciation by bringing Delia extra food: the kind she liked, not some of the other rubbish dished out by the kitchen staff. Although things had improved somewhat, food wise, after a visit from a representative of the Health Minister. It was far more edible and satisfying than previously.

Nancy's favourite story was 'The Trouble with Roman Soldiers', about a little boy showing his next-door neighbour how to lift a heavy stone statue with pulleys.

'Clever little bugger weren't he?' she said. 'That's my favourite. Some of the others are a bit creepy if you ask me. Still they're good, I've really enjoyed listening to them.'

Delia enjoyed the flattery, not just from Nancy but many of the staff and some of the inmates. Perhaps I ought to write some more, she thought. A visit to the library and a talk with Miss Watson, the librarian, convinced her. She would embark on a second book of short stories.

'Wish I had some more ideas,' she said.

'There's a second book on creative writing here, perhaps you could get some ideas from it.'

She was delighted to be allowed to borrow, this time, the Big Red Book. 'Thanks, Miss. I'll look after it.'

'I know you will.' After a pause she said, 'I don't know why we don't enrol you as a student with The Open University. You could study for a BA degree. You can use a computer, can't you?'

'Yes... don't know about studying for a degree though. How long would it take?'

'Anything from about four years to six or seven. Depends on your ability and what time you can spend doing the course. Let's face it,' she smiled, not unkindly. 'You've all the time in the world. Would you like me to make some enquiries for you?'

'Yes please.' She was warming to the idea. 'It would have to be an English degree. Or English literature.'

'BA (Hons) English Literature. That's what I got my degree in.'

Delia left the library clutching her new creative writing tome. She could hardly wait to begin reading it. She was excited too, about the idea of gaining a degree, wondering what it would entail. She did not consider the cost of the course and the text books she would need. Responsibility for finance and other things had been snatched away from her years ago when she first entered this place. Now she considered it her home, a place of comparative security and safety. She had little or no idea what went on in the world outside the hospital walls. Only the clouds. She still studied the movement of the clouds, though unaware it had been a lifetime interest: was fascinated by them, their shapes, their colours and their height in the sky. *Perhaps I can write a story about clouds. Don't know what yet, but something, some idea will creep into my mind.*

30

However, changes came to scupper many of Delia's hopes, ambitions, and ideas. Changes beyond her control and those of the librarian and the nursing staff of the hospital. Cuts had to be made, were made, to ease the financial burden of running the establishment. The cuts meant immediately that there would not be an opportunity for Delia to enrol at the Open University. Not now or in the foreseeable future was how the librarian was informed.

'I'm so sorry,' she apologised, 'to have encouraged you and now... well. It's not going to happen.'

'It doesn't matter.' Delia could scarcely contain her rage, but knew she must to maintain the comparative freedom her visits to the library gave her. 'I can still borrow the BRB... the Big Red Book can't I? Still write more stories?'

'Of course you can. I'm sure I shall still be able to print them out in the form I did for your first little booklet. Anyway Webster, off you go now, get your dinner and then happy writing.'

It was a new rule, or an old one that had been re-introduced. All inmates, Delia included, were to be addressed by their surnames at all times. The only concession made to her was the use of her maiden name as opposed to the married name she had been admitted by. Though how this helped to make financial cuts was mystifying.

Perhaps the greatest change Delia had to suffer was the loss of her single room. The hospital was forced to accommodate more inmates. From now on, Head Nurse decreed, there would be two or three to the smaller rooms and four to the slightly larger ones. Not necessarily in rows of beds, but in the use of bunk beds. This caused untold misery to the manic depressives and gave power to the more dangerous inmates. They threatened their weaker fellows with violence if they were not allowed to choose which bed, upper or lower they wanted.

Delia kept her room but it was deemed big enough for at least two beds, bunk beds. She was hustled from the room while these beds were installed and returned to find her few precious belongings were stuffed into the top drawer of a two-drawer, bedside cabinet. A temporary curtain had been erected around the toilet to effect minimal privacy, and a slightly larger closet to accommodate two sets of clothes had been installed.

She gazed with dismay at the alterations. 'That means I have to put up with someone else's smell when they use the lavatory. And watch them undress at night and everything. And listen to them snoring.'

'Sorry, Webster. Nothing we can do about it.' Nurse Johnson sympathised and secretly worried about the woman's negative reactions to the changes. He knew the fragility of her sanity and how quickly her behaviour could alter from civil to violent. He spotted the creative writing book. 'You going to write more stories for us? The last book was amazing.'

'That was the plan,' she said. Her head drooped. She pouted. 'Don't know now. How can I write if someone else is in the room?'

He smiled. 'You will. You'll find a way.'

Then he was gone, leaving her seated on the lower bunk, *her bed*, and surveying the dismal scene. She glanced through the window, saw the lumped together grumpy clouds. They reflected her mood. She wondered who she would have to share this space with, didn't much care as long as it wasn't... what was her name? Tina? Why did she not want her as a room-mate? She rolled thoughts around in her confused head. Dimly recalled an incident with a fork, but the details remained misty. It pained her to delve into things past, or to think of people she might once have known. She saw Ted Seymour in the garden below, weeding the flower beds. Didn't she used to do that? With him?

Perhaps he could share this room with her. At least he would be quiet while she wrote and talk gardening when he did speak. Maybe she could have a word with Nurse Johnson, *he* would put in a good word for her, ask Head Nurse. She nodded to herself, yes that would solve the problem of room sharing. She stood up, winced with the pain in her hip. No way could she climb up there, onto the top bunk. That was a definite no-no.

Time to go and look for Nurse Johnson again, though she was unsure where she would find him. Staff room? Could be. Or the canteen; it must be nearly tea time. She limped slowly toward the door, tried the heavy steel handle only to find it would not move. Was the virus bug moving from her hip to her hands? She hoped not, bad enough suffering pain when walking without her hands hurting. How could she write with affected hands? She tried the door handle again, it would not budge. She rattled it, called out, 'Is anybody there? I can't open my door.'

She heard a key turn and the door opened. A female nurse was there holding a bunch of keys.

'Why was I locked in?'

'New rules, Webster. We're cutting down on staff. Means you inmates aren't gonna be allowed to wander when and where you want.'

She was devastated. 'What about...?'

'What about what?' The nurse sounded impatient. 'What about what Webster?'

'Supposing I want to go to the library? How can I if I'm locked in here?'

'There's going to be restricted opening times for the library. Mondays, Wednesdays, and Fridays. Mornings only one week and afternoons only every other week. Part of the cut backs.'

Cut backs, cut backs. That's all anyone spoke of. It was more than inconvenience, it was a complete disaster. Delia sat back on her bed in despair. The nurse interrupted her gloom.

'I've come to tell you who your room-mate will be.'

Delia remembered where she was going before she discovered the locked door. 'Nurse Johnson. I want to see Nurse Johnson. I know who I want to share with me, it's...'

She was stopped in mid-sentence. 'Two things, Webster, first, you don't get to choose who'll share this room with you, and second it's Head Nurse Johnson now. He's just been promoted, he's our new God.'

'What? What's happened to the old Head Nurse?'

'Gone, retired off. Johnson's been given the position. No need to bring in anyone else. He'll be all right I expect.'

Delia became increasingly agitated. Too many changes, too quickly. 'I want to see him.'

'Well, you can't. Now do you want to know who's sharing with you or not?'

Delia shrugged. She bit her nails, her lips, stood

up again and suffered two pains. She bumped her head on the upper bunk and her hip protested as she made to move too quickly.

'Ouch.   S'pose I've got to get used to that monstrosity,' she pointed to the upper bed with one hand and rubbed her head with the other. 'Anyway, who is it?'

'Bedford.'

'Bedford? Who's that?'

'Your dinner trusty, Nancy Bedford.'

Delia's heart sank. Fancy having to share a room with that boring old fart. She sighed. 'Well, she'll have to sleep up there. No way can I climb up there not with my bad hip.'

The nurse shrugged. 'Up to you two to sort that out.'

She did not have long to wait; the nurse returned with Bedford and her scant belongings. At least, Delia thought, she won't need too much space for her bits and pieces. She was surprised though to see the ancient and scruffy teddy bear that Nancy clutched close to her chest.

'What's his name?' she asked the dinner trusty.

'Gladly.'

'Gladly? What kind of name is that?'

'It's what my mum called him. Gladly. She used to say he was boss-eyed, but he's not. Gladly my cross-eyed bear was how she put it.'

Delia managed to smile. 'Gladly my cross I'd

bear'. She imagined Nancy's mum, always pregnant, always bearing children. They were the cross she would have had to suffer. And Nancy, as a child hearing her mother speaking these words and thinking she was referring to the furry toy. Might make a sweet story she thought, and filed it away in her writer's mind.

The new regime was harsh and unfriendly. It had to be, the intake had risen to almost two hundred. Meals were taken in two shifts in the dining canteen, which meant mealtimes were altered for some of the original inmates. They were so institutionalised that just this adjustment upset them, especially those allocated to the second shift. They found it hard to cope with the longer gap between meals. Dinner had always been taken at twelve noon, now they had to wait until gone twelve-thirty.

At least sharing her room with Nancy Bedford was bearable, just. Fortunately Nancy considered Delia to be the superior of the two of them. She accepted the top bunk without complaint, took the lower drawer for her few belongings. Apart from Gladly, who sat on her pillow by day and slept in her scrawny arms at night.

'I still got my job as trolley pusher, Webster. I know we all have to go to the canteen most of the time, but... there's always someone too sick to get there. Or on Punishment Block,' she hesitated. 'So if you like... erm... I can have my crap in one of the communal lavs.' She laughed. 'So's you don't have to smell mine.' She jerked her sparrow head towards the curtained lavatory. 'Not very private is it?'

Delia followed her glance, nodded. 'Right, now that's sorted, there's something else needs to be agreed. I want peace and quiet for my writing times. Either you don't talk then or you find some excuse to be elsewhere. Understood?'

Nancy's head nearly separated from her neck as she concurred. 'Will you still read to me?'

'Of course.' Delia allowed herself a thin smile. 'But the new stories have to be written first. Still,' she added. 'You can be the first to hear them, before I get the librarian to print them off.'

The little woman, her new roommate beamed, showing wrinkles like tiny rivulets spread over her face. 'Oh brilliant. Me hearing your stories first. Magic.'

Delia stored away the woman's enthusiasm for future favours and advantage. Outside a bell clanged informing all inmates on that corridor that dinner was ready. Their doors were automatically unlocked and thirty or more women evacuated cells to head for the canteen. Some shuffled, others pushed the slower ones aside and cluttered downstairs in their need to eat.

Delia was one of the slower ones. Each step down the stairs was taken in agony and she was pleased that her new roommate stayed with her, protecting her from the stronger women. She even managed a gruff thank you.

'That's all right, Webster. Lucky I'm not on trolley duty till next shift, innit?'

The quality of food had deteriorated. Stews were once again thin, with less meat and flavourings. At least there were a fair amount of vegetables, especially potatoes. Nancy guarded her from the others, from anyone who might decide to nick her dish. Yes, she would cultivate that friendship: might be handy, especially as her hip was preventing her from getting around easily. Soon she would have to use a walking stick all the time. She hated the idea but conceded her wellbeing was in danger without one.

31

Head Nurse Johnson called a staff meeting. He was concerned the enforced changes were not working as well as they should.

'We're sitting on a volcano that threatens to erupt any moment,' he warned. 'There's too many inmates, too few of us and the cuts are having a devastating effect on leisure times, mealtimes, and the general control of running this establishment. We need to bounce around a few ideas.'

'There's a lot of them getting agitated, especially at mealtimes,' said one nurse.

'And exercise times.' Said another. 'It's almost impossible to keep an eye on all of them, see who's pushing and bullying, and who's trying to nick things, etcetera.'

Several had things to say, problems to report. Johnson held up his hand. 'Right,' he said. 'We have to calm this situation down before all hell breaks loose. I know it's going back to the Dark Age but I'm going to introduce a calming agent to their food and drink.'

'What, like bromide?'

'Exactly. This establishment is, after all, the 'last chance hotel' for all of them. None of them will ever be released. So we must make the place as safe and peaceful as we can, both for them and ourselves. Agreed?'

His staff nodded in union. He breathed a sigh of relief.   He was still feeling his way in this appointment, still slightly anxious of their possible jealousy, their opposition to ideas he might put forward, but they seemed to be with him. Good. Time to close the meeting. He thanked them all in his usual courteous way and dismissed them, except for Nurse Channers. 'Give me five minutes will you?' he asked her.

When the others had departed he asked her to sit down again. 'I'm concerned about Webster,' he said. 'She seems to be deteriorating faster than I expected. Have you noticed this?'

She shifted in her chair, a big woman, whose buttocks overlapped the seat. 'Her hip's not getting any better and she hasn't taken kindly to eating in the canteen again. Fortunately,' she added. 'She seems to get on ok with Bedford, her roommate. Trouble is with Webster... she's as crafty as they come. Even after all these years, you never know what goes on in that head of hers.'

'True,' Johnson agreed. 'I thought the story-writing improved her behaviour a lot, especially when the librarian typed out her stories and distributed them. Gave her a bit of kudos. Now with these bloody cuts,' he sighed. 'Her visits to the library are severely curtailed and studying with the Open University is a definite no, no.'

'It's a pity we can't persuade to have her hip replaced,' said Nurse Channers. 'But she seems to have this weird idea that it's a virus, a foreign virus, and I can't dissuade her from this. Perhaps the doctor can give her stronger pills. At least it would be a temporary solution.'

'Mmn, I suppose so. Anyway keep an eye on her. We can always make an exception and let her have her meals in her room. The one she shares with, Bedford? She's a trolley trusty isn't she?'

'Yes. She and Webster seem to get on with each other pretty well. I think Webster is the more powerful of the two, acts more superior anyway. But Bedford doesn't seem to mind.'

'Ok then,' Johnson stood up. 'We'll let her eat in the room and give her a second walking stick: it'll help take the pressure off her hip. Poor old crow, such a shame she won't agree to a replacement. Still,' he added and grinned. 'Can't force them can we? Even they have human rights.'

It was almost a month before Head Nurse Johnson saw Delia again and he was profoundly shocked in her decline. The once luxurious head of hair was now thin, wispy and very grey, as was her face. She was bent nearly double and only kept at that angle with the aid of her sticks.

The arthritis looked like it was spreading to her hands, and for that he had real pity. He knew how much the writing had improved her life, given her a raison d'etre, taken her mind off day to day miseries, and even given her a modicum of fame among her peers. Now her hands were swollen, with distorted fingers and knuckles. The veins in them stood out like blackened tunnels under her thin flesh and she constantly massaged them with an invisible soap.

'Walk with me, Webster,' he asked her. He waited while she stood, grappled at the end of her bed for her walking sticks, and he gave her his arm. They walked slowly from the cell, painfully (for her) down the stairs and out into a thin sunshine that peeped through the rain soaked clouds.

'It's good to be outside,' she croaked. 'Don't get out here much now.'

He promised himself to allocate her a ground-floor room. It would be a start. She looked, he thought, at least ten years older than her seventy years, much older than his spritely mother looked at a similar age. He felt pity for her, even though she was a murderess all those years ago. He wondered what had motivated her, what kind of wife and mother she had been, before and after each killing. Probably quite a good one, he thought, and wondered on the quirk of fate that made humankind both creative and destructive.

He pointed to a garden seat, her one time

favourite spot out here. 'Do you want to sit for a while?'

'Yes dear, that would be nice.'

He carefully lowered her down, then sat himself next to her. He had no fear of her. 'Look, there's old Seymour. Shall I get him over for a chat?'

She scowled. 'I don't want to talk to him. He doesn't clear them up.'

'What? What doesn't he clear up?'

'The grass cuttings. Just leaves them there. He should rake them away.'

'Oh, right.' Johnson was mystified. He was no gardener.

They sat in silence, both relieved when the sun grew stronger. They watched the steam coming off the dampened bricks of the building, off the grass with its clumps of unraked cuttings.

After another ten minutes or so Johnson decided it was time for them to back inside. He helped her as she slowly, painfully, climbed the stairs again.

'I'll get tea sent in here for you,' he said. He added, 'I'm going to arrange for you to have a downstairs room, Webster. Would you like that?'

'Oh yes. Those stairs are a daily challenge. Thank you, Nurse Johnson, sorry, Head Nurse Johnson. That will be wonderful.'

It was the last time she spoke to him, her favourite in this God forsaken place.

She realised now, was conscious, she could have, should have, been known as... the woman who never loved. If she smiled the feathered lines of her face would increase, indent. Therefore she never, rarely, only occasionally... smiled. Even then, prohibiting it from reaching her eyes, merely a straightening of her mouth.   Likewise, she refrained from showing disapproval by pursing her lips, hating the wizened effect it produced.   Instead she folded her lips inwards and glared at the recipient of her censure. She still, at times, commanded a grudging respect, but in the now of her life it counted for little, gave her scant pleasure – if any.

She walked slowly, painfully towards the window: her arthritis was not improving. Yes, she was forced to call it that. The gardens out there were still resplendent in their summer colours; the roses still bloomed though some needed deadheading, a little pruning. She'd get round to it later, maybe early afternoon when the September sun was at its warmest, when she was allowed out for her oh so painful walk.

The grass had been mown but the cuttings had been left to lie in withered lines, lengthways along the lawn. She scowled in ungrateful annoyance. As if it was her lawn, her garden, but chided herself for a moment at her ingratitude that old Seymour had cut it at all.

It was times, like this, she questioned her own

unpleasantness. Why so uncharitable? Why so unwilling to give praise, pleasure to fellow human beings? Where was the love...?

A sudden playful breeze caught some of the dried cut grass, lifted it from its furrow and ferreted it away among the rose bushes. Perhaps it would protect the ground when the first frosts came. Or a small bird might purloin it to make a nest, or a hedgehog to snuggle under it...

She smiled her straight-mouthed smile, her eyes glazing over for a moment as she wandered back in time... to Carl. Carl, her first husband, her teenage rebellion. Huge mistake. Carl the untutored, the uncouth, who laughed too loudly at social gatherings, usually at his own coarse jokes. Who received mostly tight, polite smiles in return. Carl who bullied his way through their marriage, forced his way into her body, puncturing her with his unwanted seed. He gave her the clumsy child, Maria, shortened to Mia. Shortened name that went with a brief life of barely one year. They, the hospital staff who delivered this pitiful baby, blamed it on lack of oxygen at her birth. Said it left her damaged, no life expectancy: no skills or motivation.

Delia, or Deelie as he called her, blamed him, Carl. Brainless man producing brainless idiot, and in doing so, violated her womb. Let him do the cuddling, the midnight feeds, the bathing and changing of that mewling creature. She wanted no part of it, no responsibility. The baby who would not survive had no right to her love, her protection.

Social workers tried to encourage her. Carl struggled to persuade her to open her arms, her heart.

'Chrissakes Deelie, she's our baby, your little daughter.'

Mia died without her mother's touch or love. So did Carl, ultimately die without her touch.

Delia peered upwards to the sky beyond the hotel walls, not the hotel walls, the hospital. That is what they said it was. Not hotel or prison, although they would not let her out. No, they said, you must stay here for a little while longer. They always gave that answer when she asked could she go home. She never mentioned Bob again. Her hatred had turned to dismissal. Removal from her psyche. Home was... where? She couldn't quite remember. Never mind, this would do for now. She had this, almost nice little room she shared with stupid, harmless Nancy Bedford. And the view to the garden and beyond. And the skies. She loved the skies, their changeability, and their amazing colours. They gave her paints and brushes to paint the skies, but she would grow tired and sometimes impatient enough to throw everything on the floor. The hotel, no the hospital staff did not like her doing that. And when she carried on and screamed at them they would stick her with a needle to make her sleep. She hated the taste in her mouth when she came to. Bitter it was, like rotten food. They called her by her surname. 'Webster,' they would say. 'Calm down.' She grew agitated every time they called her that. 'My name is Delia, Delia... ' And she could not remember her surname, but it wasn't Webster. Where did they get that from?

Another nurse, the really horrible one, would sneer and say, 'What name do you want to be today then? Fletcher? Manning? Fontaine, Shackleton?' And she would protest that they were not her names, nothing to do with her. She would tell them they were all mad and to leave her bloody well alone. Then they locked her in her tiny room, strapped her to the bed, and gagged her because they said she bit them. It was all lies. She never. They wouldn't listen and if she kept on arguing with them, she'd be given the needle again, have to suffer that bitter taste again.

Now she had the arthritis to suffer on top of all that other aggravation. Burned into her hips it did. And her knees. She looked at her hands, at the raised veins and the shrivelling fingers. She muttered to herself. 'You used to have lovely hands.' Not anymore. Nothing was the same anymore. Why didn't they let her go home? Where was... her home? Gerald hadn't known about the clumsy child. Mia died before she and Carl had moved into the flat above Gerald's stationery shop. The one that sold art materials as well. She wanted to purchase paints, brushes, canvasses and watercolour pads, but there was no money to spare for such indulgences. Only Carl's sneer. 'What bloody for? Who d'you think you are? Bloody van Gogh?' Surprising really that he even knew the name or the fame of such a man. Rough, uncultured Carl. Carl the bully who knew where to punch that left her gasping, and where the bruises would not show.

Gerald, quiet, polite, couth and tutored. Bookish Gerald who called her Delia always, who – years later – apologetically infused her with the twins, a girl and a boy. What were their names? She struggled back in her confused memory. Tilda and Danny, that's what they called them, Matilda and Daniel.

She smiled her straight-lipped smile, the one that did not reach her eyes. She dissected her memories. Remembered the little pub on the hill where she and Gerald had met a man whose name she did not know, the man who spoke only those three words to her, *'You all right?'* during the whole of that meeting. The man who ordered a large scotch from Gerald and did not say please or thank you. How, days later, Carl was dead and she was in Hereford with her sister Saskia and Gethin and their two boys. The sister she denied when she and that ex-policeman had married. She had told him she was an only child.   Then being discovered in her lie when her nephews came calling. Or did they? She was not sure. There were men who came to the house. In uniform. Not her nephews. Police, who put her in chains... or something. One of them hit her. They should not do that. It was against the law. She remembered he called her a bitch, said she had bitten him. As if she would... She shook her head at the much thought.

Her children had never been allowed to do anything like that. Oh no. They were properly brought up, *and* their friends vetted. No nasty ones were allowed in their lives. Not to stay anyway. There was Damien, horrible boy. And the gangrel. Funny how that name came back to her. But what was he called? Timothy, Tim Cad... something or other. Tim who fell on the railway lines and was crushed under the train. She remembered women in burkas, black, no parts of them showing save their eyes. Could have been anyone in disguise... anyone.

Some memories were stronger than others. She remembered the stew they were eating when the police came to tell her of Carl's death, recalled the strong taste of thyme that Saskia had picked only that morning and the smell of it when she brought the small bunch in from the garden, her hands covered with the soft red earth of Herefordshire. She could not, however, remember the journey back to Hampshire.   Or Carl's funeral that Gerald had sympathetically arranged. Only afterwards, leaving the flat she had shared with Carl and moving into the one above Gerald's antique shop; gradually moving into his bedroom, and into his bed.

She shifted now, in this bed with its creaking iron frame and too-thin mattress. Discomfort screamed through her arthritic limbs, but not through her mouth. No need to wake Bedford. Bad enough listening to her farts and snores, smelling her bad breath that pervaded the small room, hearing her cry out in her nightmare dreams or her moaning from an aching, aging body.

Her mind flickered backwards and forwards in time. It snatched at the few good memories and gathered anger at the bad ones, those that were the cause of her being here and not there where the good memories resided. But sometimes she could not quite remember those good memories. They disappeared into the mists of time, into the cloudy skies out there. Only one hovered. When Daddy had made her a sledge. That snowy winter when everything glistened and was so beautiful. And silent...

32

'Webster, you have a visitor.' The hard-nosed nurse in her uncompromising uniform flicked her head towards the door, indicated a woman standing outside. Delia, annoyed at being addressed by a surname, not even hers as far as she was concerned, barely glanced towards the half-glass door. She did not recognise the figure. Not really, although there was something familiar about the shadowy silhouette. Still, a visitor was a visitor in this grey, grim place.

'You can come through to the day room. Put your slippers on and that.' The nurse indicated her dressing gown hanging over the bed end. She almost protested at having to wear it. It was rough and itchy, grey as the rest of this place, but if she didn't obey, the nurse would not allow her to go through, to meet her visitor whoever she was. She struggled into the unpleasant garment, painfully slipped her veined and swollen feet into the uniform slippers, wished there were colours here. Pink fluffy slippers, soft, towelling robe white or pink or lemony; floral curtains and wallpaper, warm carpet, warm room...

'Come on Webster, I haven't got all day.' The nurse broke into her faddling mind.

'I'm coming, I'm coming. I need my sticks, where's my sticks?'

'Oh for God's sake, there! End of your bed. Now come on... '

She slowly followed the nurse's grim and unforgiving back, noted the overweight waddle and two stolid, uncompromising legs, and two feet that overlapped the black lace-up shoes. *One day you'll suffer like me.*

The door was unlocked and she was allowed through into a room furnished with bare wooden tables and plastic seating chairs. There were no flowers in vases, despite all those growing in the gardens out there; no curtains at the windows, only blinds that rattled and did a bedraggled dance when the breeze attacked them. The open windows did not quite take away the stale smell of badly cooked food and Delia wrinkled her nose: she had her standards.

A woman sat at one of the tables, her legs to one side of it as if ready to make an escape. She had one hand resting on the table and drummed her fingers in a nervous tattoo. Delia did not recognise her shape and could not see the turned away face. Her tapping sticks alerted the woman's attention; she turned to face Delia.

'Hello Mum.'

Mum? Why is she calling me Mum? I don't know her. She allowed the nurse to settle her onto the plastic seat, and decided to play along with this stranger. 'Hello dear,' her voice cracked. *Surely this person was too old to be her daughter? There was one, had been, what was her name? Tilda or something. This isn't her, nothing like her, much too old.*

'Are you all right? 'The woman rummaged in her bag, glanced over at the watchful nurse and indicated chocolates. She pulled out a gold coloured box when the grim-faced woman nodded. 'I've brought you these, your favourites.'

'My favourites? How do you...?' Delia left the sentence unfinished. Best not show irritation: show craft, cunning. They don't like it in here when you argue. Instead she said, 'Thank you dear.' She took the box and placed it on the table in front of her, stared at the wrapping and wondered how to get inside it.

'Would you like me to open them for you?'

Her eyes flickered in annoyance. 'I can do it.'

The woman who pretended to be her daughter shrank back. 'I'm sorry.'

Delia gave herself a private smile, a victory smile. She was scared of her, this stranger: you could see it in her eyes. She was tempted to say to her, 'It's ok, I don't bite.' Thought best not to. She struggled with the wrapping, gave up. 'Here you do it.' She watched while the woman found a small strip that enabled you to take off the outer wrapping with ease. Stared as she lifted the lid and took off a dark brown corrugated protective sheet to reveal a layer of sweet-smelling chocolates, some wrapped in foil, others laying there waiting to be chosen.

Delia salivated and wiped the dribble on her dressing gown sleeve, her eyes gazing hungrily at the boxed contents.

'Go on Mum, have one. They're all for you.' Her alleged daughter smiled and pushed the box nearer to the old woman.

Her gnarled fingers crept towards it, like a spider crawling towards a trapped fly, eager for a scrumptious morsel. Delia scrabbled among the paper wrappings, closed her fingers around one, then two, then a third.

'Hey steady Mum,' the woman laughed. 'You don't need to eat them all at once.'

'Who says so? Thought you said they were for me.' Her face assumed a look of anger, belligerence. She was sick and tired of always being told what she should do, what they allowed her to do. Her chocolates, she'd eat as many as she liked and damn them all, these interfering women.

'Yes of course, they are for you, Mum. Eat as many as you like.' The younger woman sat and regarded the old lady, a look of sadness spread over her middle-aged face. She could see, at the corner of her vision, the whey-faced nurse staring at her mother. Watched as the woman half stood then settled again as much as to say none of her business how many chocolates went into that dribbling orifice.

Delia grabbed the moment, and a handful of the chocolates, cramming them into her mouth, munching, chewing, and masticating. She made weird sounds as she chewed, nodding her head, until a nut cluster caught in the back of her throat, causing her to cough and splutter and wheeze in a terrifying way. Matilda stood up, knocking her chair to the ground as she did so. She moved towards the choking woman, as did the nurse. Delia made horrifying sounds as she breathed the nut clusters down into her lungs. She grabbed her own throat and fell back in her chair, her eyes bulging. The woman who was her daughter stood statue-like, transfixed, her hands hung useless by her side. The nurse, knowing nothing of the Heimlich Manoeuvre, attempted to thump Delia's back, trying to dislodge whatever was choking her. But Delia was sitting too far back in her chair for the nurse to get a proper positioning. Delia choked, her daughter stared, and the nurse stepped back and listened to the strangled sounds of an unexpected accident.

Delia died untouched, choking on nuts from the chocolate, the chocolate from a box given her by a woman who called her Mum. Her last, fleeting thought was of someone she knew a long time ago: a friend called Manda who had choked to death on nuts... the day that she herself had married a man named Robert Shackleton.

chadgreen books

More titles from our authors[†]
A POCKETFUL OF YESTERDAYS
an anthology by Joan Barlow

FROM THE MOUNTAINS TO THE SEA
Tales from Africa by Rosemarie David

THE CHAMPAGNE WRITERS OF SHROPSHIRE
an anthology of poems and stories by writers from
north-east Shropshire

READING BETWEEN THE LINES
an anthology of poems and stories
by John Cliff and Anna Newman

MISS FLINCH
a novella by Anna Newman

Coming soon[†]
THE KILLING OF ELLIE SWALES
a thriller by Olga Merrick

A RAKE OF LEAVES
a thriller by Olga Merrick

† for further information about these titles please email us at

chadgreenbooks@yahoo.com